SCARLET THIRST

SCARLET THIRST

by

Crin Claxton

2014

SCARLET THIRST

ISBN 13: 9781626393172

This Trade Paperback Original Is Published By
Bold Strokes Books, Inc.
P.O. Box 249
Valley Falls, NY 12185

First Edition: July 2014

CREDITS
Editor: Cindy Cresap
Production Design: Sandy Lowe
Cover Design By Lee Ligon

By the Author

The Supernatural Detective

Scarlet Thirst

Visit us at www.boldstrokesbooks.com

Acknowledgments

From the original version, big thanks to Kathleen Bryson, to Miss P and Rita H for language consultation, to Deni Francis for femme clothing advice and numerous comments, and to my family who have always encouraged me to write.

For Scarlet Thirst 2013, thanks to Radclyffe for asking, to Cindy Cresap for painstaking editing, to Deni for more reads and comments, to Stella Duffy for the right words at the right time, and to Campbell for your encouragement. To Mavis Claxton for avidly reading the first version, even in the doctor's waiting room, albeit with a card tacked over the cover.

And importantly, to everyone who has written to me or come up to me and told me what the book has meant to you, a huge thanks. You keep me writing. In many ways, this reprint is for you.

Dedication

For Deni. You are the joy and magic in my life.

CHAPTER ONE

I had a sudden and persistent thirst. The nagging, gnawing kind I couldn't ignore. The heaving sound of many bodies moving on the dance floor through the open doors behind me was proof I'd checked a lot of hand stamps in the last two hours.

My boss, Lois, came through the doors. The club was filling, and she was grinning like a cute, blond Cheshire cat. I figured it would be a good time to ask for an early break.

"Hey, Lois." I tried to look appealing. "I didn't get a chance to eat before I came in. Can I just nip out and grab something?"

"You need to get up earlier, Rob," Lois said sternly. A grin was creeping onto her pursed lips, though. I was safe. As I walked to the door, Marcia looked up from bagging door takings to roll her eyes at me. I sauntered past, smiling.

I stepped out onto the streets and walked well away from the punters strolling to the club. I walked for maybe five minutes before I found what I needed: a guy hanging out on the street corner ahead. He was leaning against a shop doorway, smoking. There was no one else about.

I focused in on him. His energy was calm and self-confident. He could handle the exchange, so I walked over to him reaching for his eyes, and locked with him mind to mind until I saw his eyelids drooping. Then I gently pushed him back into the doorway, out of sight.

While he drifted in a sweet dream, I sliced a small cut in his neck with my left incisor and drew his blood into my body.

I took a deep breath through my nose as the blood flowed through my system, feeling the power of the energy flowing into me. I get a little high on every feed. This feed was more about sustenance than pleasure, though, and I was sealing the wound, pressing down and drawing the energy up from my belly that stops the flow, when I heard footsteps very close.

A man and a woman stopped outside the doorway to eat kebabs. I held my new friend to me and grunted, projecting an image into their minds.

After a moment, they moved quickly away, muttering about the gay club round the corner.

"I don't mind what they do as long as they don't do it on the streets," the guy said sharply. He put his arm around his girlfriend, the irony lost on him.

The donor was still dreaming. I checked his pulse was fine and that everything was flowing properly in his body before I gently released his mind. He came to after I led us both back onto the street.

"All right, mate?" I said, walking away. All he would remember, if he ever thought about it again, was a person of indiscriminate gender passing him on the street.

Marcia winked as I returned, waving me over to her table.

"You got ketchup on your chin, Rob," she said. "Not like you to be messy with your food."

I got a handkerchief out of my pocket and wiped my chin. Marcia was right. That wasn't like me. I resumed my position as door security and kept an eye out while Marcia checked how much change she had left.

Marcia took the money, stamped their hands, and passed the punters on to me. I checked their stamps and waved them on in. We both smiled a lot. Lois ran a friendly club. She wanted women, and their male guests, to feel welcome. I'd found it hard smiling at strangers when I first started working at the club, but I did it automatically now. I didn't need to look tough on the door. The smiling approach calmed down most situations, and if it didn't, I did what I was paid to do.

The club door policy was men as guests. It was a bit of an early nineties concept. Still, it avoided problems on the queer gender front about who was in and who was out. Back in the day, I worked women-only clubs. I missed it sometimes— women all together and strong and all that. But I sure as hell didn't miss turning trans people away. There was something screwed up about back then. I understood why separatism was necessary, but felt for who got left out.

I went over to Marcia, hoping to catch up, and three Techno-babes walked in, wearing short, tight tops, their hair gelled and spiky.

I checked the women's hands as they passed into the club. I liked the short exchanges. Just the briefest of energy exchange, usually nothing more than a second of contact. In an evening, maybe several hundred people pass through the door, and that little buzz of contact with each person energizes me. I guess it's the connection to life. Like walking through a garden, touching and smelling different flowers. The essence of life in each person reaches and connects with my own life force, touching base.

Marcia looked stressed. There was never enough change, and her brow creased several furrows deeper at the sight of another twenty. Lois cheerfully headed for the bar. A woman came past me for the fourth time. She was obviously expecting a lover or a friend.

"I'm just going to the door."

"It's okay. I think I'll recognize you by now. But make sure you don't lose your hand stamp just in case, yeah?" I smiled at her. She had a nice feeling about her, a doing good in the world feeling. I watched her head off toward the main door and felt a faint prickling sensation along the back of my neck.

I turned round to the biggest, deepest, brownest eyes I'd seen in a long time. The kind of eyes it's easy to get lost in. I was fascinated by the different intensities, variation in hue, flecks of amber. The rest of her face was as beautiful as her eyes, and she was staring back at me, her hand pressed out toward me. I did what any butch would do, I took that soft and lovely hand in mine, brought it up to my lips, and kissed it. Her eyes widened. Something clicked, and I saw the scene for what it was: a gorgeous woman had come to get her hand stamp checked, and I'd made an ass of myself.

"Um…um…" I stammered. I was still holding her hand so I brought it down and looked at it. "Yes, that's fine," I muttered, trying to make out looking at her stamp had been my intention all along.

I dropped her hand. She didn't smile, but her mouth was

all crinkly at the edges like she was trying to stop herself laughing. Her eyes dipped to the floor and back up again. I was impressed with her very long, very dark eyelashes. Then she walked through to the dance floor without a word. I couldn't help but watch her go. The rear view was as good as the front had been.

"Kuh-hum." A young butch coughed to get my attention. She put her hand up and attempted a feminine pose. "Wanna see my stamp?" she joked, managing to look more like a camp gay man than a femme. I waved her in with a wry smile. I deserved to be coated. Marcia was giggling. I guessed she'd clocked my moment of indiscretion. Fortunately, we were too busy for her to be able to max on it.

I kinda pretended it hadn't happened. The femme was, after all, not the first beautiful woman I'd ever seen. I noticed her again later though, when Lois sent me inside on one of my rounds. She was talking to another feminine woman at the bar, her body moving to the music unselfconsciously, with a fluidity and grace that was mesmerizing. I didn't go over. I'd made a fool of myself already, and she hadn't come out to the door to talk to me. Anyway, I was still hooked into Selena.

At chucking out time, I was called to a problem in the toilets. The woman's problem was she'd been dumped, drank copious amounts of alcohol, and was now finding it hard to stand up. I held her while she cried on my shoulder a little, and while she vomited in the toilet a lot. Then I rounded up her mates and put them all in a cab.

Marcia was ready to go when I was done. We walked out together.

"We should rename chucking out time: chucking up time," I proposed.

She agreed, having had to fetch the mop on many an occasion. "You wanna come hang out at my place?" she asked. I declined. None of the mortals at the club knew what I was. I'd only snatched a meal earlier and needed a proper feed.

"Hey, someone said good-bye to you," Marcia teased me as I turned to go.

"Who?" I asked, hoping it was the beautiful dark-skinned femme.

"The woman you made a damn fool of yourself over."

"What did she say?"

"She said to say good-bye to the good-looking butch on the door."

As I walked home, I mused on the streets at night. Night and streets go together like a horse and carriage used to. The cool, crisp February night was invigorating. Winter convinces me the seasons are based around a vampire's needs—just when it gets colder and a body needs a little more blood, the nights get longer and there's more opportunity to feed.

I stopped for half pint here, half pint there, always making sure the human I fed from didn't feel any pain and wouldn't have any memory of the event. Selena taught me about feeding when I was a new vampire.

"I think of them as precious," she'd said one night, not long after we'd met. "I couldn't harm them in any way. At first, I hated taking blood from people who didn't know what we are. But it's the safest way. And, Rob, everything on this planet sustains something, and is sustained in turn."

"But what do we sustain?" I'd asked.

"We can heal plant, animal, and human tissue. That's how we stop the blood flow when we feed. And ultimately, we can give life."

"You make us sound nice!"

"We *are* nice, or at least there's no reason why we shouldn't be. We're another life form, that's all. You need to get past all that myth and nonsense about vampires. They want to believe we're monsters. Who knows why? Doesn't make any more sense than any other prejudice ever has."

After a shaky start, Selena's philosophy and wisdom made my first years in the Life beautiful learning experiences. She listened to my fears, and then she took them away. Selena was my first and greatest love in the Life. We spent many years together, and I wasn't sure why we were apart now.

Eighteen months ago, we'd had to leave the States. We'd been there too long. Selena had felt drawn to Mexico, but I wanted to come to England. The pull for both of us had been strong. Selena had decided we were supposed to be apart at this time. I'd taken it to mean we were splitting up. I hadn't seen her since, and I missed her.

I thought about her all the way home, calling her to me, so that by the time I'd fed and was tucked up in my dark room, I felt her with me. I stayed with Selena, spending mind-mind dream time, until my five-hour ahead time zone pulled me away.

***

Couple of weeks later, I was sitting in Babe Bar waiting for Marce to show. Eighty years into the Life, I was getting the hang of letting time pass. I sipped on a Nastro and studied my reflection in the mirrors behind the bar, thinking about the vampires not showing up in mirrors myth. Lucky that is a myth. It's the kind of thing people would notice, especially in the Village with all that glass and chrome. It's a weird thing looking at yourself when you never change. Apparently, a group of vampires four centuries ago couldn't cope with it. After a couple of hundred years, they got freaked out by still looking twenty. So they wouldn't have mirrors in the house. According to Selena, that's how the myth got started

Marcia and I were going to have a few beers and catch up. I'd had a bite on the way down. I usually picked guys for my casual feeds. Women don't hang out on their own at night as much, and I don't like to go into people's homes. Also, there's still so much fear for women on the streets, I couldn't be a part of that, not even for the tiniest second before I calmed them down.

My preference for male donors got me into some heated arguments in the heady days of vampire separatism. The ideas swept out from human politics, starting with Black Civil Rights in the States in the 1960s. As vampires, it was important to create our own images of ourselves, to respect the centuries of wisdom living amongst us. But some of it was daft. Some of those she-vampires (we couldn't call ourselves women) didn't even think we should bring anyone new into the Life. It was something we had to go through to get rid of old, set ideas. I prefer the more tolerant attitudes of vampires now. There's a lot more acceptance of individuality.

Marcia was even later than usual. She was pretty good at turning up on time for work, but socially, she was murders. I thought I might reach out, try to guess how far on route Marcia was, when the back of my neck started prickling.

I instinctively turned toward the door just as *she* walked through it. The gorgeous femme from the club didn't see me.

Her attention was on the tables to the left of the door. I had time to study her slowly from top to toe. Damn, but she looked hot in tight trousers hugging her skin so close it made me swallow. She had a cute little jeans jacket on top. Her long black hair was tied back with something that sparkled; her skin was the color black coffee is in a clear glass held before the light. She was looking toward the bar, but her eyes were fixed on a woman several barstools in front of me. Her face lit up, embracing the woman with her smile. I looked at that smile the way the little match girl must have looked through the rich peeps' window.

Out of the corner of my eye, I saw Marcia clock me.

"Hey, Rob, how ya doing?"

"Okay, Marce, what do you want to drink?" I pulled up a barstool.

"A Bud, thanks. Just need to go to the loo, yeah. The tube train was stuck in a tunnel for half an hour. I'm desperate." She walked past me, and I laughed, watching her head for the back of the bar. When I turned round, the hot and very lovely femme of color was sitting on the barstool I'd pulled out for Marcia.

"Hi." She was smiling, and there was a childlike delight in her eyes at the game she'd played on me.

"Hi." The memory of all words except hi deserted me, so I smiled. The nearness of her sent my heart tic-tacking.

"Do you work here as well?" she said after a while, arching one eyebrow delicately.

"Yes." She was waiting for me to say something else. "Night off," I managed.

"I saw your friend come in, and I was going to say hi, then I saw you."

"I saw you when you came in."

"Did you?" she said so softly I wanted to lean in to hear her better. She fixed me again in the deep brown pools of light some people would call her eyes.

"Yeah, I saw you meet *your* friend."

"Did you?" she repeated, still speaking soft. If she didn't stop, I really would have to lean in.

"Well, I feel better for that."

I registered Marcia pulling up the barstool behind me. Hot and Lovely dropped my eyes and turned to Marcia. "Hi, do you remember me from the club?"

"Yeah, sure I remember," Marcia said. "Passed on your message." She smiled.

"Why don't we all sit together?" I blurted out. "You with your friend, and me and Marcia." I sounded like an overexcited five-year-old.

"Yeah. I'd like that." Ms. Hot and Lovely went over to her friend, who'd managed to get a table so they waved us over.

"Can I ask you something?" I said.

"Of course."

"What's your name?"

She leaned her head back and laughed. The laugh collected and bubbled in her throat. I was very drawn to the dimples each side of her trachea. Concentrating on the left one, I saw a pulse flicker rhythmically up and down. I could feel the thud of it vibrating through me with a rush of sexual tension.

"I said my name is Rani."

I snapped back to reality. That must have been the second or third time she'd said her name.

"That's a lovely name," I said noncommittally because I was trying to collect myself. Rani looked disappointed. I sensed she thought I was uncomfortable with her Indian name. I was suddenly very sorry I'd been distracted by her neck.

"Tell me about yourself." I had an urge to find out something about the kind of woman she was. Rani must have picked up on my interest because she told me how she grew up in London, going to a mixed school, and how tough she'd had to be. I learned no matter how soft she looked, Rani had the hardness, strength and beauty of a diamond. I liked her analytical and compassionate mind. She was in touch with real things like injustice, and when she got fired up, the heat burned out from her. I was engaging with her mind, but the sensitivity of the way she spoke tugged on my heart. And there was a sexual pull that was hard to ignore. The attraction was several chakras high.

When the bar closed, Marcia and I walked Rani and Gulsin to their car. Rani thought this was ridiculous, especially as their car wasn't even on the way to the tube. I insisted.

"I enjoyed tonight," I told her when we reached the car.

"I'd like to see you again," Rani said. "Will you be at the club on Friday?"

I nodded.

"See you then, then." She kissed my cheek the way a tiger moth might brush against jasmine in full bloom.

***

On Friday, I was more of a flutter than I cared to admit. Marcia winked over so much anyone would have thought she had something stuck behind her contact lenses. I fixated on the entrance doors. Lois smiled at me benevolently from Marcia's table.

"What's up with Rob?" she whispered to Marce, not quietly enough because I heard her. I shook my head violently, willing Marcia to get the hint. But Marcia's lips were moving, and then Lois gave a bright laugh. I frowned at them. They giggled.

Nobody came for the first hour, prolonging my personal agony, then everyone came at once. We were dealing with a long queue that snaked round the block, when in walked Rani. She brushed my lips in greeting and then had to go through. She couldn't hang out on the door because there was no room for "friends of" when it was busy. I tried to watch her walking away, which was fast becoming a favorite occupation, but she was all too quickly swallowed up by the crowd. I had to get back into heavy hand stamp checking.

When Lois finally relieved me, my patience was stretched so tight I could have played it like a guitar. One and a half hours is a long time to make do with a peck on the lips.

I found Rani on the dance floor and slipped in opposite her. I suddenly felt shy. She pulled me to her, resting her hand behind my neck. She pressed close. her head on my shoulder and I closed my eyes, my body warm liquid dissolving. The music and the room reduced in volume, slipped to the periphery of my senses.

I drifted with Rani for a while lost in the tune, the bass, the feel of her in my arms. It made me think of lying in warm moonlight. When I felt her hands on my buttocks pushing me up onto her leg, I didn't think it was possible to get any closer, but she proved me wrong. She started a fierce throbbing between my legs. I tried to keep it together. I didn't mind being flat on my back, maybe, but not on the dance floor at the club where I worked, and not flipped so easy by a first date. Rani pressed her lips to my ear:

"I hope you haven't got any plans for later." She turned my face to her so she could study my reaction. "I'm going to keep you very busy."

I felt the need to go and find Lois, and check if she needed me to stay to the very end.

Lois said, "Rob, I'd like to meet the woman that can melt some of your cool. She deserves to get a bit more of you tonight. Take her home."

Back on the dance floor, I came up behind Rani and said low into her ear, "So would you like me to come home with you?"

She turned, her eyes brighter than the scanners spinning above us. "Your place or mine, you mean!"

"Well, your place I think. If that's okay? I'm having some work done at mine." *And I don't want to freak you out.*

"What makes you think it's safe to come back with me?" She tried to look scary and only succeeded in looking gorgeous.

"Don't worry. I can look after myself," I assured her.

Rani took me home, directing the taxi along quiet streets. We were quiet too. I looked out the cab window to distract myself, wondering where Rani was taking me. Considering the potential for danger, I was amazingly calm.

Inside her flat, Rani asked me if I wanted a drink.

"Why don't we take something straight through to your bedroom?" I said.

"Bottled water suit you? Want some beer, some wine?" Rani asked coolly. "I got some in, just in case."

I got a buzz knowing she'd been thinking about bringing me back. She handed me a couple of bottles and pulled me by the belt into the bedroom.

Holding my gaze, Rani stepped away and lifted off her flimsy shirt thing. She had a tight top on underneath, thin enough for her nipples to stand straight out from. Mmm, already she looked good enough to eat. The phrase going through my head reminded me to keep my wits about me. Rani peeled off the tight top. "Oh." A sigh came from deep within me as two round, bewitching breasts made a sudden dramatic entrance. I fell in love instantly. I knew we would become good friends.

I helped Rani with her jeans. The zip slipped apart in my

hands, and I eased the jeans down. I bent down with them, kissing Rani's legs all the way back up. I could feel the heat coming off her.

She began to sway so I helped her out, guiding her to the bed. I leaned in to kiss her, but Rani held back, licking a fine, slow line around the outside of my lips. Then she lay back against the pillows, one arm under her head, looking up at me, soft and relaxed, like she did this kind of thing all the time.

I picked the thought out of Rani's mind that she didn't like me being so fully clothed when she was so nearly naked. So I pulled off my T-shirt while Rani unbuttoned my trousers. When I was stripped down to boxers and sports vest, Rani said, "There, now we're even."

I ran my fingers along the soft skin of her stomach, fingering the outside of her knickers, slipping just under the band until Rani's breath was coming loud and fast. Her nipples were crying out for my mouth. I didn't disappoint them. Rani gasped as I sucked a nipple between my teeth. She pressed her hands into my back, stroking the skin and feeling my buttocks through my shorts. I took Rani's other nipple in my mouth and slipped a hand down her knickers, finding her slick and swollen. She started to move more urgently under my fingers then, and her knickers became superfluous. I peeled them off and threw them somewhere into the far reaches of the room. I slipped into Rani from behind and breathed in her ear, "Do you like it like that?"

Her cry answered me. She moved on both my hands, making a thorough and intimate acquaintance with them. The thrusting got more urgent, her cries louder, until I felt a strong pulsing across my fingers. She pushed me away from her and looked at me suspiciously, as if she were wondering what I might do next.

I smiled a wolf smile. Rani took a long drink of water, then tipped the bottle over me, making me jump up.

"Oh no!" she said innocently. "Now we'll have to get those wet clothes off you. You'll get a chill."

I checked her out, the energy between us tangibly smoldering. Normally, I have to know someone pretty well before they get to see my breasts, but Rani made me feel easy and comfortable. Drunk on lust, I stripped off the wet vest and sat up, letting her see my naked torso for the first time.

Rani sighed, looking at me till the tension was too much, and I finally let her into my boxers.

She explored my body. Everything tingled where she touched it. Soon she had trails of her energy sparking rivers of lust all running straight between my legs. I let her have me, spelling out a dream state, hypnotic orgasm that crashed through me.

I came to to Rani's breathtakingly beautiful face beneath me, her hair spun out, a fine black net against the white of the pillow.

I yearned to stay, yet the pull of the moon far to the west warned me I couldn't. I wished I'd waited till my night off, when we could have met earlier and time wouldn't have run out at such an awkward moment.

"You worrying about something?" Rani asked softly.

"Yes," I admitted. "This is going to sound funny, but, um, I have to go." Rani's eyebrows raised, and I rushed on. "I have to be somewhere else at six o'clock. It's a work thing. It's been set up for ages, and it's really important."

"A work thing?"

"Yeah, it's sort of work, but it's for a mate. I can't let her down. I really can't." I was talking wildly now, telling half the truth and making the rest up.

"Oh. Well, if you have to go..." Rani pulled away.

"I do." I begged her to see the truth in my eyes. "I really do, and it's not about you. I want to see you again. It's not a one-night thing for me." And then I caught myself. "But of course, if that's all you want, that's okay too."

"Oh, you'd give up so easy would you?" She was amused. Good. Amused was much better than upset.

But I had to go. "I'll call you,"

She kissed me so sweetly, so deeply I felt one of the barriers around my heart lift and dissolve.

By the skin of my fangs, I was safely in the warm darkness of my room before dawn had fully broken. I didn't sleep straight away. I lay replaying the night's events. Feeling half in a dream, and half like I was replaying a dream. Surrounded by sweetness, I went off, chasing wherever the moon had gone to.

***

As soon as I woke, I had one of those startlingly clear moments when past, present, and future resonate into one crystal realization. I couldn't walk away from Rani. Even though she was human. I wanted to sleep with her again, and very soon, human sex wouldn't be enough. I'd want the real thing. A lot of vampires would have got out then, when they could. Being crazy and impetuous, I sent an e-mail to the Night Council. They are the vampires who decide the important things, including who is allowed to come into the Life. No one knows who the councilors are. Their identities are secret so that they can't be influenced. I knew I was getting way ahead of myself, but I had to test the water and see whether I could bring Rani into the Life, if she wanted to come in. I reasoned that these things take time; it was sensible of me to start the process. I figured the Council would just say I'd need to wait till I knew Rani better.

Someone had crept in while I slept and lit a fire in my loins. All I could think of was the tantalizingly beautiful woman who'd opened a floodgate I'd successfully battened down since Selena and I split. Who to ask for advice? Marce couldn't understand because I wouldn't be able to give her all the information. I sent off another e-mail, to my long-term friend and all-round drag queen extraordinaire, Jameel.

Help Jameel. Met a human. Fancy her so much I wanna bring her in.
Am I mad?
Rob xxx

I phoned Rani, got her answer machine, and left a message.

CHAPTER TWO

I work in the Babe Bar on Tuesdays. As I strolled down Compton Street, I thought about the e-mail from the Night Council.

Dear Rob Perdoni,

At a meeting of the Night Council, it was unanimously decided that you may proceed in the direction of bringing a mortal into the Life. You have been a vampire for the prerequisite number of years. Furthermore, you are considered an important and valuable member of the vampire community, suitable to act as a mentor.

Our concern is the short amount of time you have known the mortal in question. We suggest a meeting take place between yourself, the mortal, and Adjoa in order for Adjoa to form a second opinion on the suitability of the mortal for the vampire Life. Incidentally, Adjoa would be your point of contact should a transition take place.

Therefore you have permission to reveal who you are as a first step. Please advise us of the outcome immediately.

They Who Decide

I was glad Adjoa had been chosen as the inspector. She was absolutely ancient, the oldest vampire anyone knew. She'd helped me out in the past. and I trusted her. Adjoa was to casually drop into the bar.

I was nervous. It was kinda like taking the girlfriend home to meet the folks and hoping they would like her. Except Rani didn't know that's what was happening. I felt bad about that, but she couldn't know Adjoa was a vampire unless she came in.

Rani arrived an hour later than she said she would. I went mushy and incoherent on sight and made the most of the bar being quiet to enjoy the static crackling whenever we accidentally brushed against each other.

I looked suitably surprised when Adjoa arrived, and introduced her as an old friend. To my annoyance, Adjoa took Rani off to a small, intimate table in the corner of the room, making the excuse that all the people pressing up to the bar was getting on her nerves. I kept looking over and straining to hear the slightest snatch of conversation. They laughed a lot. Adjoa looked like she was searching the depths of Rani's soul. If so, it looked like she liked what she found. Adjoa was relaxed and absorbed in Rani. Rani was animated. She was even flirting with her a little.

I'd completed a large order and was trying to spy on Rani and Adjoa when a large crowd of dykes walked in, Maria in the middle of them. She came straight over.

"Hi, Rob. I've been hearing things about you." She whispered, "I heard you're seeing a mortal."

I hugged her, but said immediately, "You have to go, Maria."

Maria spotted Adjoa, and Rani sitting with her. "Is that her? She's a looker." Her eyes were taking in every inch of my mortal girlfriend's body.

Maria didn't have a vindictive bone in her body, but she did like gossip. I ran into her a lot because she hung out on the mortal lesbian scene.

"Maria, I don't know how you found out, and I don't want to know, but you have to go. Rani doesn't know about me yet, and I can't cope."

"Oh, Rob. Wanna talk about it?" she said, looking hopeful.

"Maria, go!" I said sternly.

She made me take a drinks order for all her friends before she slipped off. I was just thinking they couldn't possibly have anything left to talk about when Adjoa came over to say good-bye. I wanted to ask her how her daughter was, but it wasn't the time and place. Adjoa was very tight-lipped about her conversation with Rani.

When the bar closed, I asked Rani if she wanted to go anywhere like an all-night coffee place.

"I've got coffee at home," Rani said with a sultry smile.

That got us moving. I hoped Rani wouldn't be disappointed conversation was my main motive. She led me through the door, the front room, and would have kept walking to the bedroom if I hadn't pulled her back.

"I really would like to sit and talk with you a while."

"I see," she said. From the glint in her eye, I knew she didn't see at all.

"What would you like to talk about?" she said, sitting very close on the sofa.

"Oh, anything," I said vaguely, and then casually, "How about films? Have you seen *The Hunger*?"

"*The Hunger*?" She was studying my hands, playing with my fingers.

"Yeah. Do you know the film I mean?"

"*The Hunger*?" she repeated, bringing my fingers up to her mouth and brushing them with her lips. "The vampire film?"

"Yes." I beamed at her. "What did you think of it?"

"Very sexy." She was tonguing my fingers now.

"You thought it was sexy?"

"Oh, yes," she said absentmindedly, in between mouthfuls, as she inserted my fingers one after another and sucked.

"So...do...you...like the idea of lesbian...vampires?" I did try to keep the conversation going, even though I was getting distracted myself.

"Uh-huh." She slowly unbuttoned my shirt.

"And *The Hunger* turned you on?"

"Oh yeah, baby, it turned me on." This she said right into my eyes as she took her clothes off for me.

The sight of her naked body shut my mouth, but not for long. Rani climbed up on me, right there on the sofa, so that her legs were hanging over my shoulders and over the edge of the couch. I spoke to her very intimately, though I doubt she heard a word I said. Rani tasted as good as she looked, and she rode my mouth like a pro, coming delicately over my tongue while I separated her buttocks and fingered her cute behind. She worked me till I was exhausted, and any thoughts of revealing my true vampire identity were driven completely out of my mind.

***

Jameel's reply was short and to the point.

Time out, boifriend. ARE U SURE? Sorry to shout, but no easy way to say it. Glad to hear u met a woman though. Don't forget to send all gory details. If you're really sure just do it. My advice: if you like her don't lie to her. Don't pretend to be human. It's too hard to keep up. But be careful. Humans are unpredictable. Don't hassle her to come in. It's her choice, remember. All u can do is be true 2 who u.r. Maybe she'll end up hating u, maybe she'll join the club. No golden rules, sorry. Let me know. I'll be thinking about u. Call me late if u want.
Jameel :) xox

I frowned at the screen, feeling very alone. Why were my closest people so far away?
I sighed. Sometimes it wasn't easy being a bloodsucker. I would have to figure this out myself.

***

A few nights later, I met Rani on the South Bank and we went for a walk by the river. I wanted somewhere peaceful, and somewhere Rani couldn't distract me like she had so impressively the time before. We sat on a bench looking out to the darkness of the river, with the brightness of the light on the buildings opposite. Festoons, strung like necklaces between Dickensian lampposts, lifted the chill of the February night. I gathered all my courage into one deep, butch breath.
"You know what I was saying about lesbian vampires last night?"
"Vaguely." Shivering, Rani turned from the river view. "I wasn't really paying attention," she admitted, pulling her coat tighter around her.

"Yes, I know," I said. "What would you say, if I told you they really do exist?"

"Lesbian vampires?"

I nodded.

She smiled. "Why? Do you know some?"

"I might." I smiled back.

"Oh no! Don't tell me you're one!" Rani held her hands up in mock horror. I looked into her eyes.

"What is it you're trying to say?" she asked after a time.

I smiled my wolf smile at her but much wider than before, knowing my two sharpened incisors would stand out. It occurred to me maybe I should have some gold inlaid, just for that extra glint in moonlight. That would be really hot in vampire clubs. It's a worry how panic can force the most ridiculous thoughts into your head. Rani was staring at me, transfixed.

"W-what are those?" she finally asked.

"My teeth, I actually am a lesbian vampire."

There was a long silence.

"Why do you think you're a vampire?" she asked eventually.

Oh no. She'd gone down that road.

"What would it take for you to believe me?"

"Turn into a bat."

"I can't do that." I held her gaze. I searched for something I could work with, some willingness of Rani's to expand her present consciousness. Her eyes were completely flat.

"Well, I'm sorry you don't believe me," I said.

Rani creased her brow. "You really do believe you're a vampire."

I didn't know where to go with that. My courage failed me. "Look, it's getting late." I wanted to let it go. "Shall I walk you to your car?"

"Oh." She looked confused. "Okay."

Rani didn't ask any more questions. She just hugged me demurely, got in her car, and drove away.

I let her.

CHAPTER THREE

Rani stared out at the river and wondered why, of all the places to go for lunch in London, Gulsin had to want to come riverside. Rani glanced at her business partner. She and Gulsin went back a long way. They ran an Internet/mail order lingerie business together, which was doing very well. *At least I've got that to bury myself in.* The gentle winter sun was sparkling off the water in an uplifting way, making it seem a different place from the cold and moody river she'd been staring at a few nights ago. Rani didn't want to be reminded of that night—of Rob, and how she thought she was a vampire. She hadn't brought herself to tell Gulsin that chain of events. Gulsin was looking expectantly at her now, wanting details of new love, excitement, and passionate sex.

"Don't tell me you're cooling off already." Gulsin scooped up a mouthful of Thai green curry and scrutinized Rani's face for clues.

Rani pushed noodles around on her plate. "Maybe she's not what I thought she was."

Gulsin looked confused. "I have to ask, what did you think she was?"

Rani, usually so talkative, found herself reticent. "I just thought she was an ordinary butch."

Gulsin's eyebrows raised to the top of her head. "Well, what *is* she then? Superbutch?"

Rani's face softened.

"Are you sure you're not just getting cold feet because someone's getting close?"

Rani considered this but didn't comment.

"You know what you're like," Gulsin suggested. "Don't want anyone to get in the way of your independent life."

Rani thought she wouldn't mention the new butch had a vampire delusion. Perhaps she'd misunderstood anyway, and it was just some kind of biting fetish. In fact, the more she thought about it, maybe she had overreacted. Rani knew Gulsin was right about Rani backing off the minute someone got serious. So what if Rob thought vampires were erotic? Rani could deal with that.

CHAPTER FOUR

Time dragged lead heavy. Which was kinda how my heart felt. I cursed myself for getting involved with a mortal. I was sure Rani had either gone to the police or had written me off as crazy. We had invisibilized ourselves to the point where mortals refused to believe vampires even existed. It made me angry, but I understood why. No way did I want to return to the slaying times. I started looking into where I might move to in case it got messy. Ironically, the Night Council sent me a cheery e-mail saying that Adjoa had approved Rani to come into the Life.

Two weeks after I'd scared Rani off on the South Bank, she called saying she wanted to meet.

"Okay, where?" My eternally optimistic heart began a light tripping motion against my chest wall. My logical and suspicious brain tried to squelch it for my own protection.

"Your place," Rani said succinctly. "How about nine o'clock? It's your night off, isn't it?"

I didn't know what to do so I fussed around cleaning the flat from top to bottom. Then I started on myself—showering, spraying cologne, ironing clothes, polishing shoes. When my heart had started tripping, my loins had woken up from their short nap. If Rani hadn't decided I was crazy, she might want to sleep with me again. I had to be prepared.

When Rani arrived, she had a good look round the flat. She went through the kitchen with a fine tooth comb. I guessed she was trying to find some food. While she looked around, I feasted my eyes on Rani. Her cute and sexy body looked lonely to me, like it wanted company.

"Aren't you going to show me your bedroom?" Rani asked. I wondered if she went through everyone's cupboards like that.

"Well, yes. Come this way, madam."

I took her into the hallway and opened the far door.

"Oh." She took a deep breath, looking round the room, taking in the huge blond birch bed, the Indonesian limed desk, the built-in wardrobe stained pale green, the blackout blinds at the window—not black on the inside but ivory pink like the first wisps of sunrise. I'd tried to create space and light in a space that completely blocked out sunlight.

"It's not what I expected," Rani said finally.

"What did you expect?"

"A dungeon."

"A dungeon? Why would you think I'd have a dungeon?"

"Well, somewhere dark."

"It *is* dark. When you turn the lights out it gets very dark."

"Turn them out then." Rani walked over to the bed and stood provocatively, one hand on her hip.

I like to please a lady whenever I can. I flipped the switch.

"Ooh. You're right; it is *dark*." Rani's voice purred a warm shower of invitation. "Why don't you come on over here and show me how this bed works?"

We did it in the dark. My body ached for her, even though it had only been two weeks since I'd seen her. I had to get her into my system again. Rani's hands were all over me. She laid me out on the bed and licked the skin over my pecs, then she moved up and across my throat, nipping the skin gently between her teeth. When she started sucking, my body arched and I stopped worrying about what she thought about me. I slipped into a dimension where sex was the only thing that existed. In fact, I did it like I might never see her again. It made the sex poignant and sweet. I opened up to her, figuring what the hell? I let her all over and inside me, only flipping on top after she'd explored me good and proper on my back. She kept sucking on my neck and pumping hard till I exploded all over her fingers.

It was around one a.m. when Rani asked, "Can I stay the night?"

"You mean can you stay all day?"

"Oh yes, it would be all day. I mean, you sleep in the day don't you? What with your...night work." She couldn't bring herself to say it. "I mean," she rushed on, "I won't interrupt you. You can go to sleep, and I'll just be here next to you."

"Yeah, like I'm gonna get much sleep if you do."

She frowned. "But don't you just go into a trance or something?"

I shook my head. "No. Actually. It's the same as me lying beside you all *night*, in your bed. Just lying there. Beside you."

"Oh." She smiled shyly. "Well, do you want me to stay?"

I kissed her softly. "Yeah, I would like it. But I'm not feeling sleepy right now. It's the middle of the night." I realized that didn't make much sense to Rani. "So that's like the middle of the day for you."

"Oh! Well, I don't feel that sleepy. I'm sure we'll think of something to do."

Sex till sunrise. Dreamless sleep, an unfamiliar presence in my dark room, warm, loving sex, being held, falling and being lifted again.

My annoying alarm clock shattered our timeless state. I woke bleary-eyed from snatching sleep and hungry. It was six p.m. Breakfast time.

"I have to go out," I said.

"Why?" She snuggled up.

"I have to. I need to... I need to...drink." I paused. "I need to feed."

"Oh." Rani went quiet, thinking.

I couldn't ignore my body's need to take blood for long.

"You don't have to go out. *I'm* here." Rani looked at me, a little unsure but amazingly calm.

I was touched. "You're saying I could take your blood?"

"Well, that would be all right, wouldn't it?" she answered with a question.

"I'm not sure." There were no specific rules that said I couldn't do it, but I was sure that drinking Rani's blood wasn't what the Night Council meant when they told me to "reveal who I was."

"It's a very unselfish thing, what you're offering," I told her. "Giving me your blood. That's, well, that's precious."

Rani smiled lovingly. I smiled back and kissed her gently on the lips. She opened her mouth and kissed me back deeply. Then she lay back on the bed.

"Go on, then," she said quietly.

I kissed Rani's neck very softly, brushing the skin with my lips. She smelled good—musky, warm. I reached into her mind. She wasn't frightened. She was waiting for something. I read that she thought I was a mortal with a blood fetish, but there was a tiny part of her ready to believe I was a vampire. She was curious to know what it would be like to go with a vampire. I sucked hard on her neck without piercing the skin, feeling Rani respond. I knew for sure she wanted this, and I suddenly needed her very much.

Quickly and gently, I sliced a small puncture wound in Rani's neck and started taking her blood into my mouth. She gave a gasp that turned into a moan. I felt the rush of sexual pleasure going through her body and relaxed, relieved she was having a good time. I allowed myself to tune into my own body. Taking in Rani's blood had accelerated my heartbeat to fever tempo. I felt an intense wave flowing hot and swift through my arteries. It was like switching a switch; Rani's blood in me took my breath away. She was giving me life.

I called out and linked with her, knowing that was as much blood as I should take. I held Rani to my mind for a second before pulling back. She lay back, breathing heavy and still moaning while I stopped the wound with my fingers.

"Oh, that's nice. It tingles," Rani said, or tried to say between breaths. I got the gist of it.

"Yeah, it does feel nice, doesn't it? It's the energy from my fingers when I'm stopping the wound."

The tiny puncture was healed. I leaned back. Rani opened her eyes. They were shining. She was high. I'd forgotten how humans are affected when they give blood consciously.

"Oh my God, you really are a vampire." Rani's eyes grew round with astonishment.

"A bone fide card-carrying blood sucker," I said. "How you doing?"

"Oh fine. That was, um, I don't think I can find words for it. It was like having sex on drugs." She thought a moment. "But actually, it's really not like that at all. I've never felt anything like it."

"But it was a good thing? You don't regret it?"

"No, not for a second." Rani stroked my cheek with a silky finger. "Am I a vampire now then?"

"No." There were several raven black hairs lying across her face, I brushed them away. "If, and it's a big if, yeah? If you want to come into the Life, I have to take your blood three times and you have to take mine."

"I get to take yours?"

"Yes."

"I like the sound of that. You flat on your back and me taking you into my body."

I was shocked at how inside the experience Rani was, already focusing on taking my blood.

"Would I grow fangs?" She was playing with me.

"They do get a little bit longer, and you would have to learn to sharpen them. However, you won't turn into a bat, and I can promise you your eyes won't go red."

"That's a relief," she said. "The red eye part. Well, Count Dracula, now you have me in your castle, what *are* you going to do with me?"

"Rani, Dracula isn't a good name to toss around in front of vampires. He was a sick serial killer. He wasn't a vampire anyway, but if he had been we wouldn't be proud of him." I stopped, realizing I'd gone on a rant. "I'm sorry to spoil the moment," I said gently.

Rani cuddled up in my arms. "So what's all that about, that thing about vampires draining all the blood out of people?"

"Well, I'm glad to say that doesn't happen often."

"But it does happen?"

"I won't lie to you. It has happened. Vampires make mistakes, yeah? When they bring people into the Life. There's been situations when a murderer's been brought in. Or there's been other cases when a vampire you've known for centuries goes off the edge. Vampires have killed in anger or jealousy."

Rani nodded, understanding.

"But they've usually killed people they know, like a crime of passion."

"So what happens?"

"We deal with it," I said.

"What do you do?"

"Whatever we have to. Most things get sorted out without taking life, well, taking any more life. But if someone's out of control, and we can't help them, ultimately, we don't have any choice. A vampire that kills humans puts us all in danger. It's not a question of morals; it's a question of survival. And a vampire killing vampires, well, obviously that's a question of survival too. We do what we have to do."

"I see." Rani lay back on the bed, thinking.

I saw from the bedside clock sunset had been and gone. Rani could open the bedroom door now without endangering me. I remembered how important it is for humans to be alone after giving blood for the first time. I suggested this to Rani.

"*You* want to be alone," she said.

"No. I want you to be sure, that's all." I took her hand. "If you do come into the Life, I don't want you having regrets three months down the line. Suddenly getting frightened of what you've done and blaming it all on me. Telling me how I put you in a trance or something, throwing every stereotype you ever saw in a vampire film at me. Believe me, I've seen it happen. I think you should take some time to think about if you want to change your mortality."

Rani considered what I'd said. Then, without speaking, she got her things together, kissed me, and left. Before she was out the door, I called to her, "Hey, Rani, you can turn back from here, remember that."

***

Two nights went by. I didn't hear from her and didn't call. Rani had to make the decision on her own. On the third morning, I went to bed and fell into a deep sleep. I was in a garden with Rani. She kissed me on the mouth and then kissed my neck. She started sucking my neck, I felt like she was pulling energy from me without piercing the skin. Running water was very loud in my ears…very loud. It sounded like someone knocking on a door.

It was someone knocking on a door. And not the street door either, my bedroom door. I woke with a start.

"Rob, wake up." It was Rani.

"Okay, okay," I shouted. At the door, I checked. "Are all the curtains drawn in that room?"

"Yes," Rani confirmed.

"When I open this door, you come in really fast. Don't muck about. It's very dangerous for me."

"Okay."

She did come through fast, almost knocking me out of the way. I shut the door behind her.

"How the hell did you get into my flat?"

"Don't ask. I got into some stuff when I was sixteen, learned things. I could have got through to your bedroom." Rani looked pleased with herself, but there was something wired about her.

I crumpled back on the bed. I was angry, and scared—not about Rani getting into the flat, about her being able to creep up on me in my sleep. Only another vampire lover could do that. I was worried I'd underestimated her, badly.

"You're worried I'm reckless, aren't you?" she said.

Oh God, was she reading minds now, or just intuitive?

Without waiting for an answer, Rani changed the subject. "I want to do it again."

All saliva left my throat. Any moisture of any kind was swiftly diverted in the direction of my shorts. Rani took off her coat and bent her head back, showing her neck. I could see the artery pulsing where her skin was stretched tight.

"Now listen, Rani." By some super vampire effort, I forced myself to stay focused. This was no light matter. "Come sit here." I patted the bed. "Not too close," I pleaded. I could smell the heat coming off her, the musk, the blood smell. "Rani, I haven't heard from you for two nights. Are you sure you want to do this?"

Rani leaned across and licked my neck.

"Rani, this is important." I made myself pull back. "I need to hear you say it."

She held my gaze. I felt a flicker of energy from her, almost like she was searching me. But that wasn't possible. It was way too early for that. Rani sighed.

"Okay, Rob, yes I do want this. I want you to suck my neck again, drink my blood, just like you did last time."

I searched inside and saw Rani was ready. She'd made her

decision.

Rani tilted her head back again.

This time, I didn't hesitate and went straight for the jugular, the vampire equivalent of wham bam, thank you, ma'am. Rani's body instantly and completely relaxed as I held her and bit into her neck. I felt an orgasm bolt through her and then ricochet through me.

I carried on drinking her, feeling like I had carried her somewhere up above the earth and was holding her in my arms, her body floating at my waist. There was the sense of eternal peace, with each moment as measured as a heartbeat. Rani fed me with every precious drop of life I took from her. She was giving me life. I was offering Rani immortality.

After I sealed her wound, I asked gently if she was okay.

"Oh yes," she whispered, holding on to me while she caught her breath. As Rani's blood raced through mine, I felt bubbles of her energy bursting through my bloodstream, like champagne might feel coursing through the system.

"When do I get to do you?" Rani broke the silence spectacularly.

I took a breath, thinking.

"I want to take your blood. Now," she said. Just like that.

I was concerned. You usually gave blood on the third time.

Is there any reason I can't do it now? She asked me *inside* my head.

I froze. I had never heard of anyone reaching inside someone's mind *before* they'd taken vampire blood

"Is there any reason I can't do it now?" Rani repeated, aloud.

I searched her eyes. "It's traditional on the third time."

"Is there a reason I should wait?" Her energy was strong. I was sure I could feel Rani's heart beating in time with mine. I heard a low, distant pulse at Rani's jugular. Already, I was getting a sense of her bloodstream. What should I do? I felt overwhelmed with responsibility.

"I have made up my mind," Rani said after a few moments. "Why don't you let me decide?"

I stared at her for a long, hard moment. Then I shrugged. "Okay I'll have to make a cut for you." I got my silver knife from the desk. "Just suck. I'll tell you when it's enough."

"Okay" Her eyes were shining; she looked excited and a little like she was going to laugh. I guessed she was nervous. I made a tiny cut in my neck and lay down.

"Whoa!" I called out as a rush of sensation hit me.

"Do you want me to stop?" Rani lifted her mouth.

"No." I laughed. "It was just more powerful than I was expecting."

"I'll try and be gentle with you," she joked.

She put her lips on me again, and I was pulled into her. I shivered as the blood was sucked from me. The release of giving, the delicious ache of exchanging blood took my breath, wiped my consciousness, and stole me clean away. I came several times in a physical sense. Giving blood is physical and emotional for me. It feels like a cocktail of chemicals sweeping my body clean.

When it was enough, I gently pushed her lips from my neck. I pressed my fingers to the wound since Rani didn't have the ability to heal yet. We slept then, curled up into each other.

I woke as Rani was stirring. She stretched, got up, and lifted the blind. I heard her thinking. *So different at night. So quiet.*

Lovely, isn't it? I thought back to her.

Rani jumped. And then she smiled. She looked at herself in the mirror.

"Am I a vampire *now*?" she asked.

"I don't know." I looked at her complexion like I was really studying it. "Well, you're not really, really pale so you can't be," I joked.

"Will I go pale?" Rani said, immediately concerned.

"Only if you don't feed," I explained. "But you'll never go really light, like those white actresses in the films. You'd just look anemic."

She looked relieved.

"But am I?"

"Are you vampire? Yes, I suppose so. It's not usual. Usually, any exchange happens on the third time. I've never known it to happen on the second."

"So what does that mean?" Rani asked.

"It means you've got to have the final exchange," I replied, trying to sound confident and like I knew what I was doing. "It will make you complete."

"No turning back?" she asked, suddenly serious.

"No turning back,"

"Wouldn't want to if I could."

The next time, we took less of each other's blood. I wasn't sure how much we should take, as I hadn't done it like that before. She started touching me while I was drinking from her. It was all new to Rani, and yet she kept taking the lead. She slipped her fingers inside me while I was linked to her mind. I was to-ing and fro-ing, first swept along with the chemicals in a trippy way as our blood mixed. Then I was brought back by a flush of physical sensation as Rani slid in and out of me, lost in the beautiful, mortal purity of letting myself feel.

I found Rani wet and wide open when she drank from me. She moved slowly over me, sometimes holding the moment. Stopping and looking deep into my eyes. Coming was a very small part of the exchange. Getting there and coming down from there were so much more important.

Later, Rani slept. I was in a drugged state, slow and dreamy but not capable of sleep. Feeling restless, I was drawn to check my e-mails.

Welcome Rani.

Glad to have you with us. About time we had some new blood! Hope to meet you soon.

Rob, well done.

My love, Selena. Xxx

As night fell and the moon began to rise, I drew the blinds and watched Rani sleeping. I was looking for any sickness or shaking. There were no signs, but she looked pale. Without waking her, I carried Rani in front of the window, and sat with her in my arms, letting the moon warm her new vampire blood stream.

Rani woke an hour later and stared out the window at the crescent of pale yellow still hanging low in the sky.

"It's going to be a lovely day," she murmured.

I gazed at Rani's beautiful face bathed in moonlight. "Night," I corrected her softly.

CHAPTER FIVE

Rani frowned at the whiteboard. She was sure it was all very important to Rob, but why she had to keep going over it now when she had the rest of her life to learn it, she had no idea. Rob was pointing at three words written at the top of the board: The Night Council.

"The Night Council," Rani read aloud.

Rob nodded in an encouraging way.

"No one knows who they are. They make all the important decisions. They're like the government, I suppose, are they?"

Rob screwed her face up. "Sort of."

Rani tapped her fingers on Rob's kitchen table. She stared at the next line written up. "Justices are like judges?"

"Yes." Rob beamed. "And they're the jury too. They're like magistrates and judges combined."

"What about lawyers?"

"They're called representatives."

"Then there's the guardians." Rani waved her hands about demonstrating. "They're like police. And you've got enforcers. They're executioners."

"Correct." Rob clapped her hands together.

"Executioners, Rob? You can't be for real?" Rani was half-convinced Rob was making all this up.

Rob ignored the question. She went through to the living room and started lighting candles. There was a huge candelabrum on the side unit and several smaller ones placed all around the room. When Rob turned the lights out, a warm hush descended.

Rani got up from the kitchen table and walked through to stand in front of Rob. The pale walls were glowing apricot in the candlelight. Rani studied the little parchment card in her hand and felt the seriousness of the moment. She took a breath and read.

I, Rani Shah, am a new vampire embracing the Life
I swear:
I shalt harm neither mortal nor vampire.
I shalt keep my council concerning the business of vampires and reveal the Life to no mortals, nor will I reveal I am in the Life, save where I have express permission to do so.
I shalt engage in no activity that may endanger the quiet existence of vampires alongside the human world.
And I shalt adhere to the decisions of the Night Council.
I, Rani Shah, on this day, the 15th March 2000, accept the code I have sworn and may justly demand acceptance from vampires from this day forth wheresoever I may travel until eternity.

Rob's eyes glowed; she held in them a moment outside of time. "Rani Shah." Her voice was formal, laced with a sweetness that dissolved on the inside of Rani's skin. "Welcome to the Life."

Chapter Six

Jameel smiled as Carlos stood and blew him a kiss. Admittedly, it was more of a pout than a wave-me-off, bon voyage of a kiss. It looked good on him all the same. "You won't change your mind, bonito?" Carlos's boyfriend Juan asked. "Maybe there are many men just waiting to meet you at the club."

Jameel declined. "Not tonight, amigo."

"Let me settle the tab," Juan said. Carlos looked discreetly away as if money was too insensitive a subject for him to discuss.

"No, no. I've got this one," Jameel said firmly. Juan shrugged, kissed Jameel on both cheeks, and they walked off across La Plaza San Nicolas. Juan's black leather shoes tapped softly on the intricately cobbled square.

Jameel let his whisky slip over his tongue while he scanned the tables outside the bar. *So many beautiful Spanish men, and the nights getting shorter with summer on the way.* The sharp malt of the whisky, the pungent smoke of tobacco negro cigarettes, the salt of plump pink prawns fried in their shells. Jameel drank in the scent of the bar and felt excitement course through him as he enjoyed the smells that made Granada Granada.

The outside tables were busier now that the nights were losing their characteristic winter coldness. The geraniums in blue and green pots set out on the iron balcony above the bar were coming into bloom. Recorded flamenco drifted out from inside. A woman's voice spun notes into a melodic cry that pulled at Jameel's sensitive soul. As the tune hit a crescendo of guitar and handclapping, Jameel felt an answering need to get up and explore the shadows of this Andulucian night. He waved an arm at the handsome bartender, who came over immediately.

"My bill, please." Jameel smiled up at him.

"Your bill is all paid, señor."

Jameel was surprised. He thought for a moment, then said, "Oh, that naughty Juan. When did he come to pay you?"

The bartender smiled at the idea of a *naughty* Juan, but shook his head. "No, no, señor, it was not Juan. It was another señor who paid me."

Jameel curled one eyebrow, delighted with the intrigue. He bent closer to the deliciously rugged barman. "Is he here?" he asked quietly.

The barman looked indiscreetly around the tables and bar. "No señor." He shrugged. "He must have gone."

"Oh." Jameel reluctantly leaned away from the barman. "What did he look like?" The bartender glanced at the bar where several men were waiting to be served.

"I'm sorry, señor. He was just a typical man, you know."

Jameel smiled. He liked to think he knew. "Okay. I'm sorry to keep you. Thank you." Jameel drained the last of the whisky from his glass and stood, glancing at the streets off the square.

Maybe his mysterious benefactor was waiting for him somewhere. Somewhere quieter. The night was suddenly full of promise. He walked toward the side street. Toward the long, sleeping shadows.

CHAPTER SEVEN

As the rain turned to light drizzle, I saw Rani come up. She steadied the middle-aged man while she wiped her mouth delicately on a tissue. Her physical strength was increasing. I took a deep breath, drawing in the sharp scent of oak, the lighter tang of birch, and the dark smell of earth rising from the brown leaf bed beneath my feet. The smells of the night forest invigorated me, stirring my senses.

The man's dog waited patiently. I appreciated his love and loyalty. He sensed no threat to his master. He was waiting for him to wake up and carry on with their walk. Rani sat the guy against a sturdy old oak tree, and the dog nuzzled up to him, resting his nose on his master's lap.

I felt Rani's energy as she came toward me. I smelled the blood on her. She was smiling into the night, maybe at me, maybe at herself. She was flushed, and her eyes were shining.

"C'mon." As soon as she stepped up to me, she grabbed my hand and pulled me farther into the forest. Behind a row of silver birches, she stopped, looking in the direction of the dog walker and listening. I was pleased she was checking the safety of the guy who'd just given her lifeblood. For me, it's a matter of principle, and I felt a rush of warmth that Rani had the same concern. I heard a far off rustle and a scamper as the dog got to continue his walk.

With a quick glance at me, Rani turned again, still holding my hand, and set off almost at a run. Wet branches brushed my face and bracken tugged at my boots, but I followed her anyway. The smell of the new blood flowing in her veins pulled my pulse to hers like a magnet.

I slowed. My throat was dry and my heart beating fast. Not from the run, from lust. She turned. "Can't keep up, huh?" She teased me, her tongue on the tip of her front tooth, then circling her left incisor.

"Yeah, I can keep up," I shot back "But I'm hungry…"

Rani's eyes locked into mine, and I felt my head start to go back, my neck come up. With some effort, I straightened up. Rani was smiling, pleased with herself. She was so beautiful she took my breath away. The rain had stopped, but the branches above us dropped tiny drips of rainwater. The warmth of our body heat and our vampire energy seemed to turn the drops of rain into steam. Rani stood in front of me, her long hair glistening, her eyes glowing in the misty light.

"Can I?" I asked.

She waited. She wanted me to ask.

"Can I share with you, Rani?"

She took my hand, this time placing it on her neck. I stroked the line of her collarbone and then put a finger on her jugular pulse. She surged under my fingertip. As the drizzle fell once more, I bent my mouth to her neck and took her inside me, our blood flowing and mixing.

I drifted, lost in the scent of rain and earth, the rhythmic, steady drip of raindrops falling from the wet leaves above our heads and Rani thundering through my veins.

Satiated, I couldn't help but grin. Clouds scudded across the sky above, throwing us in and out of dappled moonlight. We had shared blood in a small glade. A large oak tree had been uprooted at some time in the past, and now it sprawled across the forest floor. I took off my leather jacket and covered the damp bark. Rani sat beside me.

"I enjoyed that," she said.

"It's a big night, Rani. First blood."

"So how did I do?" Rani squeezed my leg.

"You did good, girl. You dealt with it well. You can go out on your own now."

Rani looked pleased with herself. She had good reason to be. I had been around, in case she got into trouble, but she hadn't needed me. The first time a vampire feeds alone is called first blood, and Rani had passed with flying colors.

"Did I do better than any of the others?" Rani's voice was teasing, but there was seriousness in it too.

"What others?" I asked.

"The others you've brought into the Life."

I was still thinking about what a big night it was for Rani, and how we would celebrate it.

"How many have you brought in, anyway?" Rani asked after a minute.

I didn't want to get into that. "Um, one," I told her. "You."

"Oh," Rani said with surprise. "Oh," she said again, sounding disappointed.

"Wait here." I jumped to my feet. "This is a big night. I've got something in the car for you."

I walked back to where we'd parked the car, priding myself on moving as silently as any of the nocturnal wood creatures. Epping Forest had become a regular haunt of mine since my return to London.

Tucked away in the boot of the car was a cool box. I opened it and grabbed the perfectly chilled Laurent-Perrier and two chilled champagne flutes.

I crept onto the clearing as quietly as I could, hoping to surprise Rani, but the glade was empty. I put the champagne by the fallen tree. The clouds had moved on, leaving a clear sky for the plump, waxing moon to perform from. In the bright light, my jacket was still lying across the bark of our makeshift seat. I looked around the glade, searching the perimeter of birch and beech trees. Silver birch bark reflected moonlight into the shadows.

I sensed Rani was amongst the trees somewhere, but I couldn't see exactly where. So she wanted to play hide and seek, did she?

I started moving silently through the birches. I pulled back branches and peered into holly bushes, but there was no sign of her. Hearing a rustle in the undergrowth, I went to investigate.

I followed the noise farther along a thin trail until it went very quiet just in front of a tangle of blackberry bushes. I was working out how to walk into them without getting torn to pieces when something very cold, very slimy went down my back.

I leapt round with a cry, pulling soggy leaves out of my

shirt.

"Right, you've had it!" I shouted at Rani who was doubled up with laughter. She screamed and ran off as I charged toward her. I was gaining on her and could hear her giggling, but that just spurred me on.

I caught up to her in front of a large oak tree. She turned to face me, crying with laughter, and breathless.

"I was just practicing creeping about," she said, leaning against the tree. "You know I have to practice. I'm amazed I managed to creep up behind you."

I should have put soggy leaves all over her, but what could I do when she was being so beguiling? I found her soft lips, explored her warm, wet mouth. She opened up to me instantly, and I was suddenly crazy for her again. She was like a drug. I opened her jacket and pushed her top up, quickly unhooking her bra one-handed so that her breasts got to feel the cool night breeze.

I felt the moan in her throat, and that spurred me on to push up her skirt and slide my hand up her leg. That's when I discovered my gorgeous, lingerie-selling girlfriend was completely knickerless.

I pressed my leg between hers and started to bite into her neck. I couldn't take a lot of blood this time, so I made sure she had plenty of physical sensation, giving her my thumb to ride from behind. I supported her with my other hand and lifted her completely off the ground, resting her legs around my waist. I got her pushed up against the handy oak tree, letting it take some of her weight and giving me more room to maneuver.

Rani started calling out, a long series of ahhs, that punctuated the forest hum beautifully. She moved on me like a martial arts expert, graceful, strong, and ethereal. I valiantly kept lifting her up and down and sucking until she sang out one sweet, long, melodic note that cut through the still night air sending a flutter of wings upward and a rustle through the forest floor.

We found our way back to the champagne eventually. Rani sat on my jacket, and I sat beside her. The moon was hot. She had spread out, seeming to take the space of the whole sky for herself.

"I haven't forgotten that I'm the only one you've brought

out," Rani said, her glass held out expectantly. I was fumbling with the wire closure of the bottle. I turned to her to see she had taken her top off completely. Her body was beautiful bathed in moonlight; the silver blue light flattered Rani's complexion.

"In. Brought *in*," I said and popped the cork. The champagne flowed over both glasses and ran sticky rivulets down Rani's bare legs and my trousers. We locked eyes as we drank, and Rani put a hand on my wet patch.

"Champagne on your trousers, or are you just pleased to see me?" she breathed into my lips and came in for a champagne kiss. "More please." She had pulled away and was now thrusting her empty glass toward me.

The moonlight energized and invigorated me. It was April, over a month since Rani came into the Life, and the full moon nights were starting to feel warm again.

"Why am I the only one you've brought in?" Rani's voice was slightly slurred, as if she were talking in her sleep.

I sighed and opened my eyes. "Well, for a start, you have to be fifty years of age before you can bring anyone in."

"What does that mean?" Rani snapped her eyes open and sat up. She always sounded impatient when I said something about the Life she didn't understand. I felt relaxed. And horny. I didn't feel like giving a history lesson. I knew Rani needed answers, but the night was so laid back.

I snuck a look at her. She was waiting expectantly.

"You can't make a mortal into a vampire before you have been a vampire yourself for at least fifty years," I explained as clearly as I could.

"But you've been a vampire for eighty years," Rani said.

"Sure." I sighed. "I never wanted to bring anyone in, till I met you." I looked up at the moon.

"Oh." Rani smiled. Her hand found mine, and she stroked my skin lightly, very softly. "So you didn't meet anyone in the last thirty years?"

I studied her, amused, wondering what it was exactly she wanted to know.

"But I don't get to know many mortals. Not really well." Uh-oh. Rani looked pissed off now. "Look, what I mean is, I don't get close to many mortals. I can't tell them what I am. Can I?"

Rani stared at me, listening hard now.

"You know what I mean. You're going through this right now."

Rani flinched.

"It's a serious thing coming into the Life. It's *very* serious bringing someone in..." I trailed off, unwilling to drag us both down.

A slight breeze stirred the air. The moon was high in the sky and gloriously warm.

"Oh, you're such a worrier!" Rani looked at me, laughing. "If you're going to get this serious every time I have a few doubts, I don't know if I'll tell you about them."

"So there's nothing bothering you?" I asked.

Rani pulled me down to the forest floor and poured the last dribble of champagne into my mouth.

"Don't you think you'd know?" she said, so close her nose brushed mine, before her tongue searched between my lips and began stealing the wine back, drop by drop

CHAPTER EIGHT

Jameel pushed open the door of his little house in Albiacín, invigorated from his nightly feed. He had fed down in Granada town. A sweet man had *donated blood*, as Jameel liked to think of it, in a quiet street near the bus station. Jameel licked his lips. He had been very tasty. Like Rob, Jameel preferred to feed from men. And, of course, he grinned to himself. There were so many more men on the streets at night than women. Selena would probably give him a lesson in feminism if he dared to mention that to her. But she wasn't around.

Jameel had enjoyed the walk back up to the old Moorish quarter of Albiacín. Now he strolled along steep, narrow streets. Pale golden light filtered softly down from black iron lanterns, attached to the rough-hewn walls of houses each side of the street. Spring was in the air, and spring came very sweetly to southern Spain. Jasmine was starting to bloom; the cicadas were clicking more joyfully.

The sound of crickets always reminded him of the little village in Bengal where he had grown up. Two hundred years had passed since he'd had to leave. Jameel had been fifteen, a poor farmer on a tiny plot of land. That year the crop had failed, and Jameel couldn't pay the tax. A tax collector, in Jameel's language a *zaminder*, hadn't been very understanding. In fact, he had beaten Jameel and left him near death. The *zaminder* would himself have been beaten if he hadn't done anything. That was the way the system worked.

Jameel had been found by a vampire who took pity on him

and nursed him back to health. The vampire had been passing through Bengal and offered to take Jameel with him, traveling. Jameel had agreed, hoping to make his fortune. Later, the same vampire had brought Jameel into the Life, and during the first twenty years, Jameel did make his fortune through clever trading in spices to the West.

As Jameel closed his front door, he sensed immediately there was something different about the house. He lived alone, yet he was sure someone had been there while he had been down in the town. Jameel looked carefully around, his acute senses warning him something was out of place.

Propped up on the windowsill was a postcard of Albiacín. Jameel walked over to it. It was one of the hundreds in stands outside tobacconists all over Granada. This one showed Mirador San Nicolas, a place Jameel often visited to sit in bars with friends. He turned the postcard over. A block handwriting Jameel didn't recognize read in English: *Meet me at Plaza Larga at 5 a.m. Perhaps we can see the sunrise together.*

Jameel shivered at the thought of the sun, but he felt relief. This person didn't know he was a vampire. Whoever it was did know he spoke English though and knew he went out at night. Jameel studied the card, his eye flicking to a tiny drawing of Cupid in the bottom left corner, Cupid complete with bow and arrow and looking quite camp, Jameel thought. He smiled to himself. *Looks like I've got an admirer. How interesting.*

He looked at his watch. *Three a.m. Two hours to kill*

***

Rani felt an unreasonable anger. It growled in her belly and jarred with every movement. She stood outside her flat on Albion Road willing herself to go in. Inside was her old life, a life that had changed so completely she could never go back. The thought of going inside filled her with rage, and fear. Searching for a meal, she had drifted from Rob's flat in Wood Green to her flat in Stoke Newington. *To do what? To stand outside in the rain, apparently.* She looked up at the first floor flat and almost yearned to be inside, leaning out the window looking down. Almost.

She'd last been to her flat a week ago. That had been one

week after her first blood, and she'd still been a bit high from it. When she had walked into her flat, she had been greeted by piles of letters on the floor, stacks of e-mails and endless voice mail messages. She knew there would be more messages inside. Gulsin, her business partner, had been leaving messages on her mobile all week. Rani hadn't told Gulsin about her change of circumstances, just said she was involved with another project during the day. So far, Gulsin hadn't asked too many questions, but Rani dreaded the day she started to.

She couldn't face any of that. Angry at herself, Rani got into her black Ka. Buying a tiny, parkable car had seemed a responsible thing to do a year ago. Now, as she floored the accelerator, she wanted to trade it in for a Mazda MX5.

Rani made it back to Wood Green in twenty minutes. Driving at speed had eased the restlessness inside her, but she couldn't shake her feeling of irritation. It felt like PMT— something she'd never feel again. For some reason, that annoyed her too. It was just another thing she'd lost. And losing her period *was* something she missed. *How ridiculous for vampires not to get periods.* It cut through her realizing she would never give birth. She didn't remember agreeing not to have children.

She parked up, then prowled outside Rob's flat. Now she was here, the thought of going inside made her feel trapped. *Seems I have an obsession for the outside of houses tonight.* The rain was driving down hard, and it was less than an hour till sunup, but still she hesitated. She didn't want to *have* to go in. She was used to being able to come and go as she pleased, night or day.

There was no moon in the sky. It was new moon time or, as Rani preferred to think of it tonight, dark moon time. Rani surveyed the impenetrable clouds above her for the glimmer of stars. There was nothing but sheets of rain pouring from a swirling, black ocean.

By the time her hair was plastered to her head and her mascara run clean from her lashes, she'd had enough. She let herself in the communal door, slipping the Yale lock with her credit card—for her own amusement, seeing as she had a full set of keys in her pocket. As she mounted the stairs, a throbbing pain started in her jaw. Her incisors were hurting again. Rob had insisted this was normal and that she definitely didn't want to go to the dentist about it. Rani reached Rob's flat door and was digging for her keys when, out of habit, she pushed the door. It opened inward; Rob had left it on the latch again. Rani tutted.

A haze of smoke filled the normally fresh, light living room. Rob was lying stretched out on the sofa puffing on a long spliff. Rob didn't smoke much. She disliked the smell and taste of tobacco. It seemed tonight was different.

"What happened to you?" Rob asked bluntly.

Rani took perverse pleasure in knowing she must look awful. All the same, she resolved to check how she looked in the mirror at an early opportunity.

"Got caught in the rain," she said blithely, shaking off her jacket, actually Rob's leather jacket, and throwing it over a chair.

"Drink, darling?" Rob got up, passing her the spliff, and stood attentively waiting for her answer.

Rani nodded, and Rob went to the kitchen.

"Red wine?" she called out.

"Yes, please," Rani said from the bathroom. She checked her appearance, shuddered, and began reapplying. Rob was in a good mood. Rani could hear her whistling. A fact Rani found annoying. Rob didn't seem at all concerned that it was nearly sunrise before Rani came home.

Rani tossed her lipstick in the direction of her makeup case. She grimaced, exposing her painful incisors. They did seem a little longer. Rani stared at herself for a moment. She wasn't sure if fangs suited her or not. Oh well, too bad if they didn't.

"So did you have a good night?" Rob called out from the front room. Rani flinched at the intrusion into her private scrutiny.

"Um-hum," she muttered, knowing full well Rob wouldn't hear. She sighed and went into the other room. Rob was holding out a glass of wine to her. Rani took the glass and then walked to the window. Thankfully, the blind hadn't been drawn yet. She opened the window a fraction, just to get a little fresh air into the room.

Rob watched her, putting out the spliff. "So what did you

do?" she asked.

Rani answered with her back to Rob, scanning the sky for any signs of sunrise. "Had a meal. Went to my flat." Rani was about to tell Rob how she'd gone there and couldn't go in, but Rob started talking.

"I'm glad you brought that up. I've been thinking; it's about time we sorted your place out. It's really not that hard. I know someone who'll do all the work."

Rani turned round. "What are you talking about?"

Rob walked toward her, wrinkling her handsome brow as she tried to work Rani's mood out. She gently leaned past Rani, opened the window further, pulled in and fastened the shutters, closed the window, pulled down the roller blind, and Velcroed it light-tight.

Rani grimaced and strode to the front door, fastening all the locks and putting the screen in place. Rob followed her. "I'm talking about doing all this kind of thing to your flat, making it safe for you to stay there."

"Oh, I see," said Rani dangerously, anger rising in her the way a hot spring rises swiftly through earth. Rob took a step backward. Then, saying nothing, she walked to the kitchen and poured herself another glass of wine. Rob wouldn't provoke Rani. As far as she was concerned, Rani was in a bad mood and should be left alone. To Rani, this was like lighting the blue touch paper and retiring. Rob's smoldering passion, her ability to hold everything in until she exploded, was as irresistible to Rani in bed as it was provoking in an argument.

"So you want me to move out!" Rani strode up to the sofa, forcing Rob to sit down to get out of her way.

"Well, yes, "Rob said with forced evenness. "It is a bit *cramped* in here. What's the matter? Don't you want your own space? I know I do." The last she half-muttered under her breath.

Rani walked away. She felt so trapped she wanted to scream. Yet the thought of Rob pushing her out made her crazy. "Yes, I do want my own space!" Rani shouted.

"Good then, that's good, because that's what we both want then." Rob looked and sounded like she was dealing with a mad woman.

Rani glowered. Let her think she was crazy. Rob obviously

didn't remember what it felt like—knowing she was different from her friends and family, not being able to be honest with them. Maybe Rob didn't know many mortals, but Rani did. Her whole life up to now had been mortals. And they were already asking questions. Rani's flat was overflowing with messages, e-mails, letters, all wanting an answer. It annoyed her, and it hurt. It hurt as bad as her bloody teeth were hurting.

"I know someone, someone in the Life, who can sort your flat out for you if you like," Rob said quietly.

"Oh, you would!" Rani screamed.

Rob looked truly shocked. So shocked Rani's anger left her as quickly as it had risen, leaving her feeling like a deflated balloon. "I'm sorry," she muttered. She sat next to Rob. "I can't bear to be in my flat. There's a message from nearly everyone I know…all the humans, I mean." She stole a glance at Rob. "I don't know what to say to them." Rani leaned back against the sofa, feeling sad.

Rob put her arm around Rani and held her close. "It'll get easier, honey," she said. She gently stroked Rani's hair away from her face. "We'll work it out together."

Rani let herself be held. Rob's breath in her hair was warm, soft, and felt a lot like coming home. She knew Rob couldn't solve all her problems for her, but she wanted to believe it wouldn't always feel like this. This knife-edge pain lodged deep in her heart.

***

Rani wanted to see the old estate in Bow, so she took a slight detour on the way to her mum and dad's house. She drove in and stared at the 1930s five-story series of blocks built to form a square, split into two rectangles by another long block in the middle. Red brick walls, white casement windows, and the classic uniform council door spaced at regular intervals, punctuated the long walkways.

Once you entered the estate, it surrounded you. Rani felt a curious mixture of bitterness and nostalgia. She noticed many of the windows and doors now had hard, black iron bars in front of them. Rani guessed to try to prevent being broken into—so easy with the walkways giving access and the way no one ever seemed to notice anything.

The Shah family moved out eight years ago. Rani, with her college education and articulate politics, together with her father's proud determination, had meant the Shahs were at long last, impossible to placate and ignore. They got a housing association house three streets away. Shoba Shah, Rani's mother, finally got the garden she'd always wanted.

Ahmed, Rani's father, had tried to get someone to listen to him for years, standing before the estate manager painstakingly detailing the harassment. Rani remembered the hardness of the plastic seat beneath her, the harshness of the estate manager's eyes, and the strong, straight back of her father as he patiently read details from a little red notebook.

The Shahs and three other families were dark islands in a sea of white. A dedicated few of the watery Londoners made it their mission to agitate the Southeast Asian and Caribbean families on the estate. These unfortunates were afflicted with the disease of racism—a hereditary disease, passed down from parents to their children. It manifested as taunts and name-calling, various objects shoved through the Shahs' letterbox, the occasional smashed window, and complaints about the smell of spices—this from families who regularly filled the walkways with the stinking, pungent smell of boiled cabbage.

It could have put her off white people for life, Rani reflected. And here she was going out with an eighty-year-old Italian. *Life is strange.*

She noticed a shimmering pile of smashed car window glass and was transported to her seven-year-old self. The little girl who thought the constant glinting of glass in the streetlight was like frost on a country road. She'd imagined that every night the estate became a magical wintry landscape, and that a wonderful, beautiful but icy Snow Queen visited. Of course, every morning it changed back, except sometimes pockets of frost remained. One late afternoon as her mother had tended her window boxes, Rani had told her what happened when they were all asleep.

"That's wonderful, beti," her mother had said. "Never shut down that part of yourself, that part that sees beauty in everything."

Rani pulled her coat tighter around herself, turned the

ignition, and drove out of the estate.

Two doors away from her mum and dad's house, they were having a wedding. An arch, placed on the front path, bloomed with flowers and fairy lights.

Rani rang her parents' doorbell. Minutes later, her mother appeared at the front room window, her face lighting up when she saw it was Rani. "Oh, Rani, beti, I am so happy to see you." When the door opened, Rani's mother held her close for several long, warm minutes, then she pushed her gently away so she could inspect her. Luckily, she smiled and nodded approval. "I like that salwar kameez." Her mother rubbed Rani's silk sleeve between her finger and thumb, reminding herself of the quality of the fabric. "We bought that suit on Green Street didn't we? I thought it was too expensive. Designer Punjabi suits—really!" her mother threw over her shoulder as Rani followed her to the kitchen.

"Where is Pita?" Rani looked around the sparkling kitchen for her father.

"He's working the late shift. I don't mind so much. It's good money."

"Oh." Rani was disappointed. "I wanted to ask him something about my computer."

Rani's mother sat at the kitchen table. "Oh yes, he's an expert at computers now. Once, it was enough to be a good telephone engineer, but now he must keep going on these training courses. He's too old for training."

Rani laughed. "He's not, Ma!" she protested. Rani didn't understand why her mother, a woman in her late forties, insisted on describing herself and Rani's father as if they were old.

"Some sindhi gosht, beti?" Rani's mother was up and heading for the stove.

"Oh no, Mum, I'm...I'm not eating meat."

Her mother turned, surprised. "Oh. Well..." She considered this. "That's not a bad thing, beti. I'm still mostly vegetarian. My body likes it that way. Okay Some dahl then, I can make it in a jiffy."

"What! But you always say you can't hurry a good dahl. 'The flavor's in the cooking time,' remember, Ma!" Rani reminded her.

Rani's mother waved the suggestion away like an annoying mosquito. "A quick dahl is better than going hungry."

"I'm sure it is, Mum." Rani tried to get her mother away from the lentils. "But actually, I'm on a macrobiotic diet now."

Her mother stopped pouring lentils into a sieve and stared at Rani as if she'd just said, "I'm living on the planet Mercury now." Finally, she shook her head, tutting. "You youngsters with your faddy, faddy. You have the luxury for all this macro...what is it?"

"Biotic. Come and sit down, Mum."

Her mother reluctantly sat down, frowning. Rani felt terrible. It was an insult to come into her mother's house and refuse food.

"So how are you?" Rani broke the silence.

She shook her head from side to side. "Tik, taak. Okay, I miss you, beti."

Rani stared into her mother's eyes. "I miss you too. I've been so busy with the business."

"Oh yes, the business. That's good. People need knickers."

Rani smiled, acknowledging with a warm feeling in her stomach how lucky she was. Not only was she able to be out to her family, but they were cool about her lingerie business—a double result, as long as she didn't go on about either topic to the relatives.

Rani and her mum sat talking for several hours, easily incorporating Rani's dad when he arrived home tired after his shift. Rani forgot her irritation, her scared feeling. Laughing and joking with her parents, she slipped back into being beti, the daughter, allowing herself to be appreciated and loved.

When she left, very late, she carried the feeling with her, a warm shawl lying lightly across her shoulders.

CHAPTER NINE

I was happy in London. I hadn't been entirely sure it was the right thing to do when I came back a year ago, but I was sure now. Everything had worked out. I had somewhere to live, a job, friends—some of them mortals even—and a partner. A rather gorgeous, exciting partner.

I thought Rani needed distracting. I understood she was going through a difficult time. Trouble was, I didn't have all the answers. Vampires sometimes had a bad passage into the Life. But some of them didn't have any problems at all. I didn't tell Rani that. She had this thing about learning things. She expected to know stuff she couldn't possibly know.

I e-mailed Jameel for advice. He was the oldest queen I knew and the kind of person you could ask anything. For some reason, I didn't ask Selena for help. I hadn't heard from her since her e-mail welcoming Rani into the family.

I got on to Rani to get her flat lightproof, but after we got into a tussle about who would do the work, I dropped it. I knew a reliable vampire, but Rani wanted to get one of her mortal friends to do it. I thought that was too risky.

I also thought Rani should put some energy into her lingerie business. Her partner, Gulsin, was getting increasingly impatient with the amount of time Rani had taken off. I had suggested Rani think about dissolving the partnership. It just wasn't safe, with a mortal. Rani had hit the roof. It wasn't about money. I could keep us if necessary. I wanted Rani to start sorting her life out. And Rani had far too much time on her hands. When the invitation came, it was the perfect distraction.

One clear, moonlit night, I picked up the mail and, along with several bills, was a crisp parchment envelope addressed to *Sir Robert and his beautiful new bride.*

"Oh no! How did he find out!" I said.

Rani was making coffee in the kitchen. She came through with a cup for me even though I rarely drank it.

"How did *who* find out *what*?" Rani twinkled. I loved her all light and bubbly.

"The Count," I muttered. Without even opening the envelope, I knew it was from him.

"The who?" Rani's interest was piqued. She sipped black coffee from the whitest of espresso cups and looked over my shoulder.

I pulled out an ivory card. It was a heavy card with a fine, silky surface, and red writing on ivory with a gilt border.

You are cordially invited to the Bloodsuckers' Ball
On Saturday, 25th April
From twilight until your appetites are exhausted
Traditional dress appreciated
The Count & Countess await your pleasure
(and your RSVP)

"What's a Bloodsuckers' Ball?" was the first thing Rani wanted to know.

"That's the Count's sense of humor. We've been invited to a vampire party."

"Really?" Rani arched her eyebrows, looking at me like I'd suggested we go to an orgy—and that she liked the idea.

"Yes." I smiled at her. "Should be quite fun. Wanna go?"

"Do I want to go!" Rani threw her hands in the air. "You ask a femme if she wants to go to a ball?" She leaned in closer. "You ask me, practically a *virgin* in the Life, if I want to go to a vampire party? Of course I want to go."

The Count wasn't the kind of vampire I wanted Rani to meet. But there would be lots of other vampires there, and it was about time Rani met some.

"So where is it? There's no address on the card. Who's the Count, and *who's* the Countess?" Rani rattled off a list of questions.

"Which of those do you want me to answer first?" I said, flopping onto the sofa.

But a misty look had come over Rani. "Never mind any of that," she cried. "I've just thought of something far more important. The twenty-fifth of April is next week. What am I going to wear?"

CHAPTER TEN

In the deepening purple of twilight, Rani looked through the car windshield at a perfectly round moon rising in the cloudless sky. It was April full moon, the night chosen for the ball. Rob stepped out of her Saab and walked round to open the door for Rani. She looked fantastic in a black dinner jacket and trousers,

Rani smoothed down her short, black cocktail dress and accepted Rob's arm with a smile that matched her diamanté choker in brilliance. Rob whispered, "I'm so proud to be seen with you."

Other partygoers were arriving up and down the posh street near Hampstead Heath, commonly referred to as Billionaire's Row. A group of handsome males strolled toward them. Rani could tell a butch from a hundred paces, and indeed, two of them were butches. Like Rob, all four had black suits on, white shirts, and black bow ties. The twilight glinted off their sunglasses. Rani noted a pair of DKNY, a pair of Police, and two pair of Armani glasses. She pushed her own pair of original 1950s shades a little further up her nose and smiled graciously as the group stood back to let her walk in front of them.

"I know why they're doing that," Rob muttered in her ear. "So they can look at you from behind."

They turned into the winding driveway of a huge house. Big stone steps flanked by columns led up to the large front door. Rani felt excitement swell in her till she felt like a ripe mango. It was all getting too much—the promise of a vampire ball, the freshness of twilight, attractive butches in designer sunglasses, mansions in Hampstead, and she hadn't even rung the bell yet. Rob laughed, and Rani suspected Rob had read her thoughts.

"You forgot to screen, honey," Rob reminded her. Rani didn't care.

"There is no bell. Only a knocker," Rob said in a mysterious voice. Obviously, she was encouraging Rani's excitement.

As Rani tapped the knocker, it opened with a slow creak. In the dark hallway, a man in a butler's uniform smiled and gestured them inside. "Hi, Mike." Rob shook the butler's hand. "I see the Count has roped you into this evening of amateur dramatics."

Mike was a small, thin man with wiry energy. He laughed. "You know how theatrical he is. I said I'd play butler for him."

"Hope he's paying you well."

Mike just laughed again and turned to Rani. "I am very pleased to welcome *you* to the ball, Rani, isn't it?"

"It is," Rani said with a gracious smile. She was delighted he knew who she was.

"Follow me, please, lady and sir." Mike slipped back into role and led them to the entrance of a very elegant room.

"Sir Robert and the b—"

"Just Rob," Rob interrupted Mike's announcement.

He bowed to Rob, then turned back to the crowded ballroom. "Just Rob and the beautiful Lady Rani," he announced loudly with a slight smile on his lips.

Heads turned in their direction. Curious faces took in Rani from top to toe as Rob led her into the large, impressive room. They stopped to take a glass of sparkling wine each, proffered from a silver tray by another uniformed man. He stared at Rob coldly. Rob stared as coldly back.

"Who's that?" Rani asked when they were out of earshot.

"Todd," Rob said with distaste.

"Come again?" Rani said.

"Is that an invitation?"

Rani held her provocative stare.

"The man's called Todd. They all have their nicknames," Rob said disdainfully.

"Who do?" Rani often wished that Rob would just tell her the whole story at once, so she didn't have to get information out of her piece by piece.

"The Count's people. A lot of these guys work for him." Rob waved at the people in uniform. "And half the guests are on his payroll," she added with a low growl.

A lot of effort had gone into making the room look like a ballroom of old. Flickering candles in chandeliers hung from the ceiling and from sconces on the walls. The walls were pale, and the red candles threw soft pools of amber light directly onto them. Hard, sticky drips of wax had settled on the chandeliers, on the sconces, and had dropped onto the floor. Flowing voile draped the large windows, which had been opened so that the night breeze stirred the drapes. A long table covered with a starched white linen tablecloth and more candles ran along one wall. It was lined with glasses and a vast selection of bottles, as well as plates and trays of something that guests were picking up and putting in their mouths. The music was as new as the atmosphere was retro. Fresh garage and hip-hop, spun by two DJs, with live rappers, vocalists, and dancers.

Rani was impressed. She surveyed the room, picking up on the buzz of interest their entrance had made.

"Well, I suppose we'd better greet the hosts." Rob was looking over at a small group of people by the French windows. "You wanna meet the Count?"

"Okay." Rani made sure she looked her best as they crossed the floor. The group stopped talking as they approached. When Rani and Rob were very close, people stood back one by one to leave a space in front of a woman and a butch—or transman. Rani wasn't sure. The woman was tall and imposing; she wore a long black dress cut tightly around her waist and breasts. Large portions of skin were visible for such a long dress. A veil completed her outfit, but it was slung off her face now. She was beautiful. Rani had no doubt people would find her attractive. She smiled at them, though Rani couldn't find the smile in her eyes, only on her lips.

The butch turned as Rob and Rani reached them. She was good-looking, tall, with an assured manner, wearing a black tailcoat and trousers, white shirt, white bow tie, and a black cloak. Looking for all the world like a blond Bela Lugosi in *Dracula*.

"I am so pleased to meet you, Rani." The Count extended a manicured hand toward Rani. As she took it, the Count flipped over Rani's hand and kissed it, looking into Rani's eyes.

Rob coughed like something had stuck in her throat.

"This is the Countess Leah." The Count waved toward the tall woman with a flourish. Leah extended one hand to Rani, without smiling, quite as if she expected Rani to curtsy.

"Pleased to meet you," Rani said confidently, brushing Leah's hand with the lightest of handshakes.

Rob shook the Count's hand firmly. "Count," she said crisply.

"Robert," said the Count dryly. "It's been a long time. Haven't seen you in, oh, fifty years, isn't it?"

"I saw you in San Francisco five years ago," Rob remarked coolly.

The Count looked thoughtful. " Oh, yes. That little soirée in frisky San Fran. But that was such a select gathering, I'd quite forgotten *you* were there." She paused for a time, during which no one spoke. "But then, of course, you were there with Selena," she said eventually, as if that explained it. She turned to Rani again, openly studying her from top to toe.

"Well, well," she said softly. "How lucky we are to have such delightful new *blood*." She managed to inject the word blood with so much sexual tension Rani felt herself flush between her legs, and a slow throbbing began, quite outside her control.

"Stop playing with the girl, you naughty boi." Leah tapped the Count lightly on the wrist. "That's boi as in b-o-i," she said smoothly. "Need me to explain, honey?"

Rani smiled to herself, amused that this femme was trying to teach her the term butch boys sometimes used.

"School's out, Leah," said the Count. "I'm sure Rani knows *everything* about naughty boys." She looked into Rani's eyes, and Rani felt her whole body yearn to lean toward her.

"Well, we would love to stay and chat." Rob physically stepped between Rani and the Count. "But it would be rude not to circulate, don't you think?"

The Count stared at Rob without speaking, a strange air of triumph flowing from her. Rob bowed to Leah, turned, and walked away. Rani caught up with her on the other side of the room.

"So who do you want to meet now? There's some really nice people here." Rob spoke as if nothing had happened.

Rani pushed Rob down into a deep and elegant armchair and squeezed in beside her. "Oh no, you don't, *boi*. No changing the subject till I get the cou. What are you holding back? Tell me everything." She waved a waiter over and took two glasses of champagne from his tray. The night was getting better and better. Posh houses, sexy butches, a sad old femme, but never mind her, and *intrigue*. Hurrah.

"There is no story," Rob said. "I don't get on with the Count. I told you that."

"How come you never told me she was butch?" Rani persisted in her information-seeking mission. Intrigued by the Count, and in all things vampire, she wasn't going to let this drop.

"Didn't I?" said Rob innocently.

"You know damn well you didn't."

"Well, I think he's butch. He used to define as butch in the 70s, but then he was a womyn for a while in the eighties and used female pronouns and everything. Now he likes male pronouns again."

Rani looked at Rob, more confused than before. "So, are you saying the Count identifies as a man now, then? Is she a female to male transsexual?"

Rob seemed amused. "Don't be daft. The Count wouldn't give you some easy definition like that!"

Rani looked askance. She had made a study of butches and found herself almost exclusively attracted to them. That was fine. However, Rani wasn't sure about the male pronoun thing. *Why would some gorgeous butch want to be referred to as he?* As much as she didn't like the Count, Rob seemed very comfortable with using male pronouns. *Interesting...*

"So tell me why you don't like the Count." Rani stroked Rob's trousers with the tip of her shoe.

Rob looked around cautiously. "This isn't the best time and place, Rani. This is his party, man. I have to be careful what I say." All the same, Rob came in close to Rani. "We never got on. He didn't like me being with Selena."

"Well, you're not with her anymore, so what's the

problem?" Rani said, tossing her head.

"He knows I don't approve of him or the way he treats people."

"Like what?" Rani persisted.

"I'm not going to slag him off. You can make up your own mind, in your own time," said Rob. "I can't tell you to stay away from him."

Rani sensed Rob wanted to. She looked over at the Count, who caught her eye and smiled. Rani thought that if sharks smiled, their smiles must be something like that. She looked away. "Be careful, Rani. He's a player, and look who he models himself on—Count Dracula." Rob wrinkled her handsome brow.

"Well, I didn't like the femme much."

"Leah?" Rob's tone of voice changed completely. "Oh, she's all right really. She's very sweet when she's away from *him*."

Rani raised her eyes. Rob could be such a fool.

Rob got up then and took Rani by the hand. "C'mon, let's circulate. I want to show you off."

Rani felt as nervous and anxious to please as when she had first come out as a lesbian. Fortunately, the party crowd seemed eager to meet her. They were certainly curious about her. She answered a lot of questions as they went from one small group to the next. What her background was, how she met Rob, what she had thought about vampires before, and what did she feel about them now. Well, right now she thought they were very nosy. One thing she was realizing, with some relief, was that vampires came from all walks of life, all races. She had been pleased to spot some black and brown faces in the crowd when they had first arrived. She sought those faces out, curious herself about their journeys. Even if she didn't get to speak with them, she exchanged a smile, instinctively connecting.

Rob was deep in conversation with a man she had known in the States. Bored with the conversation, Rani went over to the long table to see what people were putting in their mouths. On closer inspection, the objects were canapés—small, round slices of some kind of meaty substance.

"Can I tempt you?"

Rani recognized the Count's voice before she turned round. Somehow, she had come up behind her without Rani noticing.

It was on Rani's lips to reply, *I don't know. What did you have in mind?* But she stopped herself. "Would you like a black pudding canapé?" Amusement danced in the metallic blue of her eyes.

His eyes, Rani mentally corrected herself. Rani shook her head. "No, thank you," she said very definitely. She had heard of black pudding and shuddered at the thought of it.

"Were you vegetarian?" the Count asked, those steely eyes had a hold of Rani's. She felt she couldn't have moved her eyes away even if she'd wanted to.

"Yes. Primarily," Rani said.

"Ah," the Count said as if that explained a great mystery. It made Rani feel very important. "I think it's hardest on vegetarians, coming into the Life."

"I suppose so." To be honest, Rani hadn't felt much beyond the urge to feed. She wasn't killing to sustain herself, so her conscience was clear. Apart from the first time, when blood had tasted strange to her, she'd never had any problems with drinking it.

"This may be more to your taste then." The Count had moved along the table toward trays of shot glasses. "What's your pleasure, O or A, Rhesus positive or Rhesus negative?"

Rani saw that the shot glasses were filled with blood. The Count held a glass between his finger and thumb and brought it close to Rani's nose.

"What do you think of this? Light on the nose, this one. Can you catch the salt? Just a whiff of it, and then it's gone, don't you think?"

Rani had to agree the blood didn't have a strong smell. It pulled her though; suddenly, she felt hungry.

The Count tipped the glass toward her mouth, gently pressing it against her lips.

"Take a little sip, just a small one. Suck the blood gently back though your teeth. Let it slip down your throat, and tell me what you can taste."

Rani did as the Count suggested. She closed her eyes and tasted earth, cherries, sunlight.

"Very good." The Count smiled down at her when she opened her eyes. "That's excellent. I might get you to work for me as a taster. You have a skill for it. You know the mail-order business already don't you? That could be useful too."

Rani was startled. "How do you know?" she blurted out.

The Count just smiled. "Finish your blood," he said patronizingly. He was looking far too pleased with himself for Rani's liking. She did finish the blood though, hungry now, and took a glass from another tray. She drank it straight down. Instead of looking disappointed that Rani wasn't playing his tasting game, the Count looked more pleased than ever.

"Have as many as you want, Rani. If you see something you like, take it. Why wait?"

Rani felt uneasy. She looked around, wondering where Rob was. She couldn't see her anywhere in the room. The Count followed her gaze.

"Now just where has that boi gone?" he said aloud. "How *are* we spelling that word now? Remind me." He winked a long, slow wink. Rani felt a wave of fondness for him again.

He leaned in very close and whispered in her ear. "Perhaps Rob saw us talking."

Oh God, of course. Rani realized that must be why she couldn't see Rob anywhere. Suddenly, it wasn't funny. Rani felt a wave of concern for Rob. Even if this Count person was exciting, he wasn't Rob.

Rani began to search the ballroom, quite calmly at first, but with growing panic when she didn't find her. Rob must be in another room.

Rani went out the big door and back into the hallway. She was hoping to see Mike; he had been nice to her and maybe he'd seen Rob. But Mike was also conspicuously absent. *Who's greeting the guests then?* Rani thought as she walked along a deserted corridor. *Surely, everyone didn't always arrive early to a vampire event.* She shuddered. What an awful thought. *Well, I don't care if they do all arrive on time. They'll just have to get used to me coming late.* She was completely unprepared to change the time-keeping habits of her previous lifetime.

Rani stopped outside a big closed dark oak door. She listened for a moment, unsure if she should open it. Maybe guests were supposed to stay in the main room. *Well, if that's the case, Mike should have been back there stopping me going anywhere. It's not my fault if he isn't doing his job.* She opened the door cautiously.

Inside was a small, comfortable sitting room. A roaring fire filled the plain, large, stone fireplace. The walls were light; velvet and more voile dressed the windows and hung from parts of the walls. A polished wood floor was clothed in several sheepskin rugs. An ornate screen intrigued Rani. It was decorated with paintings that looked very like Indian miniatures. Rani studied a picture of a serene androgynous figure sitting in a tree playing the flute while beautiful bathing women, all with long hair and copious amounts of jewelry, asked him to return the clothes he had stolen from them. Though they were bathing, the women all had saris on. Rani recognized it as a painting of Lord Krishna and the Gopies.

As Rani looked at the detail in the painting, the panel moved. Standing behind it was Leah with a python cradled around her neck.

"Hi, Rani," she said casually, as if standing behind a screen with a snake was the most ordinary thing in the world.

"Oh," said Rani.

"I was just feeding Kadru,"

Rani saw that Leah was holding a small live rat.

"I do think it's a shame the tidbits have to be alive when Kadru eats them. But that is nature, isn't it?" Leah lifted her hand, and Kadru swung her muscular head toward the rat. The snake stared at the animal, and the rat looked up at the python. Leah opened her hand so that the rat was just resting there, and still it didn't move. The python swooped and swallowed in one graceful, accomplished movement, leaving Leah's hand empty.

"Remind you of anyone?" Leah said smoothly.

Rani wasn't sure if Leah meant the snake or the rat, but she got the gist.

"Care to look into Kadru's eyes? It's really quite energizing," Leah held the python's neck and swung her in Rani's direction.

"I don't think so!" Rani said, more primly than she meant to. She wanted to ask Leah if she'd seen Rob, but she didn't want to admit she'd lost her.

Leah came out from behind the screen and walked to a small padded sofa.

"I noticed you and the Count hit it off," she said, as if in confidence. As if, in fact, she and Rani were friends and this was something exciting to discuss. She patted the empty space beside her on the sofa. With some suspicion, Rani came and sat with her.

"If I were you, I'd tell Rob," Leah said. Kadru was curled up in Leah's lap now. She flicked her tongue toward Rani's hand, tasting her scent. Rani knew that a small rat would not be enough to satisfy a python for long and shifted down the sofa.

"Tell Rob what?" she asked Leah.

Leah smiled at Rani, looking remarkably like Kadru for a moment. "This is the thing, Rani. Vampires have a very different morality from what you're used to. Monogamy s'nogamy. When you live as long as we do, it really isn't practical to be with one person all your life. I'm trying to do you a favor here. Perhaps you've heard of non-monogamy. It was something lesbians did in the nineteen eighties, I believe. Well, we do it, my dear. And we do it very well. Rob will have picked up on the attraction between you and the Count. It's much better to have these things all out in the open. Like I say, I'm just trying to help." Leah stroked Kadru's back with long, smooth movements. "I could have great fun teaching you. I mean," she corrected herself, "we could have great fun together, learning things. I love people who are fresh out of the grave."

"You love *what*?" Rani didn't like the sound of anything Leah was saying, especially the last part.

"Fresh out of the grave, my dear. That's what we call new vampires. Sweet, isn't it? Know what we call the people who bring them in?"

Rani shook her head.

"Grave robbers!" Leah beamed at her. "See? It's such fun learning, isn't it? That's what I love about new vamps like yourself. So much you don't know, yet still so full of chi—um, I mean, mortal ideas."

Rani was sure Leah had been about to say another word. She wasn't going to ask her though. She didn't feel like being initiated by Leah tonight, or any night soon. She got up. "Thanks for the chat. Think I'll go back to the party now. Leave you and Kadru to do…whatever you do."

She walked to the door and opened it.

"Think about what I said, Rani."

As light streamed in from the passage, Rani turned to find Leah and Kadru framed in firelight, the flickering intensity increasing the shadow of both their smiles.

Rani headed straight back to the ballroom. She had lost her nerve for exploring. Who knew what she might find if she kept wandering around alone—an attic full of bats maybe. But when she got back to the ballroom, it was almost deserted. Concerned more that vampires were sad party frumps and finished their events really, really early, than the fact that she still hadn't found Rob, Rani went up to a shot-drinking trio and asked where everybody was.

They said that the fireworks were about to start in the grounds. Declining a "Bloody Mary, you'll like it; it's the *real* thing," Rani went through the large French windows and with relief saw Rob talking to someone on the patio.

As she walked over, she recognized the woman as Adjoa, the friend of Rob's she'd chatted to for ages one night, before she'd come into the Life. Adjoa was wearing an African suit and head wrap. Rani appreciated the clothes, especially with nearly everyone in black dresses and suits.

"That's what I thought the invitation meant, when it said 'traditional dress appreciated,'" Rani said as she reached them. "I nearly wore salwar kameez."

Adjoa smiled. "Of course, I thought that was what they meant too. It warms my blood to see you again." Adjoa kissed Rani and then stood back and scrutinized her. "Rob, are you making sure the girl gets enough sleep, enough blood?" she said sharply.

Rob protested she *was* making sure.

"She's looking after you?" Adjoa turned back to Rani, pulling down Rani's eyelid and peering into her eye.

Rani nodded with difficulty while Adjoa continued to look for signs of ill health.

At that moment, a firework shot hundreds of meters into the air. Silver shooting stars cascaded into the blackness, followed by small explosions that turned the stars into a huge star cloth of shimmering pinpoints of light. A collective "Ah" sighed from the assembled vampires.

More stars, gold and silver, lit up the sky for a minute, then intense blue, red, and green rings appeared, starting as one dot that multiplied into bigger and bigger circles. A convoy of silver streaks traveled upward from the ground to the sky, like comets in reverse. They transformed into orange-gold flowers tipped on the very edges with tiny blue dots. A row of Catherine wheels spun a sparkling, rhythmic dance at ground level. Rani's heart swelled at the beauty of it. Rob put her arm around her and held her close. The smell of gunpowder hung stiffly in the air, now hazy with smoke. A spluttering concoction of green and pink flares whizzed upward, small and solitary in the dark sky, only to explode into showering, darting silver worms.

The display ended with a fierce wall of pulsating flame only thirty meters in front of them. The crackling, unnaturally bright fire seemed magically suspended in mid air. As the last flame flickered and died, the crowd burst into applause.

Leah appeared on the lawn in front of everyone as the applause faded.

"Just when you thought it couldn't get more exciting, everybody, if you follow me you can welcome our guest of honor. She has just arrived, with impeccable timing as ever!"

"Who is it?" Rob asked Adjoa, as they walked round to the front of the house, but Adjoa shrugged, as mystified as everyone else.

There was a carriage on the front drive. As the vampires assembled on the large front steps, the driver leapt down and opened the carriage door. An unmistakably feminine leg swung out, followed by an arm encased in a long cream glove, which took the driver's hand. The guest of honor bent to clear the carriage door and stepped down. She had a mask on a stick in front of her face.

She walked elegantly up to the steps in a long, cream satin gown, split to the thigh, and scattered with diamonds. She stopped in front of Rani and Rob.

"Surprise!" she called, swinging back the mask.

Rob's jaw dropped. "Selena!" she said and then broke

into a brilliant smile.

Rani saw the Count looking surprised too, surprised that Selena had walked right past him.

"But I thought you were in Mexico?" Rob said.

Selena beamed at her. "I was, but then you told me about Rani, and I wanted to come and visit you anyway, so here I am."

"Lovely," Rani said crisply. "Where are you staying?"

CHAPTER ELEVEN

Jameel had the beautiful boy above him pressed hard against the toilet wall. Jameel was going down on him, and he was so good at it the boy had dropped his head back, exposing his neck. Jameel laughed and forced his own concentration away from the neck, back on giving this man the best head he would ever have.

Jameel took him deep inside his mouth and worked him till he stopped getting off on where he was, till he forgot where he was, lost control, and had to be held up. Other men came in and out of the club bathroom. Jameel ignored them. He had all night to party, and right now he needed a drink. The boy pulled him back and stole a kiss before he'd let Jameel leave. Jameel took that as a thank you. The boy was keen to stay. He was combing his hair and admiring himself in the beautifully mirrored club toilets when Jameel breezed out the door.

Jameel liked sex with mortals. He liked the whole gay mortal club scene with its lack of words and high proportion of body language. It was all the drugs Jameel needed. He walked to the bar through the crowd, enjoying the smell and the heat of a room full of men.

He got a drink and looked around. Carlos and Juan were in the middle of the dance floor, dancing and flirting with other men. Jameel shook his head, laughing. They were such a couple. Flirting, kissing, and the occasional fumble was all either of them would do with another man. He thought it was sweet. He watched them from the bar while idly scanning the crowd for his own interest.

Carlos saw him and waved. Jameel indicated his glass, and Carlos nodded. He spoke to Juan and they both came over. Carlos said he was going to the bathroom. Jameel smiled and went to get the drinks in, shamelessly using his magnetism to get the barman's attention.

Jameel was happy. Carlos and Juan were becoming good friends. They were mortals, but decent guys, and fun too. He stood at the bar companionably with Juan allowing the sensations of the room to vibrate through him. He was well into a "Who's the most handsome man in the room and why" game with Juan by the time Carlos got back.

Carlos kept trying to get his attention, but Jameel had just noticed an exciting man who looked like he could be Indian. "He's probably gitano," Juan mouthed. Jameel was staring at the gypsy man when he felt Carlos shake his arm. Jameel turned. Carlos's normally olive complexion was pale and his skin looked cold and clammy.

"The toilets," he said. "Juan says you were with someone in the toilets."

Jameel nodded.

"Something's happened." Carlos seemed reluctant to say exactly what.

Jameel had a bad feeling. He started walking to the toilets, ignoring Juan's hand on his shoulder trying to stop him.

Outside the bathroom, two bouncers were preventing anyone going in.

"But I've just been here. Minutes ago. Can I help?" Jameel used his magnetism again.

"Maybe he knows the guy," one bouncer said to the other. Then he turned to Jameel. "Okay, but when I open the door, don't go in. Just look from the doorway. The police are on their way."

As the door opened, Jameel saw all the mosaic mirrors covering the bathroom walls had been smashed. Every single one. Most were still fixed to the wall with huge cavernous cracks in them, but some had been smashed into tiny pieces. There were shards of mirror everywhere. On the floor, a crumpled body lay amongst the glass. Jameel stared into the fixed, glassy eyes of the boy he had had sex with only twenty minutes before. A large, glinting shard of mirror protruded from his chest.

By the time the police had finished with Jameel, it was the early hours of the morning. Carlos and Juan had insisted on seeing him home. Jameel was shocked. Even though he had seen death a fair few times in 200 years, he still reacted to the fragility of mortal life. The man had probably been twenty years old. To Jameel that was hardly time to grow up. He was glad Carlos and Juan had insisted on getting a cab and dropping him off.

As the cab climbed the twisting, cobbled streets of Albiacín, Jameel asked them if they wanted a nightcap.

Carlos said, "I think we all need a little whisky, for medicinal purposes."

Juan insisted on paying the cab, despite Jameel's protest, so Jameel left him to it and went to unlock his door, feeling relieved he would soon be in his own space. The door swung open at his touch.

Jameel *knew* he'd locked the door when he'd left earlier. He'd been careful ever since the mysterious postcard had appeared in his house. The bad feeling started up in his gut, and Jameel cautiously walked into the little sitting room.

All the blackout stuff had been slashed. Jameel couldn't see that anything had been taken and nothing else had been damaged. He walked quickly along the corridor to his bedroom and found the same thing in there. On his bed lay several shards of mirror.

He felt a hand on his shoulder and turned to see Juan full of concern. Juan reached out his arms to Jameel, and Jameel received the hug, thinking quickly about what he was going to do. He had about an hour left before sunlight would slowly creep toward his house. He glanced out the window at the sky, hoping to see clouds. But there were just the first pink streaks of dawn. Carlos stood in front of him when he turned round. "You must come to our house," he said, his delicate face creased with concern.

Jameel shook his head. They didn't know what he was, but perhaps they could help. Juan could turn his hands to just about anything. Ah! He remembered the roll of tape Juan had given him a few months ago. Gaffa tape it was called. Juan swore by it.

"I need to repair this material and make my door secure," he explained.

"But come to our house!" Juan said. Carlos nodded vigorously.

"I have to stay here," Jameel insisted.

"Well, okay then. What shall we do?" Juan asked.

While Carlos helped Jameel stick the blackout blinds back up, Juan sorted out the front door. Complaining about the lack of anything remotely useful in the tool cupboard, Juan improvised with some large pieces of 4 x 3 wood he found out back and several screws.

"But you have nothing here, Jameel," Juan said. "Not a bradawl, not even a drill. I will have to screw all this by hand, my friend."

Jameel shrugged. "Why would I keep anything when I can always find someone eager to come round and show off his tool?"

It took a surprisingly short time to repair the damage. And then, Carlos and Juan left, making Jameel promise to phone them if he felt weird about anything. Jameel screwed the barriers Juan had made against the door, and then retired to his bedroom.

He didn't sleep for a long time, going over the night, wondering who had broken into his house—and why.

CHAPTER TWELVE

A *shadowy cloaked figure stood in front of the open windows in darkness. The curtains were blowing, and so was the cloak.*

"I am the Count. I have lived forever, and I have eternity ahead of me. I play with life, so I never become too serious. First comes seriousness and then comes boredom. And boredom is dangerous. For any vampire I've known to be severely bored winds up dead.

Come to me. Come at night when our powers are strongest and the mortal world is dreaming. Let go of your human past, Rani. Stop thinking like those ignorant fools with seventy or eighty years to their name. Let me introduce you to a life where you can immerse yourself in complete self-indulgence, absolute pleasure.

Rani, I can spin ecstasy for you in ways you can't imagine. Certainly in ways you've never experienced. Perhaps you think that mortal lesbians spend a long time in bed. My dear, you've no idea what is possible when you've had several lifetimes to learn how to completely please a woman...

I think that you have not been properly introduced to the joy of vampire sex. Certainly not if all you've known is Rob.

Rani sat bolt upright in bed. Rob lay sleeping beside her. Rani looked at her guiltily, the dream still ricocheting in her head.

"Rob, you need to read this e-mail from Jameel. It doesn't look good." Selena burst through the door.

Doesn't she even bloody knock? Rani snatched the covers

to her naked body and glared at Selena.

"Sorry, I forgot," Selena said quietly, backing out of the room.

She could have plucked the thought out of Rani's head, but that would be an extremely rude thing for a vampire to do. Maybe she'd just read the look on Rani's face.

Rani showered and dressed quickly. Feeling hungry, angry, mixed up, and throbbing from her dream about the Count, she just wanted to get out as fast as she could.

Selena was sitting at the computer in the front room. Rani bustled past her, picking up her jacket, some money, and makeup.

"I'm sorry, Rani. I saw this e-mail from Jameel. It's very worrying," Selena said.

Rani noted that Selena was opening Rob's e-mails. Not that it was Rani's business, she supposed, but it said a lot about Selena.

"Look, Rani, do you want me to find somewhere else to stay? Maybe I'm in the way."

"It's up to Rob, not me," Rani said shortly.

"What?" Rob appeared in the doorway to the bedroom, her hair disheveled.

Selena and Rani looked at her.

She looked back at them for a while and then murmured, "I thought we could all go out somewhere tonight. What do you think?" She beamed at them happily.

Rani just tossed her head and hit the front door without saying a word.

She walked fast. Without noticing, she headed for her own place. Once there she decided against going in. Instead, she headed for the graveyard around the corner.

The immediate silence was so quiet every rustling leaf was audible. Traffic was a faint, far off rumble. In the distance was the clickady-clack of a train.

The part of night that fell immediately after twilight was a favorite time for Rani. Birds were sleeping; people were mostly indoors, places emptied, like this disused graveyard in the grounds of a church.

Rani sat on a bench. She knew she should go and feed, but she was reluctant to give up her solitude. The thing she loved best about being a vampire was that she could do exactly this: sit somewhere quiet, on her own, in the dead of night without any fear whatsoever. Well, in theory without any fear. Old habits died hard, and Rani was too new at this game not to be a bit cautious when out alone. She didn't want to put her immortality to the test.

Two bright eyes glared out from the lower branches of a yew tree. A small bundle dropped soundlessly to the ground. A cat was exploring the churchyard too. It sauntered toward her, sniffed the air, and obviously decided against coming over.

"I can't smell that bad. I've had a shower," Rani said.

"You smell very good to me," came a voice from the shadows of a large vault.

Rani recognized the voice immediately. She'd heard it in her sleep a couple of hours before. Wondering if the Count would go so far as to turn himself into a bat, Rani felt a delicious, shivering tension in her body.

"We meet again." The Count walked toward Rani's bench. She saw he wasn't wearing the cloak costume, but was wearing a leather jacket and jeans.

"Hmm." Rani looked him up and down. He looked pleased to see her. "What a coincidence."

The Count sat next to her. He leaned in until he was very close. Rani felt hairs standing up all over her body, and she didn't mind a bit. The Count had come to find her, and they were all alone.

"I thought I'd save you the trouble of looking for a bite." He took something out of his jacket pocket and offered it to her. "Drink up, then I'll take you for a ride."

Rani took the small glass bottle. It contained about a pint of dark liquid. The label said Chateau Nosferatu AO.

"Go on. It's fresh today." The Count took back the bottle, screwed open the top, and waved it under her nose.

Rani's stomach tightened in hunger as she smelled the blood. She trusted her body's reaction and took a drink. It was fresh blood all right; Rani steadily drank the contents. It was different drinking blood out of a bottle rather than from the neck. She thought she preferred her blood warm, but it was an interesting experience. She could get used to it.

"Feeling satisfied?" the Count asked. "I'll take that." He

took the bottle back without waiting for an answer. "Now, let's get some air." He stood.

Rani didn't. "What's wrong with the air here?" she asked, teasing him.

He reluctantly sat back down. "I don't like graveyards very much."

Rani had to laugh. "I wouldn't have been surprised if you'd told me you lived in one."

The Count pulled a face. "No, thanks." He looked at Rani. "Don't tell me you like them?"

Rani shrugged. "What's not to like?"

"There's nothing to do and the feeding's terrible."

"Oh? Is it?" said Rani, amused.

"You would know this, if you came to graveyards very much," the Count declared. "The feeding's bad because the only mortals that come to graveyards at night are thrill seekers. And I've yet to find one that didn't taste terrible."

Rani laughed out loud. "And why's that?"

The Count shrugged. "Because they will put anything in their blood. The best blood, in my opinion, comes from pure living vegetarians. The kind of girl *you* were, before you came in." The Count moved very close to Rani. "I would definitely have wanted a taste of you. Maybe I would have come to your bedroom. Flown through your open window." He looked at her intensely.

Rani felt sure he knew about her dream. She swallowed, trying hard not to show how sexual she was feeling. It was probably not a good idea, hanging out with the Count. She couldn't help being attracted to him, but Rani was sure Rob wouldn't like it. Rani felt a wave of affection for Rob, now that she thought about her. The wave was too small to overpower the lust she was feeling though, and the thrill of the unknown. The Count was just too damn intriguing. When the Count got up, held out his hand, and said, "Come on, Rani, let's go have some fun," Rani took his hand, letting him lead her out of the churchyard.

A sleek, self-satisfied Harley Davidson lay gleaming under a streetlight on the road outside. The bike was black from the rear wheel arch to the fuel tank. The rest was chrome— the two long exhausts; the kick start; the handlebars; the front wheel laces, and the rear wheel hub. The turn signals were chrome bullets with orange lenses; the mirrors stood to attention while the long black seat begged Rani to sit on it. The Count grinned. He pulled two black helmets out of a nearby hedge.

"Put this on," he said.

"Worried I'll bump my head?" Rani was so in the mood for teasing now, she couldn't help herself. She wanted to run her hands along the leather seat, and if she had to hold on to the Count and run her hands along his leather jacket, well, then. She was just going for a ride. And she *was* going. There was no way she was going to miss out on the chance to ride a Harley.

"The police will take less notice of us if we're wearing helmets." The Count sat astride the bike. "Come aboard the Night Train."

Her skirt slipped up her thighs as she straddled the bike. The Count stared unashamedly at her legs over his shoulder. "She's a Harley Softail, Night Train model. 1450cc, twin cam engine." He turned the key and kicked sharply with his right foot. The engine roared to life between Rani's legs, and she couldn't have cared less how many cc's it was, as long as it carried on feeling just like that. The indicator blinked awake and the Count glanced briefly at the road before moving the bike out. Rani put her arms loosely around his waist and looked over the Count's shoulder as the bike purred along, hardly making a sound.

They cruised along quiet streets, the vibrations strong and steady beneath her. Rani relaxed, seeped in pleasure. They came up to some traffic. The Count swung the bike out, passing on the right. He revved and they picked up speed. Rani felt as if the bike was lifting up beneath her. Her stomach and pelvis lifted.

Air streamed past Rani's face, and objects started blurring on the left and right. There was nothing up ahead, but Rani noticed they were on the wrong side of the road, driving now at high speed.

The Count swerved back toward the left side, as if he read her thoughts, but drove very close to a black cab. The cab driver hit the horn as the bike brushed close enough for Rani to touch it if she'd wanted to. She saw the driver's angry, shocked face as the bike veered away to the right again.

Now they were speeding down the road straight into an oncoming car. Rani held back a scream. The Count seemed to be speeding up. She gripped his waist tight, though she actually wanted to punch him.

They were heading straight for a red car, bearing down at them at the same crazy speed they were riding. Rani had a horrible feeling neither driver would swerve. That she was helplessly caught in a game of chicken, and people would end up dead. At the last possible minute, beyond the point Rani felt anyone could stop in time, the Count swerved sharply left.

They narrowly missed a blue hatchback coming up the inside lane. The Count turned left, right across the hatchback and through a red light, weaving round a pedestrian crossing the road. Rani knew that she was staring wide-eyed and open-mouthed at the poor guy just the same way he was staring at her.

"Stop!" she shouted into the Count's helmet as he continued down the road at breakneck speed.

Immediately, the bike slowed, turned into a side street, and hit a series of speed bumps at about forty miles per hour.

"I said stop, not slow down," Rani said sharply after the sixth time they sailed into the air and came down with a bump.

The Count sighed. Rani felt it rather than heard it. However, she couldn't have cared less. He stopped the bike, kicked the rest into place, and switched off the engine. He took his helmet off and then turned, "I invented that craze you know. That craze of bikes riding on the opposite side of the road. Good, isn't it?" He grinned.

Rani wondered if the Count was maybe a little messed up in the head.

"Oh, come on." He started undoing Rani's helmet. "You've got to admit, it's fun scaring the mortals, isn't it?"

"You're crazy."

"Am I?" He seemed delighted she thought so.

"I don't want to go round scaring people," Rani said.

"I'm doing them a favor," the Count said. "Giving them a cheap thrill. They don't do much in their short lives, most of them. If it weren't for people like me, they wouldn't have anything to talk about."

"Well, I've had enough." Rani stepped off the bike.

"Oh, Rani!" The Count was off the bike too in a second, his blue eyes looking as big and sorrowful as a puppy's. "Okay, I've got the message. Please." He reached for her hands. Rani let him take them. The Count sighed deeply. "I think we've got off on the wrong foot." He looked sweetly down at Rani, and she was astounded by the depth of blue in his eyes. "I'm very misunderstood," he said sheepishly.

Rani took a deep breath, thinking. She was a sucker for the underdog. Maybe this vampire had worked that out already, but there was something so appealing about those eyes, something soft and sensitive in them...

"Come on, Rani. Let me make it up to you. I want to take you somewhere nice. I'll drive carefully, I promise." He paused. "Trust me."

Rani had a sudden flash of the snake from *The Jungle Book*. Mowgli on a tree branch getting completely hypnotized. Somehow, even though she knew that, she couldn't say no to the Count. Not when he asked so nicely.

He was true to his word. He drove carefully and courteously through Finsbury Park and then Hornsey. The bike started to climb and then the Count turned off the main road and into the grounds of Alexandra Palace, parking the bike at the top of the hill on the edge of the main car park.

They walked to the grass and stood watching London spread across the lower horizon. Tall buildings like the Post Office Tower and Canary Wharf stood out from the hundreds of tiny lights marking houses in streets stretching in every direction.

"It's lovely." Rani sighed.

"You must have come here with Rob," the Count remarked.

Rani hadn't, even though Ally Pally was near Rob's flat in Wood Green. *So why hasn't she brought me up here?* Rani felt how romantic it was.

"I don't want to talk about Rob right now," Rani said. Then she realized the implications of what she'd said. She wondered what the Count would make of it.

He looked delighted. "Let's take a walk,"

Away from the main road, he leaned against a tree. He didn't say a word, just looked at Rani. Looked and looked.

Till Rani felt like her feet were pulling her toward him. She shivered as he unzipped her jacket. It fell to her feet; her arms slipped out of it. Rani's nipples stiffened with a combination of the cold air and the Count staring. This guy wasn't going to take his eyes off Rani. He noticed everything that revealed how turned on she was. His hand was on the top of her thigh and moving up. A soft cry escaped her lips, and the Count smiled.

"You have no idea what pleasure is," he murmured.

He breathed into her ear, nibbled on the tender lobe. At the same time, he cupped her outside her panties, his fingers pressing against her. Her legs felt weak, and she didn't know how long she could stand. She hadn't meant this to happen. Rob came into her mind briefly, then Rani pushed her firmly away. There was nothing she could do now. This was too strong.

She pushed herself against the Count's fingers, against his body. She turned into his mouth and kissed him, holding him behind the neck. He kissed her back, until she felt weak, until she felt dizzy. He pulled away, looked at her, smiling in the flitting moonlight, then went down on his knees, took her knickers completely off, and put his mouth to her. He was licking her, sucking her. His fingers were inside her, kind of holding her up, and pushing inside her. She opened her legs wider. She was being lapped and sucked and...oh my God, he was biting her. There was no pain. It felt fantastic. Her stomach lifted. She felt thick and swollen and full of juice... juice for the Count...for this crazy guy. "You can...have...it," she moaned.

I'm taking it, she heard the Count say inside her head.

Her fingers pulled on his short hair, so hard she must have pulled some out. She rode his mouth—his great sucking beast of a mouth—sucking her into somewhere she never knew existed. The boi wasn't wrong about pleasure. She came like a steam engine charging down the track. She thought she would fall, but she was lifted up. She gave herself, gave every last drop...

Her toes were curled inside her strappy shoes; her heels had sunk into soft earth. She slowly came back to herself. She put her clothes back on and pulled her heels out of the ground.

As her brain clicked into gear, she needed to ask something. "So are you a woman or a man? Or…" she added as an afterthought, "a butch?" The question sounded shocking in the still air. Rani didn't want the Count to take offence.

"That's a funny question to ask now." His eyes twinkled. Still kneeling, he looked up at her. He wiped his mouth to emphasize the point.

After a pause he said, "I was born a woman. I feel like a man. I suppose I am a butch, probably, I am trans, you know, a third gender. Does it matter?"

Rani didn't suppose it did. She didn't want to ask or know anything more. Not right then. She sank down next to him and bit into his neck. His body shuddered in response as she quickly and expertly brought him to orgasm.

You're mine now.

Rani was sure she'd heard the Count say, "You're mine now," but it was in the far reaches of her mind and she couldn't be sure.

"Now." The Count reclined, healing his neck with one hand, reaching into his jacket pocket with the other. He pulled out another bottle of blood, unscrewed it, and proffered it to Rani. "Just to make sure you've had your full quota for the evening." His voice was a little breathy, but he sounded as in control as ever.

Rani drank some of the Chateau Nosferatu O+ 1978. It tasted smoky, rich, and it felt solid and nourishing going down.

"Is your pocket like *Mary Poppins's* bag?" Rani asked.

"Like *what*?" The Count looked confused.

"You just keep bringing stuff out of your pocket," Rani remarked. "Is it magic? Bottomless or something?"

The Count laughed and shook his head. He had a satisfied, dreamy look about him. Rani felt she was stealing time now.

"It's only one little pint bottle. I stashed the empty one on the bike before."

Rani smiled. Mixed in with the afterglow, thousands of endorphins running, dancing through her bloodstream, she felt the beginnings of anxiety. She was starting to wonder just what she'd done.

"Time to go."

Rani was startled by the Count getting to his feet. She

looked up at him for a second, and then accepted his hand to help her up.

They walked back to the bike. They didn't hold hands or walk especially close. The Count did tie Rani's helmet strap under her chin, though, before driving off.

Rani made the count drop her around the corner from Rob's flat. With a hard knot of guilt in her stomach, Rani walked briskly away, not daring to look back.

***

Jameel called soon after he landed at Gatwick Airport. "Hello? And which deliciously exciting vampire is that?"

"This is Rani. Who is that?"

"Rani, eh? Thank God. From your pause, for a moment I thought I'd got the cleaner. The mortal cleaner and that I'd just let it out of the bag she was cleaning in a nest of vampires. And of course, she'd be compelled to rush into the bedroom where you and Rob would be sleeping unaware and try and stab you through the heart with the end of a sharpened mop. That or she might just take her clothes off and get into bed with you, I guess. Which do you think it would be?"

There was a pause.

"*Who* is this?" Rani repeated, laughing.

"This, my dear, is Jameel. Can't you tell? Namaste, honey. Can't you feel the common bond we share, our sub continental heritage, coming through the satellite waves as we speak? Did I tell you, by the way, I nearly called myself Rani once?"

"No, you haven't told me that. But then this is the first time we've spoken," Rani said.

"Oh. Well, I'm sure you're dying to know so I'll tell you. I nearly called myself Rani because you can't have too many Asian queens in my opinion." Jameel paused to get the full benefit of Rani's laugh.

"I think we're going to get on," she said.

"I'm sure of it. Now, you can expect me in about two hours. I'm on the so-called Gatwick Express, and quite frankly, centuries have gone faster, my dear. The twentieth century went very fast actually, don't you think? Oh sorry, Rani, I forgot you're new. See, it's like we've been friends forever, and I haven't even seen your face yet. Reminds me of an old boyfriend of mine. We only ever met through the hole in the wall between two cubicles in a public toilet. Anyhoo, can't wait to meet you properly."

After a stunned silence, Rani said, "Me too. I think!"

***

When Rani told Rob about the phone call, she was delighted Jameel was on his way.

"Damn! I wish I didn't have to go to work," she said, hunting on the top of her desk for the loose change she'd thrown there the night before. "But you'll be here, won't you?" She turned and smiled at Rani. Rani shifted from foot to foot. She would happily have gone out and left Selena to meet him.

"Oh, but Jameel will be disappointed if you're not here," Selena said, walking into the bedroom without knocking again. She stood smiling expectantly at Rani too. Rani had no idea vampires could be so gawpy.

"Don't you want to meet my friend?" Rob asked. Rani didn't say anything. She felt she couldn't refuse.

When Rob had gone, Selena confided in Rani that she'd hoped to spend some time with her anyway. "There's no reason for us not to get on," she said.

"I guess not." Rani sighed inwardly. Truth was she was disappointed that lesbian vampires seemed to have the same obsession with exes that mortal dykes had, except it was worse. Before, she'd had to cope with five or ten years of previous relationship. Now, it was eighty years. That was ridiculous. Selena and Rob had been through everything together since 1924. How could she possibly compete with that?

They went out to feed. Selena wanted to do that together as well, but Rani was going to burst if she didn't get a moment to herself. She needed to think about what she'd done last night, and how she was going to tell Rob. Or what she should tell Rob. If Leah was to be believed, vampires were generally non-monogamous. But even if that were true, Rob hated the Count. Why, Rani didn't know. She really wanted to know, but putting that aside for a moment, Rani thought it was likely vampires were more fluid about relationships.

Look at Rob and Selena. They haven't ended their relationship. Oh, Rob may think they have, but I've seen the way she looks at Selena. How she looked at her the night before last, when Selena came out of the shower with just a towel on. And Selena, she acts like they're still together. Though she doesn't seem at all bothered that Rob's going out with me. Rani had looked very hard, and she couldn't see any attitude coming from Selena.

It went round and round in Rani's head. But even after she'd fed and returned to Rob's flat, she still didn't have a clue what she was going to tell her.

When Jameel arrived, he greeted Selena warmly, holding her close. Then he looked Rani up and down and declared the day she'd come into the Life should be made a public holiday for vampires, especially for vampires with a good sense of style and beauty. Rani knew he was flattering her, but sensed a genuine warmth from Jameel.

They sat in Rob's light and airy front room. Selena wanted to talk about what had happened to Jameel in Spain. Jameel was resisting.

"It's soooo tiresome, Selena. And I only have to go through it all again with Rob later."

"Jameel, I don't care how tedious you think it is, I want to go over everything that's happened since you moved to Granada." Selena's stern tone made Rani smile.

Jameel pouted mournfully, but he grinned devilishly at Rani when Selena wasn't looking.

"I just don't think it's fair to involve Rani." Jameel put his hand up in front of his face. "She doesn't look the sort of girl to cope well with tedium."

Selena rolled her eyes. "Well, that's unfortunate, isn't it Jameel? Seeing as she's just become a vampire."

Jameel looked away. "Whatever."

"Come on, Jameel, give it up. You know you want to," Selena said persuasively, smiling at Rani.

Rani couldn't dislike Selena nearly as much as she wanted to. When Rob wasn't around, she quite liked her.

Jameel shook his head. "I can see resistance is futile, you big Borg."

"Huh?" Selena frowned.

Jameel turned to Rani. "You have to excuse my uncultured friend. She doesn't watch *Star Trek*. I don't think she knows that humans have invented television."

When it was obvious from Selena's face she wasn't playing ball, he sighed. "Okay, honey, you got it. I'll dish the dirt."

Jameel told Selena and Rani how he'd met a guy in some club toilets, how later the guy had been killed and the bathroom all smashed up. How, when he'd got home someone had been in and destroyed all the blackout stuff in his place. He told them about the pieces of smashed mirror on his bed. Selena listened carefully.

"Any idea who did it?" she asked.

Jameel shook his head slowly. "Haven't a clue. Thing is, I've met hundred of boys."

"Mortals?" Selena interrupted.

Jameel nodded. "But I haven't had a conversation with any of them." He grinned. "I hang out with Carlos and Juan. They were with me at the club, so they couldn't have done my place over."

"Is there anyone you've made an enemy of?" Selena asked.

"No one. Not in Spain. Anyway, I resent the implication. A nice girl like me doesn't make enemies." Jameel patted the back of his head.

"I can think of one person who doesn't like you—Todd."

Jameel laughed loudly. "That little butt plug. I don't really think this is his style, do you?"

Selena arched an eyebrow. "Oh, don't you? You know his full nickname is Sweeney Todd. You know why, don't you?"

Jameel shrugged. "I've never been interested in any of that gangsta stuff."

"He's called Sweeny Todd because he carries a cutthroat razor."

Jameel rolled his eyes. "So messy! It's so much easier to use an incisor, don't you think?" he said to Rani.

Selena glanced at Rani. She looked like she wasn't sure how much to say. "This guy is very nasty. The Night Council think he's murdered several mortals and he may have killed at least two vampires."

Rani remembered the Night Council were people secretly chosen to make judgments on things that affected all vampires.

"Okay, so Todd wouldn't like it that I gave evidence," Jameel said. "But he's waited a long time to get back at me, hasn't he? Anyway, nothing was proved, so why would he bother?"

Rani was intrigued. "What did you give evidence about?"

Jameel and Selena looked at each other. "She'll find out eventually," Jameel said. He moved closer to Rani on the sofa. "Are you sitting comfortably?" She nodded. "This is a tale of murder and intrigue, gay men and drugs. Are you sure you want to hear it?"

She nodded again.

Jameel took a deep breath. "Well, then," he began. "I was living in San Francisco. I had a close friend. He was a mortal and he had his faults, but he really was a nice guy when he wasn't smoking rock." Jameel paused, remembering his friend. "One night, I was dancing and generally looking beautiful on the dance floor at my favorite drag club. I was getting many admiring glances of course, when my friend, Ben, pulled my arm and marched me off the floor, very excited. He wanted to give me some E; said he'd got it at a knockdown price; there was a new dealer at the club. I didn't take too much notice. Maybe I did some E, but obviously not very much." He looked at Rani quizzically. "Has anyone told you about drugs?"

"What? Just say no?" Rani joked.

"Well, you can if you like. No, you need to know that amphetamine-type drugs, the fast ones, are really fast for you now."

"Really?" Rani was surprised. "But spliff hardly has any effect on me now. I don't really bother with it anymore."

Selena nodded. "Yeah, the sedatives, tranqs, et cetera, work less. Our metabolisms are different from mortals. Don't ask me the science of it."

"So, because of that," Jameel continued, "I only took half an E, and we had a good night. Till I found him cracked out in a corner. That wasn't unusual by then." Jameel sighed. "Anyway, a couple of weeks later, on my way to the same club, I saw Todd outside. I withdrew behind a parked car, wondering what he was doing there. He's hardly a friend of Dorothy. In fact, Dorothy's never met him, I'm sure. I watched him—a little specialty of mine, Rani, if you ever need a spy—and after a few minutes, it was clear he was selling to the punters. Some bouncer types came over, and he melted away, so I went into the club. I wasn't especially concerned. We all have to make money somehow. Around a week later, it got more serious when the usual dealer, a mortal, turned up dead. Mortal papers said it was a gangland execution."

"Do you think it wasn't?" Rani asked.

"Ben told me he'd come across them having a row, a few blocks from the club."

"And the mortal dealer got his throat cut," Selena added.

Rani shuddered.

"So," Jameel went on, "when the Council sent some members of the guard, that's like our police force, because they'd heard rumors about Todd, I gave a statement. And that's the story."

Rani thought a moment. "Is this guy the same Todd who was at the ball?" she asked Selena.

Selena nodded. "Yes, he was there."

Rani frowned. "But Rob said he worked for the Count."

Jameel and Selena exchanged a look.

"Yes, he does," Jameel confirmed. "And that's another reason, Selena, why I don't think he's behind this. The Count adores me. He wouldn't let anyone do this to me."

Selena thought about that. "I agree. But the Count may not know about it. I think Todd's a bit of a law unto himself."

Rani felt excitement creep through her body now they were discussing the Count.

She asked Jameel, "So does the Count hang out with *goondas*?"

Jameel laughed loudly. "The Count is a *goonda*, my dear."

Selena rolled her eyes. "I'm sure the Count would be delighted to hear himself described so."

Rani was piqued. How come Selena knew the Hindi word for gangster?

"Anyway, we're getting off the subject." Selena seemed keen to change it back.

"Maybe so, but I think we've dissected it enough for one evening," Jameel said. "Now tell me, Rani, Rob said you're last name is Shah." He put one hand under his chin, tilting his head back expectantly.

"That's right," Rani said. "My mother's Hindu, my father's Muslim."

Jameel's smile licked both his ears. "Oh, my dear girl, we are so going to get on!" Then he slapped his knees with excitement. "Hey, I've got an idea. Why don't we all go to Rob's club? Surprise her?"

The club was jumping. They reached it at the busiest time. Rob was making sure a long queue all had hand stamps. Rani spotted her short, dark hair; slow, confident walk; cheeky, slightly crooked grin and felt her body respond. Rob was so smooth when she did security. She was quite charming, and just a little bit tuff. Music spilled out from the doors to the dance floor; bass grooved through Rani's body. She was suddenly ready to party.

Rob was looking the other way when Rani waved her hand stamp in front of her face, brushing Rob's cheek ever so lightly. Rob looked round startled, then broke into a big smile. She took Rani's hand and lifted it to her lips, laying a butterfly kiss on her. Rani looked at her with a look that said, *Keep that up and you're on a promise, baby.*

"Hurry up. You're holding up the queue," Jameel said haughtily.

"I hope you're not going to cause trouble," Rob joked, looking stern

"Who me?" Jameel put his hands up to his chest in a gesture of innocence.

"I've missed you." Rob grabbed Jameel in a bear hug.

"Move along, you lot. There's people waiting here." Selena pushed Jameel to emphasize her point.

"Oh no, another troublemaker. I'll have to keep my eye on you lot," Rob said.

"Who do you need to keep your eye on?" Lois, the owner of the club, wondered, stepping over to them. "Friends of yours?" she asked Rob. "I know this one." She wagged her finger at Rani. "Where've you been, stranger? No, don't tell me the gory details." She laughed and then turned to Rob. "Go on, take a break. I'll take over for a while."

Inside, the floor, walls, and ceiling vibrated. The dance

floor was a heaving, pulsing mass of bodies. Rani headed straight into the densest, hottest section of the floor. She exhaled, lifting her arms and expanding her chest. She felt herself start to relax and get that good vibe flowing. Rani could dance to anything, all night, losing herself. She didn't worry what she looked like. She closed her eyes and let the music take her. The DJ was mixing seamlessly, tune to tune. The bass was phat, oozing. Rani felt it through the floor; she felt it in her pelvis as she worked her body.

Someone knocked into her, rhythmically. Rani opened her eyes to find Jameel bouncing against her. She took his hand and they half bounced, half bhangra-ed, women's style, circling each other, hands raised, and then dancing back to back, all hips and arms. Selena squeezed in beside them and Rob too. Rani saw they were dancing together, and she wasn't having that. She pressed herself into the tiny space between them, smiling at them broadly, not minding at all that they both pressed back. She was used to this kind of crazy physicality from lesbians. That was one of the things she had always loved about the women's community—how physical things can get, how easy women get with each other's bodies; friends, lovers, and everything in between.

Rob was all hips and crotch. That was her dancing style. When she moved her arms, it was like she was working out. Most of the action was lower; she rotated and shook her tush, bending her knees to get maximum movement. As Rani watched, Rob held herself with one hand and bent the other behind her neck, grinding so hot Rani couldn't resist. She eased her body in close, pushing Rob's hand harder against herself. They both laughed. Rani took a big, sweet breath, feeling good. Rob wrenched her hand from underneath Rani's thigh and put it around Rani's waist. Their bodies connected like sea flowing onto shore. Rani stared at Rob, amazed at how good-looking she was.

Rani knew at that moment she wasn't going to say anything about the Count. There wouldn't be any point, she reasoned, because she wasn't going to see the Count again. Rani smiled at Rob, slowly running her tongue over her lips, loving how she could turn her on. Rob smiled back, that cocky smile that went straight to Rani's underwear. Rani remembered them dancing like this the night they'd first slept together. She remembered how crazy she'd been for Rob. She felt a rush of affection, knowing Rob had been patient with her lately. Well, she could make it up to her, Rani decided.

She ground close, pushing her thighs into Rob's and squeezing Rob's buttocks between her fingers. Rob's breath was hot on Rani's neck. Rani drew back, teasing. She looked Rob in the eyes. Oh, she was so going to get laid when they got back home

CHAPTER THIRTEEN

Some joker put me opposite the Count. I was here as a favor to Jameel who'd wanted this "little soirée," as he'd put it, to take his mind off what had happened in Spain. It had sounded like a good idea—a get-together with his friends. Unfortunately, his friends included the Count. Everyone seemed to like the cocky gangster except me. Selena, Jameel, and now Rani liked him. She'd been going on and on about him ever since the ball. Fortunately, she'd shut up about him lately.

We were getting on better. Maybe she was settling into the Life. We'd had a very long, very lovely session after we'd got back from the club. I loved her confident sexuality and I was beginning to take Rani into my heart. The age difference between us wasn't such a problem as before. I had no idea where our relationship was going. I was happy to let everything happen in its own time.

The soirée was in a private dining room in a big hotel on the Strand. The room was all wood paneling and plush leather seating. I was appreciating older buildings more and more. Knowing this building had seen time pass like I had was comforting. We were grouped along a dark wood table. The Count was opposite me, with Jameel on his left. Rani was on my right and Selena the other side of me. Leah sat opposite Selena, next to the Count.

We were smartly dressed. The Count and I were in dinner suits. Fortunately, he wasn't wearing his embarrassing cloak. Rani was in a midnight blue lengha. Both the long full skirt and sleeveless tight top were rich with gold embroidery. The top showed off Rani's sexy midriff. Selena wore a black velvet dress with a lace bodice and sleeves, and Leah was in an off the shoulder red satin dress, with rubies glittering at her neck. Jameel looked splendid in a long, dark wig, very tight vinyl dress, and high heeled boots up to his thighs.

There was candlelight, wine, beer, soft drinks, hot drinks, crystal, and fine china. *Madama Butterfly* was playing softly in the background. It was all very elegant. Any other group would have had food, I supposed. I didn't think we were all going to *eat* together. Least I hoped not. I didn't want to get down and dirty with the Count. Having to stare at his smug face across from me was bad enough. The thought of his incisors thrusting toward me made me shudder.

Selena nudged me. Everyone was staring.

"What?" I said.

Jameel leaned across the table. "Where you at, boyfriend? *We're* playing a game if you care to join us. That's if we can possibly compete with whatever's going on in your head."

I shrugged. "What are you playing?"

Jameel smiled. "We're playing the game where we say what our favorite food used to be. What's yours?"

"What? I only get one?" I asked.

Jameel sighed. "Come along. It's not that hard." He curled his long red nails around his wine glass, tilted his head back, and sipped till the wine was gone.

"Here, pretty one." The Count offered Jameel one of his blood-in-a-bottle concoctions. Jameel bestowed a smile on him, and he filled Jameel's glass with something claiming to be Nosferatu AB, 1992.

"Spaghetti alla Rustica," I said. "Plain and simple. Fresh spaghetti, tomato sauce with lots and lots of garlic."

"Oh no, not garlic!" Selena shrieked in a good imitation of a heroine in a melodrama. Everyone laughed.

"Where did that idea come from?" Leah asked.

Jameel, Selena, and the Count all looked at one another. As three of the oldest of all vampires, they automatically consulted one another before turning to anyone else. I don't think they even realized they did it.

"I know that mortals believed, long ago, that garlic would

help cure rabies. They used to say it would help against the biting of a mad dog. It was thought to protect against evil as well," Selena said.

"Maybe they thought cutting off our heads and stuffing our mouths with garlic would put us off it," the Count said dryly.

Rani reacted in horror. "What do you mean? Did that really happen?"

"It certainly did." The Count looked like he was about to launch into a potted history.

Fortunately, Selena butted in. "Garlic's good for the blood, that's for sure. Why they'd think we wouldn't like the smell, I haven't a clue."

"I find it quite sexy, actually," the Count said, not seeming at all bothered that Selena cut in on him.

"Oh, you find anything sexy," Leah said with a sideways glance at Rani. I guessed that was a dig at Rani. She narrowed her eyes at Leah. I'd already worked out the Count fancied my girlfriend. He seemed to make a habit of that.

Selena coughed. "Well, I miss olives. I have one every now and then, just for fun. Love the salt."

"I miss salt too," Jameel said. "Don't you think blood is less salty these days? I'm sure of it."

I agreed.

"It's these bloody low-salt diets!" the Count complained. "But not to worry. I'm working on a special batch of extra salty Nosferatu. Shall I put you down for some, Selena?"

Selena smiled at him. "Yes, please." I could tell she was amused at the Count's initiative. That was always something she'd liked about him. He was always ready to take advantage.

"What about you, Rob?" he asked me. "Need any more salt in your diet? Or have you had all the *new blood* you can handle?"

I glared at him.

"Well, I know what I miss," Jameel said quickly and loudly.

"What?" said Selena and Rani simultaneously. They obviously both wanted to move the conversation away from me and the Count. Leah, however, looked quietly amused.

"Spices, chili in particular." Jameel turned to Selena.

"You know how you have olives every now and then? Well, I have a little chili. Oh, Rani, you must take some occasionally. It's amazing."

Rani smiled. "Really? Okay, I will. You're right. I have been missing it. It's like my body craves it."

"Oh, my goodness," Jameel exclaimed. "We can't have that. Right then, as a special mercy mission let's take some together, tomorrow."

He was like an excited schoolgirl.

"Is it a private chili party, or can anyone join in?" the Count asked suggestively.

"Darling, I know you *want* me," Jameel pouted. "But you have to wait your turn. Tomorrow, I'm all Rani's."

Jameel was as clever as he was sweet. He diffused tension as quickly as the Count could build it.

"I miss Tarka dall," Rani said. "And chapatti with a tiny bit of butter—not ghee," she emphasized. "A bit of butter on it, hot and melting."

"Umm." Jameel was practically salivating. "Tarka dall, good choice, Rani. Now, Leah…" Jameel peered round the Count to talk to her. "What was your favorite dish?"

Leah smiled enigmatically. She indicated that the Count should fill her glass with Nosferatu.

"Hmm, that's easy. My favorite dish has to be chicken," she said, looking right at Rani.

The Count chuckled, also looking at Rani. I let out a sigh.

"Now I wouldn't go so far as to cook it. That seems a little cruel. But I'd certainly want it warm," Leah continued. She shared a laugh with the Count. Selena shifted awkwardly in her seat.

Rani looked at me. She knew something was up, but I didn't think she knew that chicken was a derogatory term for humans. Rani gave Leah a look. She'd got her number. I smiled to myself. There was no need to worry about Rani.

Leah and the Count were notoriously mortal-phobic. In the separatist 1980s, they were in the vanguard, fighting for vampire rights and building up a case against humans. To them, everything separated into vampire equals good, mortal equals bad.

Jameel went to the side table and brought a couple of

bottles of wine back. "More Claret anyone?" he said, he voice a bit too bright. "Right, what can we play now?"

"Hang on," the Count said. "I haven't said what my favorite dish is."

Jameel looked at him sternly. "Okay, but play nicely."

The Count looked like butter wouldn't melt on his lap. "I have to be honest though, don't I? And it's true that I am partial to a tender bit of chicken myself. It's finger licking good, after all, and I know Robert will agree with me." He folded his arms and sat back, smiling smugly. "It's an enjoyable sport, bringing a chicken in, wouldn't you say, old boy?"

"That's enough," I said.

"Yes, that's enough of that game." Jameel began to fill people's glasses. "I said *play nicely*," he hissed at the Count. Selena shook her head and went to the side to make herself a cup of mint tea. The Count held up his hands in an innocent gesture. I was gratified to see Rani was looking contemptuously at him. *That* took the smug look off his face.

Selena sat back down with her tea. "Count, is that guy still working for you? The guy who's good at getting things, um, Todd I think his name is."

The Count grabbed the bottle of claret from Jameel, who'd left him out. "Todd? What do you want with him, Selena?"

"Well, I just wondered if he was working for you in England, or if he's working abroad at the moment."

"Why?" The Count sat back, studying Selena.

I felt a prickling sensation at the back of my neck. Actually, it wasn't prickling. More like someone very softly stroking the shaved hairs there. I turned to Rani. She wasn't doing anything. I could tell it wasn't her energy anyway. She didn't even look like she was listening to the conversation. She had a faraway look to her.

Someone was stroking my foot now, really stroking my foot, not just sending the impression of it to my mind like the neck thing. My eyes darted to the Count. I hoped by whatever's holy it wasn't him.

"I just need someone to get stuff for me, that's all," Selena said.

"I can get you anything you need, Selena. You know that," the Count said.

The thin end of a stiletto slid up my calf to the knee. Definitely wasn't the Count then. I looked at Leah. She smiled at me sweetly.

"Yes, I know you can, Count, but I need things in Mexico, and I heard Todd worked abroad these days?"

"Oh?" The Count sipped his claret, looking at Selena over the top of his glass. "Who told you that?"

The sensation of my neck being stroked started up again. I frowned at Leah, though I was impressed by the trick. She was indicating the Count with her eyes. I looked at him, not understanding. Then Leah looked at Rani. I glanced at Rani. She looked strange. As I watched, she started to flush. Not so you'd see. Blood rising to the surface of her dark skin wouldn't be immediately obvious to the eye, but I could feel she was turned on. I looked back to Leah, and she immediately tipped her head toward the Count. With a start, I realized the Count was doing to Rani what Leah had been doing to me. And Rani was definitely getting off on it. *What a clever parlor trick.*

Isn't it? Leah slipped into my mind.

"Todd does work for me abroad. That's what you want to know, isn't it, Selena?" The Count came to the point. "He works in Europe mainly, so he's no use to you in Mexico."

"Right. Which countries?" Selena persisted. "I might have friends there."

I hoped for her sake she wasn't about to go undercover any time soon. The Count stared thoughtfully at Selena. "France, Germany, Italy, Holland, oh, and Spain. Well, we've all got a friend *there*, haven't we?" He turned to Jameel. Jameel smiled graciously. I felt Rani hold my hand. I squeezed her hand back and then dropped it to pick up my drink. I reasoned with myself not to make too big a deal out of the situation. I shouldn't really begrudge her a bit of psychic fondling with the Count.

"Do you realize Rob has slept with two out of three women in this room?" Leah changed the subject dramatically.

I spat out a mouthful of red wine. It sprayed the white tablecloth beautifully. Jameel, however, coughed in an offended way.

"Oh, sorry, Jameel. Two out of four women. Well, fifty percent isn't bad is it?" Leah continued. "We could always up the ante. What do you say, Rob? Want to go for three out of four?" Leah pouted at me and then blew me a kiss. What was she up to now?

"Mind you, that's not as good as the Count. Now, he's…" Leah paused dramatically. "He's often in that position at parties." Leah turned to him and ran her finger slowly down his throat. "Due to your ferocious appetites, aren't you, darling?"

The Count chuckled again, a low, growling chuckle. "I'm not one to boast."

"No, you pay people to do that for you, don't you?" I said, sick of the way he strutted about playing Lord of the Manor. As far as I was concerned, everything he touched was dirty.

The Count stared at me. I stared back cockily. I'd known him too long to be intimidated.

"Tell me." The Count smacked his lips. "Have you met Rani's family yet?"

I narrowed my eyes.

"Maybe they don't want to meet you. Maybe they've heard things, heard you're a little strange. Maybe they're too *chicken* to meet you."

"I'm warning you," I said very quietly.

"How many are there?" He leaned across to Rani, as if he was really asking her. Then he turned to me. "Ah, but I'm sure you don't like to count your *chickens*." He burst into laughter at his own joke.

"Shut your mouth." I'd really had enough of him.

The Count laughed in a superior way. "Breeding will always come out, won't it, Rob?"

"Well, we can't all have your way with words. When it comes down to it, you're a very high and mighty piece of garbage," I said, trying to regain my control.

"Okay, Rob, let's try to keep it civil," Jameel interrupted me.

"I'm tired of playing games," I told Jameel.

"Yes, I can see that." He sighed. "But I don't think the party will survive one of your plain-speaking moments."

"Everything can't just be about fun, Jameel." I was mad now and not listening, even to friends.

"Well, it certainly isn't when you're around, Rob," the Count said snidely.

"And when you're around, why is it I get sick to my

stomach?" I asked him.

"I don't know. But you always have had a weak stomach, haven't you, Rob? Or is it that you're just weak? Not able to stand on your own two feet—"

"Okay, I think this has gone far enough," Selena's quiet, firm voice interrupted.

I knew what he was getting at. How jealous I used to be of his relationship with Selena. Vampires aren't supposed to feel jealous. The Count bringing it up then was the final straw.

"You have to needle don't you, Count? You can't leave anyone alone. I see you have Leah playing your games too. I think it's very sad you two are obviously that *bored.*"

It was out of my mouth before I could stop myself. There was a stunned silence for a second. Jameel covered his face with his hands.

"What did you say?" The Count was coldly furious.

"That was very ungallant, Rob." Leah was clearly shocked and offended.

I kept quiet. I'd already said the worst thing anyone can say to a vampire. Vampires believe that boredom drives vampires to suicide, commonly called "lying in the sun." Vampires who have gone over are seen as weak or mad, and as turning their backs on the Life. Ever since Desdemona Dresden's popular book *The Long, Slow Death: Vampires, Boredom, and Suicide,* boredom had become a dirty word. To say someone was bored was to imply maybe they were suicidal, which made them weak, mad, and a traitor.

Leah and the Count were on their feet.

"Thanks, everybody, for a lovely evening," Jameel said, sarcasm flitting in his normally bright voice.

I looked apologetically at him. I hadn't wanted to make things difficult for Jameel.

"Well, we all have to go now anyway," Selena said diplomatically, looking at her watch. "It's getting near time, people."

The Count was helping Leah into her coat. I went to get Rani's and Selena's, then I thought I'd better help Jameel into his coat first. He acknowledged the gesture.

"I'm sorry, Jameel," I whispered into his ear, too quietly for anyone else to hear. He rewarded me with a smile that would warm anyone's heart.

"You're too impetuous, boi." He wagged his finger at me.

Rani came and got her coat out of my hand, winking at me. She looked like she'd got a kick out me rucking with the Count. Selena came over too, and insisted on putting her own coat on.

"We haven't got time for your funny little ways, Rob," she said, waving me out the door. She'd been like that ever since she found feminism in the 1970s.

The hotel had recently started valet parking, due to the craziness of parking in London. We were waiting outside for our cars to arrive when I noticed a car slowing as it approached. It wasn't my Saab. It was a nondescript hatchback. It didn't look like the kind of car the Count would drive. I looked away, wishing the valets would hurry up, when a screeching of tires made me turn back.

The hatchback was heading straight for us. The car mounted the pavement, burning rubber, the engine revving, metal flashing. Rani and I darted behind the car with Leah and the Count. Selena and Jameel were pressed flat into the entrance of the hotel. As Selena tripped on the steps, something sharp on the car caught her. The flesh on her arm opened and blood streamed out. The car's bonnet missed them by millimeters. It hit a bollard, shuddered, and then sped off down the road.

Staff rushed out of the hotel. Suddenly, there was talk of ambulances and police. We didn't have time for any of that. Dawn had begun. Fortunately, our cars arrived. The Count dealt with the humans. We got Selena into my Saab. I asked Rani to drive, as I wanted to help Selena.

"She'll need this." Leah pushed some bottles of blood through the window. With the mortals looking on, for once, I was glad his Nosferatu looked like small bottles of wine.

Rani drove off with the three of us in the back. Jameel held Selena's wound together while I focused my energy on healing it. It was a deep wound, but as the light got bright enough for all of us to need sunglasses, we were making some headway in sealing it. Jameel had to take over as I tired.

"You okay, Rani?" I put my hand on her shoulder from behind, wanting some contact.

"Sure." She nodded. "Will Selena be all right?" She

glanced in the rearview mirror.

"Yeah. The wound's healing. She just needs some blood now."

"Did you see who was driving that car?" Rani asked.

"No. All the windows were tinted weren't they?" All I could remember was dark glass.

"Surely not the windscreen?" Rani thought aloud.

"I saw in the windscreen," said Jameel quietly. "Whoever was driving was wearing a mask. A Halloween mask of a vampire."

CHAPTER FOURTEEN

Rani shifted on the sofa, listening to Selena pontificate. "I think whoever it was knew we were vampires. They wanted us to get stuck out there. Either caught up in some human-police situation or wounded and weak so we'd be vulnerable at sunrise."

"Oh, for goodness sake, Selena!" Rob was getting ready for work and sounded impatient. "You've been going on about this for three days. Why can't you think it was just some drunken idiot?"

"You never want to see what's right in front of your face," Selena said.

Rani watched them, thinking they were like an old married couple. Jameel raised his eyes at Rani and giggled. They were sitting around in Rob's front room, deciding what to do with the night. There was talk of going to Rob's club.

"If it's all so dangerous, *why*..." Rob emphasized, running a tiny amount of gel through her very short hair. "*Why* are you going back to Spain, Jameel?"

Jameel looked over at Rob. "Because I *live* in Spain."

"There's nothing to say it's anyone in Spain anyway," Selena said. "Jameel's only been in Spain five months."

"What you saying, Selena? This only started since Jameel went to Spain?" Rob stopped fussing with her hair.

"I think maybe this has something to do with Ben's death," Selena answered. She turned to Jameel. "You think Todd killed Ben. I know you do. I can see why. Todd could easily have made it look like suicide."

Jameel sat quietly. Rani suspected he was thinking about his mortal boyfriend in San Francisco and his horrible death.

"I don't get you going back to Spain," Rob said. "We can look after you here. You don't know anybody there."

"I'm going back with him," Selena said.

Rob looked at Jameel and Selena for a long moment. "Well, it's up to you," she said.

Selena put her arm around Rob. "I was always going to go to Spain, Rob," she said gently. "I'd love to stay here, but it's way too cold for me this time of year. Why don't I come back when it's warmer?" She smiled beguilingly. Rani noted how easily Rob was won over. "Anyhow, someone should be with Jameel."

Rob took a deep breath and then hugged her.

Rani sensed that Rob was disappointed Selena was leaving. Rani wasn't. She liked Selena well enough now, but she was happy it would soon be just Rob and her again. She decided she'd give Rob and Selena some time together. She had loads of work to catch up on anyhow.

She drove over to Stoke Newington, grabbing a bite on the way. She took pride in feeding herself. *I'm all grown up now*, she joked to herself as she walked away from the guy slumped against a wall outside the pub. She released her mind lock and he came to. Rani heard a thought inside his head that he must have had more to drink than he realized. He decided to go home and sleep it off.

Gulsin was waiting for Rani when she got to the flat for the face-to-face business meeting she'd decided they needed. Gulsin filled Rani in on developments and orders. High Class had a new sheer, high shine control top line of tights that promised to suck you in while making your legs look sexy and attractive. Their erotic lingerie supplier had sent details of a line that featured lacing as its main concept. The satin bustier laced up the front as well as at its cutaway sides; the tiny g-string had lace on each hip, and the stockings were lace-topped. Full-length laced gloves were available to complete the look in black, red, and the summer season's colors of hot pink and turquoise. Rani and Gulsin discussed the merits of this set and other delights, particularly whether their clients would want them enough to fork out lots of money.

"There's some letters on the computer I didn't quite finish, and they need printing out." Gulsin wound down the meeting. "Be good if you could get them in a post box tonight. If you make the parcels up, I'll take them to the post office tomorrow."

Rani agreed. "Get off, Gulsin. Go and have a life!"

"Hey, I saw your mum yesterday." Gulsin put on her jacket. "She said she's not seeing as much of you as she used to."

Rani smiled sadly.

"Still, when you've got this other project of yours sorted, you can spend more time with your family, can't you?" Gulsin said.

Rani had forgotten for a moment the distance between herself and her old friend. She felt it now.

She hit the sound system, turned it up, sat at her PC, and burned through letters and orders. She took a break and went to the post box round the corner with a stack of mail.

Walking up to the box, she couldn't help noticing a Blood Transfusion Service van across the road. It was a mobile blood donating van. She was surprised to see it there so late. Checking her watch, she saw it was nine o'clock. Very late for people to be donating blood. Mind you, it looked all locked up. Rani idly wondered if there was any blood stored on the van.

A guy walked up to the driver's door and opened it. Rani recognized him as Todd, the man from the ball that had looked so coldly at Rob. Rani stepped behind the post box, not sure what to do. Maybe she should follow the van. She might be able to find out something about Todd that she could tell the others.

"Fancy meeting you here."

Rani turned to see the Count standing behind her.

"Oh, hello," she said.

"Have you ever thought of cutting out the middle man?" he asked, eyeing the stack of letters in her hand.

"Huh?"

The Count took the letters out of her hand and posted them. "I'm thinking of starting my own delivery service. With people that come and collect your parcels at a civilized hour. You'd find that useful, wouldn't you, Rani, with your business? I bet you've got parcels waiting at home right now."

Rani had a horrible feeling he'd been looking at her lingerie.

"Well, I'll keep you informed on that one." He took hold of her hand. "I see you've seen the van. Come and have a look round."

The Count's fingers in hers seemed to have a direct effect on her heartbeat, which accelerated as he led her across the road. Rani wondered why the attraction was so powerful?

He reached in the pocket of his gray Armani suit, took out a set of keys, and unlocked the back door.

"Have a look round," he said. As the door opened, Rani remembered she was annoyed with the Count. He'd upset Rob at Jameel's soirée, and insulted Rani's mortal family and friends (she'd realized when Rob had explained "chicken" to her).

"I'd love to play in your van, but I've got work to do," she said shortly.

The Count looked at her with huge innocent eyes. "Surely you're not still mad at me, are you?"

"Oh, I'm not mad at you. I just haven't got time for your games tonight," Rani said, looking away.

"What, not even a quick one?"

Rani laughed, despite herself. Her resolve was melting.

"But you insulted my family."

"My dear Rani." His fingers traced subtle lines on Rani's wrist. "I apologize if I offended you. My intention, I assure you, was to wind Rob up. You know how competitive we bois can get around beautiful women."

Rani sighed, not entirely believing him, but her misgivings were satisfied for the moment.

"I suppose I could take a quick look."

As Rani stepped inside the van, she heard the driver's door slam and footsteps. Todd appeared at the door just as the Count switched on the light.

"Ah, Todd. You've met Rani, haven't you?" the Count said to him.

Todd stared at Rani without smiling and nodded slowly.

"Ready to go, boss?" His voice was very quiet, understated.

"There's been a change of plan." The Count winked at Rani. "Listen, why don't you go and get the van in Docklands, unload it, and drop it off at the depot? Here." He tossed another set of keys to Todd. Todd caught them and stood in the doorway without speaking.

The Count looked at him then said, "Oh, yes. Take the bike. It's round the corner. The helmet's hidden under the hedge of a pretty house nearby with a blue front door."

Rani had a feeling he meant her house, though she hadn't seen the bike.

Todd nodded and left. The Count shut the door.

"Well, what do you think?" He gestured at the interior.

Rani thought it was very much like a place where you went to give blood. Black couches, syringes and sachets for blood, wipes, etc., posters explaining the benefits of giving blood. "Why have you got the keys?" she asked.

The Count's eyes crinkled in amusement. "It's my van. Do you like it?"

Rani supposed so. "What do you do with all the blood?"

"What, all this?" the Count said, opening a long steel fridge full of red sachets, all neatly labeled. "Feeling peckish?"

The scarlet rows, hanging like fruit for the plucking, drew her thirst.

"I sell it, of course," the Count answered her, taking one of the sachets out of the fridge. "Three hours out of the body. Can I tempt you?" He picked up a sharp and pricked the sachet. One drop of blood appeared proud and alone on the cold plastic. Rani's mouth watered. She started to breathe shallowly. *I'll just take the blood. I've got to eat.* The Count held the sachet toward her. She started to reach for it.

"Ah-ah!" He snatched it back. "If I give you this, what will you give me? I wonder..."

He stared her up and down, confident and sure. The longer the Count stared at her body, the hungrier Rani got. He took the drop of blood from the plastic with his finger and pressed it to her lips. A shiver ran clean through Rani. She told herself the night was cold. The smell of blood was strong; the pounding of her heart was making her light-headed.

"You look dizzy, my dear. Perhaps you should lie down." The Count touched her very lightly, and her body moved to a couch.

The Count picked up the sharp again and pricked the sachet all over one side. He held it over her, squeezed, and drops of cool blood fell on her lips and ran down her throat. She opened her mouth and drank in the gentle, red rain. *Sweet scarlet thirst.* The Count's voice inside her head was soft, soothing. She felt stroked, held.

"May I?" The Count lifted one of the drops of blood off her throat and held it up. Rani didn't speak. She couldn't trust herself. Fleetingly, she thought of Rob. The Count came level with her head. Rani stared into the eternity of his eyes. "May I?" he repeated.

Rani felt everything shift. Nothing was as it had been. Nothing could be relied on.

"Yes," she whispered. Then, "Yes," again.

He unbuttoned Rani's blouse, baring her to the breast, and then circled a nipple. The Count smiled as it stiffened. He took it between his finger and thumb, squeezed it, lifted his other arm, and drops of red rain fell onto Rani's face again.

You want me. Admit it. My blood is inside you. It runs in yours. You crave me. You always will.

Sand sifted beneath her as the Count's sweet, seductive voice spun away reason. There was nothing between this moment and sinking into ecstasy.

"Okay, I want you." She closed her eyes, laid her head back, and waited for the sharp, exquisite pleasure of his teeth on her neck.

"I like a bit of human stimulation. How about you?"

Rani opened her eyes, surprised as the Count unzipped her trousers. She raised her hips to help him take them off, and peeled off her thong herself.

"That's better," he said.

Rani smiled, and then her smile got broader as the Count unbuttoned his trousers. He was packing and standing proudly to attention.

"Let's do it like the humans do," he said with relish, jumping on the couch.

He slipped expertly inside her and Rani opened wide, taking the silicone deep inside. He moved back and forth. Rani moaned loudly, unable to keep quiet. The Count pressed into her, licking her neck. Rani opened as wide as she possibly could and pushed her throat into his mouth. Finally, she felt him bite through her skin and begin to suck.

He thrusted fast and they pumped on the couch as the Count sucked the blood from her neck. Everything slipped away. There was nothing except the sensation of being full in every part of her body, gorged, ridden high toward climax. Rani didn't want to come, wanted to stay pressed onto the couch forever. In a sea of wet, unable to stop herself, she flooded into massive orgasm. The Count held her, still moving inside her, still sucking on her neck until Rani squeezed every last drop out of it, until the last shuddering moment faded gently away.

"Are you aware quite how loud you were?" the Count asked, laughing. "I should imagine the whole street's standing outside."

Rani flushed, but she didn't care. She felt incredible. There was a knock on the door.

"I wonder who that is," the Count said, standing and buttoning himself in. Rani pulled on her top and trousers before the Count walked to the door. As he turned the handle, it opened.

"Not the whole street, just me." Leah stepped up into the van.

Rani didn't know what to make of this new direction.

The Count looked at his watch. "You're a bit early, darling."

"Oh, sorry, didn't spoil anything, did I?" Leah had a devilish look.

"Not at all." The Count grinned. "I was just showing Rani my equipment." Leah's eyes glowed. Rani saw the Count was more of a player than she'd realized. It didn't bother her, but she saw she'd need to keep her wits about her.

"So are we going to spend the rest of the night together?" Leah asked. It was the friendliest Rani had ever heard her be.

The Count looked at Rani for an answer.

"Sorry, I've got things to do." Rani shrugged. She wasn't ready to play games with both of them. She was just about handling the Count—oh, and Rob, of course. She spotted her thong lying under the couch, bent to pick it up, and smoothly slipped it in her pocket. "See you around," she said nonchalantly. At the door, she paused and turned. "Nice van."

She pouted at the Count and sashayed out, letting the door shut behind her.

Rani laughed as she walked up the street, enjoying the look of surprise on their faces when she'd left them.

She went into her flat. She was in no state to go to Rob's club. But she could get a helluva lot of work done. She had a fantastic amount of energy suddenly. She decided she'd stay at her flat, sleep there, and see Rob tomorrow. Maybe by then she could work out just what it was she wanted.

CHAPTER FIFTEEN

On the plane to Malaga, Selena pondered on the attacks directed toward Jameel. She was thinking of a way to broach the subject when Jameel spotted his favorite trolley dolly.

"Now where was *he* hiding when I came in?" he said to Selena.

"No doubt he was busy counting tea and coffee or something," Selena said.

She wondered how long she should leave it before she put some of her theories to Jameel. She was dying to solve this mystery. She just needed to get some more information out of him.

"So, which one do you fancy?" Jameel could always be relied on for light gossip.

Selena followed his gaze. He was looking at the three air stewards.

Selena checked them out.

"Well, I don't fancy the one wearing trousers," Selena joked.

Jameel smiled broadly. "No, he's not butch enough for you is he?" He winked. Then he leaned closer. "Actually, don't take this the wrong way, but I meant the women!"

Selena pretended to look shocked. "You're not suggesting I'm a…" She gasped. "*Lesbian*, are you?"

"I think you might be incurably homosexual," Jameel said gravely.

"What gave me away?" Selena asked.

Jameel looked her up and down. "Big thumbs."

Selena slapped his arm. Still, she looked at her hands. "Are they?"

Jameel gave her his best superior look. "You wish!"

She turned away. "Do you think there is a gay gene?"

"Plenty." Jameel flicked through the in-flight magazine.

"Really?" Selena turned back. Maybe Jameel had some scientific information she hadn't heard about.

"Yes," said Jameel. "I've known at least five in my lifetime, all gay, all called Jean."

"Oh, for goodness sake!" Selena noticed there was an article in the magazine about shopping in Madrid. That looked interesting. She took her copy out of the pocket in front of her.

"You haven't told me which one you fancy," Jameel said nonchalantly, flicking pages.

Selena answered without looking round. She was fixing to memory that the Salamanca district was good for designer clothes shops, and that El Rastro had a big flea market on weekends. "The blond one," she said to shut Jameel up.

"Short blond hair or long blond?" Jameel asked.

"Hmm?" Selena was engrossed in her magazine. "Short blond. The one with the nice legs."

"Good choice," Jameel said.

"Anything to drink, ladies?"

Selena looked up into the amused face of the short blond-haired stewardess standing next to them in the aisle. Selena glared at Jameel and ordered some sparkling wine. The stewardess smiled at her in a very unoffended way. Jameel tittered to himself for a good five minutes till the plane started to bounce around a little. The fasten seatbelts sign flashed on, and the sweet looking steward came down the aisle checking seatbelts.

"You should have that a little bit tighter, miss." He bent down, adjusting Jameel's belt. He nodded at Selena and then moved along with a wicked smile to Jameel. Selena raised her eyebrows.

"I don't know how you do it!" she said.

"It's hard being this gorgeous, but someone has to be," was Jameel's reply. He was looking particularly lovely in tight jeans, a red T-shirt, and a denim jacket. His blond wig contrasted strikingly against his complexion. He had removed the wig temporarily while going through passport control to avoid complications.

"It's different with women," Selena said.

"What is?"

"I can't imagine a woman being so obvious about fancying a total stranger."

"It's true. Men are dogs. Thank God!" Jameel tapped the end of Selena's knee while making his point.

Selena loved the female-male combination of Jameel. He was tough and sensitive, liked style and beauty, and Selena adored him. He was one of her best friends.

"Maybe you just haven't met the right women." Jameel always lived in hope.

Selena thought about Jameel and the steward. "You've got a thing about mortals, haven't you?"

Jameel smiled enigmatically, though there was a cloud in his eye.

"It must have upset you, that man dying in Spain," Selena said.

Jameel didn't say anything. Selena pursued the conversation. "Did it make you think of Ben?"

Jameel looked down the aisle, but his focus was far away. After a long silence, he turned back to Selena and nodded hesitantly.

Selena clasped Jameel's arm, wishing she could do more to ease his guilt and pain. She turned the pages of her magazine, but her mind was on Jameel and the mortal who had died in the States.

When Jameel met Ben, he had a history of using drugs but was off them and in Narcotics Anonymous. Jameel hadn't meant to fall in love. Ben was a mortal, and it was only supposed to be a casual affair. But Ben had been charming, handsome, and sensitive. He'd made Jameel feel special, and more than that, he'd made Jameel feel powerful, like nothing in the world could touch him, or hurt him. Ben found out about Jameel by accident because Jameel had been careless.

He had been feeding in a cruising area. Somehow, he hadn't noticed Ben. When Ben confronted him about it, Jameel had told him, and Ben had been brilliant. Carried away on a wave of enthusiasm at being able to be himself, Jameel wanted to bring Ben in. He sent an application to the Night Council. Ben had been very excited about the idea; Jameel couldn't see any problems.

Then two things happened. The Council wanted longer to consider the idea, and Ben started smoking rock again. By the time the Council made up their minds, Jameel agreed with them. It would be crazy to bring Ben into the Life. Their relationship never recovered, and Jameel had a potentially messy problem—a mortal who knew what he was.

Soon afterward, there was the incident with Todd and giving witness against him. Then one night, two mortal policemen had come to Jameel's apartment and told him Ben had taken a drugs overdose. Apparently, Ben had surrounded himself with candles before he took a massive amount of barbiturates. Somehow, while Ben was comatose, the flat had caught fire. By the time the firemen got his body out, he was beyond resuscitation.

"Do you think of Ben much?" Selena asked.

"All the time," he said quietly.

Jameel had thrown money at Ben's funeral. Ben didn't have any family, at least none who wanted to know him, and not many friends. Jameel wanted him to have the best. Jameel ordered the most expensive coffin, closed casket, as Ben's body had been burnt in the fire. Ben was driven to the cemetery in a horse-drawn hearse, surrounded by white lilies. Jameel had worn a simple black dress with a black veil and had wept as Ben was lowered into the ground. He'd thrown black roses onto the coffin as earth showered from above. He'd blamed himself.

"Do you still think Todd had anything to do with Ben's death, or do you think it *was* suicide?" Selena stroked Jameel's arm. All of Jameel's friends had been incredibly gentle with him since Ben's death.

"Do you know Todd came up to me at the funeral…*at the funeral*," he emphasized, "and said I'd killed him."

"You never told me that before," Selena said. "What did he mean, anyway?"

Jameel paused, like it was hurting him to say it out loud. "He said Ben should never have found out about me before I was sure about him. He said I shouldn't have broken up with him while he was so vulnerable. Selena." Jameel gripped Selena's hand. "He said Ben spoke to him the night he died, and Todd had tried to find me because he thought Ben might do something stupid. He *did* come up to me, but I refused to have anything to do with him. I refused even to talk to him. It was at that club, and there were mortals about, and I thought he was going to try and stop me giving evidence."

Selena gently pulled Jameel's hand off her arm and held it. "So let me get this straight. Todd came up to you, you refused to speak to him, and he just walked away?"

Jameel nodded, haunted with grief and guilt.

"Well, he didn't try very hard then, did he? And what could you have done? Jameel, if someone wants to go, they'll do it eventually, whatever you do. It was horrible for you. I know. We don't have to deal with death very often, remember, particularly suicide."

Selena wished she hadn't brought the subject up. Trouble was, Jameel never wanted to talk about it. An announcement cut into their silence. The plane was about to touch down. Selena was thankful for that.

The mood lightened after they landed in Malaga. Selena was excited to be in Spain, and Jameel was pleased to be back. Plus, the steward had slipped a phone number in his hand as they'd left the plane. By the time they'd passed passport control and customs, and Jameel had fixed his wig back on in the toilets, they were both laughing and joking about Selena's chances with the blond stewardess.

"I think she bats for our side," Jameel said as they stepped through the doors into arrivals. "It might have been a trick of the light, but I think she was packing. I know that's unusual in a skirt, but I quite like it."

"You're making it up!" Selena laughed.

"No, I tell you—" he broke off, his attention taken by a man waving at them. He was holding up a sign that said *Jameel Patel*. Patel was the last name Jameel was currently using. Jameel walked over to him while Selena followed with their trolley.

"Señor Patel?" the man looked at Jameel quizzically. He couldn't help looking him up and down.

"Flowers for you, señor…ita." He produced a bouquet from the chair beside him and gave them to Jameel.

"So who's sending you flowers, and to the airport? That must have taken some organizing," Selena said excitedly.

But Jameel just stared at the beautiful cellophane wrapping. Even covered, the scent of the white lilies was glorious. Jameel's eyes were fixed on a small white card. Selena read it over his shoulder: *Te compadezco.*

"What's that in English?" she asked.

Jameel's voice was shaky. "You have my deepest sympathies."

***

The Count's office door was wide open. He was obviously expecting him. Todd went to knock, but the Count saw him and waved him in.

"All the vans are back, boss. The blood's being unloaded now. Looks like people have been especially generous today."

The Count smiled wearily. "Glad to hear that, Todd. Have a seat." He gestured toward the empty leather chair in front of his desk.

Todd shook his head. "I won't if you don't mind, boss. I've got a few things to do."

The Count sighed. "Okay, here's the thing. You know how you're not supposed to go to San Francisco."

Todd nodded. They both knew he had been banned from visiting San Francisco since the warning from the Night Council.

"Well, I've got a problem," the Count continued. "I need someone to make sure the West Coast shipment gets there. I need someone I can trust."

"Why can't Mike take it?" Todd asked. Mike had been responsible for all the US shipments since Todd had fallen from grace.

Todd had never thought it was necessary to take all the US shipments from him, but the Count had thought it was best. He'd said the company needed to be seen to comply with the Council's demands. Todd suspected it was the Count's way of rapping his knuckles for the trouble in the States.

"Mike was picked up by a couple of guardians an hour ago at twilight."

"Why?" Todd asked.

"Yesterday, his face appeared on a website that claims to identify members of the mortal Mafioso. A photo of him with his current identity appeared at midday, Greenwich mean time. The guard were alerted anonymously at fifteen hundred. By the end of sunset, two guardians had picked Mike up and taken him in for questioning." The Count stared at Todd.

Todd stared back impassively.

"We need to find out how this happened. I don't like it," the Count said quietly. Todd knew that tone of voice. It meant the Count was furious.

The Count opened a drawer and pulled out some airline tickets. "Still, that can wait for now. The shipment is a bigger problem. I need you to go with it. Will you do that for me?"

Todd was under no illusions the Count was making a request. He knew an order when he heard one. The Count was aware Todd would be in serious trouble if anyone found out he'd broken the conditions of his warning. He'd decided the shipment of blood was more important.

"Okay, I'll go." Todd kept his voice was level. There was no trace of emotion in it.

The Count looked relieved. "Then it's noted. You've done me a favor."

The Count pushed the tickets and a second envelope across the desk toward Todd. "All the details you need are in there."

Todd picked up the envelopes, nodded, and went to leave.

"Todd." The Count stopped him. "Make sure you're not seen."

Todd turned. "And what if I am?"

The Count blinked once, coldly. "Then you're on your own."

Todd left. Outside the door, he smiled to himself. He'd expected no less from the Count. Business would always come first for him. As Todd walked along the corridor, his smile got broader. He thought of the suitcase packed full of ecstasy waiting in his flat. Then he thought of Mazzioni in San Francisco. The Italian was going to be one happy capo. Right now, he had a lot of desperate punters and no E. Shame how the supply had dried up in San Fran, when in London there was so much the price was rock bottom. Todd's smile was very broad indeed.

***

Traveling Business Class softened the blow for the long, complicated journey from San Francisco to Malaga. The guardian pulled down the blind covering the window, even though there was no chance of any sun in any time zone this plane was flying through for the next thirteen hours. An air stewardess approached. The guardian declined any food, accepted some Scotch, and prepared to settle in. The air stewardess leaned in discreetly.

"I believe you have special requirements, um, your condition?"

The guardian nodded. It was standard practice for vampires traveling long haul to inform the air companies that they had erythropoietic protoporphyria, a human blood condition where excess porphyrins are produced. The buildup of porphyrins in tissue leads to skin photosensitivity—sensitivity to sunlight. Normally, the stewards were too embarrassed to want to talk about the disease.

"I don't think there'll be any problems on this flight,"

The air stewardess smiled in a sympathetic way. "I'm surprised how many of you there are."

The guardian frowned. "I'm not with you. How many... what?"

She looked a little flustered. "Oh, I didn't mean anything. It's just, I thought the disease was quite rare, but you're the fourth person I've met on this route this year. Oh, and there was someone last December too. I remember her especially as she was an Asian lady wearing a blond wig." The air hostess looked thoughtful. "Well, I think it was a wig," she reflected to herself. "It must have been a wig."

The guardian's eyes slid across the name tag on the stewardess's shoulder. "What about the others, Mary? Do you remember anything about them?"

Mary thought, looking up and down the aisle to make

sure no one else needed her attention. "Well, I'm not really supposed to…"

"I may know them, that's all. There's a worldwide support group I run."

"Oh, I see." Mary didn't seem to need much excuse. "Well, there was a little old lady in January. I remember her because I caught her drinking red wine in the toilets." Mary giggled.

The guardian knew who that was. Ethel had come into the Life late. She lived in New York and visited London regularly.

"And the others?"

"A gentleman, in March. I think he was quite short and thin. But I don't remember him very well, I'm afraid. And just last week on the London to New York flight, another gentleman. I don't know how to describe him except, quite bad-tempered looking."

"Black, white?"

"A white gentleman with sandy hair, quite tall."

"And they were all in Business Class?"

Mary thought. "Yes…No, no, the man in March, he was in Economy. It caused a few problems because he insisted on keeping the blinds pulled down and another passenger objected. I don't think he was very well, actually."

"Why do you say that?"

"He was shaking, and he was so very pale. I know that's part of the disease, but, really I was worried for him. When we got to London, he insisted on traveling straight on to Spain, even though he wasn't very well."

"He traveled straight on to Spain? He didn't stop over in London?"

"Yes."

The guardian realized Mary was glad someone else had the same concerns she'd had.

"I had to phone through to Iberia to let them know he would be on their flight."

"What time was the Iberia flight?"

"Six thirty. I remember that because that's why I had to phone them. It was very tight to get him on their flight as we touched down just before six."

A businessman two seats up the aisle pressed his call light, and Mary shrugged apologetically. "I have to go. If you need anything, don't hesitate to ask."

The guardian thought about the other vampires traveling on this flight. Ethel had been one of them, Jameel was clearly the one in December. And that figured. December was when he moved to Granada. But who was the man traveling to New York last week? And even more of a concern, who was the vampire traveling economy? The flight from London to Malaga was two and a half hours, so the sun would have been up when they'd arrived in Spain. It might have been okay if it had been a cloudy day as only direct sunlight was fatal. But then, it was southern Spain. That was extremely dangerous. This would take some further investigation.

Chapter Sixteen

Jameel clicked on Internet Explorer, then dial up connection. The modem brr-ed and ding-donged into life. He clicked favorites, and then the GayChatFun tab, logging in as Scarlet Lady. He entered the Back Room, and scanned the users Buffboy was there. Great.

Jameel typed a greeting to the other users, watching the conversation unfold on his monitor.

ScarletLady: Hey boys and girls, what's up....or should that be who's up who?

NoClone: nah it's too cold here for any of that Rascal, wdn't work in Philly anyhow

DirtyRascal: lol, Clone...that's 2 bad. Better luck next time.

MsLAYneous: hey ScarletL

QueenoftheCastle: Hey Scarlet, whassup Girlfriend?

ScarletLady: sadly nothing at all's up, Queen, that's why my ass is back in this back room.

The private conversation box pinged up. Jameel was happy to see it was Buffboy wanting to talk in private. This was just what he needed, a little cyber flirtation with his cyber boyfriend. When reality was too damn painful, Jameel had just the escape route he needed. Thank heaven for the wonderful invention of the computer and the World Wide Web. It was a little strange sometimes, and a lot like biting on air, but Jameel found cybersex hit the spot when he didn't want to engage with anyone real.

Buffboy had come into his life just when he needed him—when Jameel had only been in Granada a couple of weeks and hadn't known anyone. He met Buffboy in one of the chat rooms on Gaychatfun, and they'd hit it off. They had cybersex once, twice, then regularly. Jameel didn't have a number for Buffboy, and they'd never suggested trying to meet IRL, in real life. They only knew each other as ScarletLady and Buffboy. Neither of them wanted a real connection. They did have each other's e-mail address, which was a nice, different way to flirt. But mostly, they met in chat rooms.

Buffboy always seemed to be around when Jameel, or Scarlet Lady, needed him. Though if he wasn't, there were plenty of other hot boys to distract Jameel in the slow hours of the night before dawn. Jameel typed into the text box and hit send.

ScarletLady: Missed me have you? I thought you were ignoring me.

Buffboy: Don't be huffy, I was in a private convo with Bigboy, didn't C U cum in.

ScarletLady: Thought it'd be sumthing like that. Well…is he as big as he claims?

Buffboy: He was when I'd finished with it.

Buffboy: but I don't want to talk about that. Where have u been?

ScarletLady: Been away from a computer for a few days. Thought about u once or twice.

Buffboy: Only once or twice? I didn't cum in yr dreams

then?

ScarletLady: Surely u wd know if u did.

Buffboy: Go anywhere nice?

ScarletLady: London.

Buffboy: Hope u were careful in all that fog.

ScarletLady: Where u at boy? There's more fog in LA than London — u about a century out of date.

Buffboy: sorry, guess I don't know it very well.

ScarletLady: well, Buffboy whatcha been doin, making yrself more buff?

Buffboy: U got it, been down the gym, pumping hard.

ScarletLady: I like to think of u like that…tell me more.

Selena coughed from the doorway to get Jameel's attention. "Don't forget I need to send an e-mail tonight before dawn. And I need to call Rob back."

Jameel rolled his eyes to the ceiling. "You pulled me out of the back room to tell me *that*? For goodness sake, you've only just got up."

"It's important, Jameel. I'm sorry."

"Okay, okay." Jameel waved her away. "Give me half an hour. I work fast," he said with a wicked grin.

The webcam phone icon came up, flashing.

"Damn! Now what?" Jameel clicked on it.

"Serve's you right for having two lines!" Selena laughed. "I don't know how you cope."

A blurred view of Rob's empty living room came up.

"What's going on?" Selena asked Jameel.

Jameel thought for a moment. "I know," he said. "She's put a call to us on timer and then forgotten about it."

Before he could disconnect, Selena called out loudly, "Hey, Rob, you there?"

Rob's tired but smiling face appeared on the hazy screen. Selena thought it looked like Rob was wearing a pair of rabbit's ears. She decided it must be a trick of the camera.

"Hey, you guys. That is you isn't it, Selena? I can just about make you out in the blur," Rob said.

Selena nodded, budging Jameel up so she would be picked up by the Web camera perched on top of Jameel's monitor. It looked like an oval eyeball, something a robot might have carelessly misplaced.

"What's happened now?" Rob's voice came out reasonably clearly from the tiny gray speakers.

"There was another incident," Selena began.

Jameel cut in. "Hey, Rob, any chance I can call you back? I'm on another call."

Rob appeared confused. "Got to go to work." She shrugged. Her shoulders moved up and down one frame at a time. It looked like she was doing everything in slow motion.

"Why not call us when you get in, Rob?" Selena said.

"Hey, hot stuff, come back to bed." Rani's voice called sweetly from off camera.

Jameel and Selena laughed. "That's our Rani," Jameel said.

Rob's blurry head turned back to face them. "Gotta go. Call you laters." She clicked off.

"Now, if I could have a little privacy, pleeeeese," Jameel implored Selena. "Half an hour, I promise."

Selena made a wry face and went through to the sitting room. Jameel turned back to Gaychatfun. He hoped Buffboy hadn't started without him. Their last lines stared up at him.

ScarletLady: well, Buffboy, whatcha been doin, making yrelf more buff?

Buffboy: U got it, been down the gym, pumping hard.

ScarletLady: I like to think of u like that. Tell me more.

Buffboy: First I strip right down to shorts and a muscle T.

Then I lie down on a bench, grab the biggest barbell and push that sucker, hard as I can. Say, why don't u cum to the gym with me right now. We cd have some fun in the locker room.

Buffboy: What's up Scarlet. Not playing hard to get now r u?

Buffboy: HEY SCARLET. You talking to someone else?

Jameel quickly typed in a reply, hoping Buffboy hadn't closed the connection while Jameel had been talking to Rob.

ScarletLady: Sorry Buff, I got a call. Got rid of them as fast as I cd. Still up for some hot locker room action?

Jameel tried a couple more times, but there was no answer from Buffboy. He must have gotten fed up waiting and started chatting to someone else. That or he got booted off. Jameel swore, then called out, "Selena, you might as well come do that e-mail. Then maybe I can have the computer to myself."
Selena appeared smirking. "That *was* quick!"
Jameel just sniffed on his way out.

***

Selena had to be careful. The wording of the e-mail had to be accurate, intelligible to the right people, and completely uninteresting to anyone else, including Jameel.

When we spoke you said you might come and visit. I would like that very much. Now is a good time to come, as I'm not doing very much for a week or two. Ring me with the details if you like. Aunty Jo has my number.
Selena

That looked okay to Selena. She pressed Send.

***

A warm flush of sexual excitement spread through Rani's

body as she shook off sleep and stretched. The blinds glowed pale golden; a gentle heat radiated from the windows. Rani could smell early summer, sweet and lazy in the air, the energy of afternoon sun buzzed through the room. Rani was sure it had been a hot day. She sensed sunset was close. The night was just beginning.

Rani turned to Rob, still sleeping. Her long, black eyelashes fluttered gently. Rani ran a finger across Rob's left shoulder, causing Rob to stir with an "Mmm." The sheet shifted down the bed, and Rani got a chance to ogle Rob's naked chest. Rob needed to be woken, Rani decided, slipping out of bed. Rani wanted to play with Rob—tousle her hair, paint tattoos on her body, make up her face while she slept. The thought of Rob with lipstick on made Rani giggle as she searched through her wardrobe.

Rani's white boa lay invitingly across the shoulders of her black cocktail dress. Hmmm. Rani plucked a single white feather from the obliging boa and advanced soundlessly on Rob.

Pulling the sheet down further, Rani stood beside Rob and flicked the feather across Rob's chest, stomach, thighs, darting about Rob's body light as a Fairy Queen bestowing kisses. Rob's body rippled and swirled under the feather touch until finally her eyes shot open. Rani grinned down at the bewilderment in Rob's eyes. The bewilderment faded fast.

"What are you up to?" Rob said, narrowing her eyes suspiciously.

"Nothing," Rani murmured in a sultry tone, shrugging innocently. Rob's eyes had already left her face and were traveling over her naked body. Rani's nipples stiffened, and a shiver went through her, even though this was entirely what she'd planned to happen.

"You look a bit hot." Rob was kneeling in bed now. "I think you'd better lie down and cool off." She pulled Rani by the hand, back to bed. "Oh!" Rob's face changed as she discovered the feather hidden in Rani's hand. "I see. So that's what that was. Well then, madam, I'll just take charge of this." The feather disappeared into Rob's hand and Rob stepped out of bed. "Close your eyes. I just need to get a few things."

Rani wanted to kiss Rob sweetly and deeply when she

looked like that—teasing, confident. Relishing the suspense, she closed her eyes and pressed herself against the cool sheets. A cupboard door opened, and then Rob slipped something over Rani's head—an eye mask. Rani smiled, a soft "ha" slipping from her throat. A butterfly kiss hovered on Rani's lips for an instant, then the air around her was still.

Drawers opened and shut, then the wardrobe door; hangers slid along the rail, clothes rustled, and music permeated the room. Sub bass speakers, situated under the bed, sent a sexy bass throb through the mattress, while tweeters built into the wooden bed surround directed the treble into the center of the bed. Rani was in R & B heaven as slow soul tuned her senses into sensual, sexual serenity.

"Now, Ms. Shah, I'm conducting research on behalf of the Suckers Science League." Rob's voice broke through the music, close to Rani's left ear. "I'm going to test your sensory perception. See if you can guess what I'm touching you with."

"Okay," Rani said huskily.

Something smooth snaked across Rani's stomach, moved in wavy lines up, across her breasts, along her throat, and when it finally reached her face, Rani was certain. "Silk," she murmured.

"Very good."

Immediately, something else brushed against her arm. It felt soft and light. It flickered down her legs, between her legs, and all over her body, though the flickering was concentrated between her legs. It was an unusual sensation. Rani had no idea what it was.

While the soft flicking continued, Rob rubbed a substance across Rani's breasts. Cold at first, Rani's nipples stiffened, then with Rob's fingers rubbing the gel, they grew warm. Rani luxuriated in the warmth radiating across her breasts, then she heard a spritz, and warm water fluttered lightly onto her thighs. She spread her legs, enjoying the soft anointment. Her body felt wonderful. This new life felt so good something shifted inside. A door that had been locked and bolted creaked open. Rani pulled off the eye mask, suddenly wanting to look at Rob.

Rob was kneeling between Rani's legs. A plant spray in one hand, a pair of small bunny ears in the other. Rani bit her lip, laughing. No wonder she hadn't guessed what the furry brushing was. "Who said you could go in my dressing-up bag?" she asked.

Rob didn't answer. Instead, she smiled an adoring smile and put the bunny ears on her head. Rani laughed, pulled Rob to her, and kissed her, wanting her badly. Rani was swept along on a new sensation. Her heart was suddenly engaged and turned on. Rob broke off the kiss, instead putting her mouth to Rani's neck. Her hand slipped between Rani's legs, stroking her.

Rani's body wanted Rob. She wanted Rob. Damn! She had fallen in love with Rob. As the first flush of orgasm hit her, Rani pulled Rob's mouth from her throat, looking her in the eye as she came. She defiantly searched Rob's eyes and found something beautiful there, something that lifted her heart out of her body.

Rob put her arms around Rani, holding her, and they lay together watching the blinds turn from amber gold to pale lilac. A loud buzzing from the webcam in the living room interrupted their intimacy.

"Let's ignore it," Rob said.

But Rani had already moved on from the moment. "We're going to get up anyway," she said, giving Rob a little push.

"Oh, Rob," she called at the last minute, but Rob didn't hear her. Never mind, Rani thought. Whoever it was would have the joy of seeing Rob in the bunny ears she'd forgotten were still on her head.

At first, Rani bathed in a state of bliss, a drugged-up, feel-good feeling that washed over her and made her feel lucky, like everything was right with the world.

"Hey, hot stuff, come back to bed," she called out, wanting to get her hands and her fangs on Rob. While she waited, she pondered on this new situation. Rob really did it for her, but it wasn't just lust. The feeling was serious. The sex had been amazing, and Rani realized it was the first time she had felt that depth of love while having sex.

Part of her yearned to just be with Rob. But that would mean giving up the Count. She sighed. It was too much, trying to work out what she needed when everything was changing.

She pushed her thoughts aside and headed for the shower.

***

By the time Rani got to her flat that evening, she had a plan. Her plan was to say nothing to Rob about the Count. It was only sex with the Count anyway. She figured that vampires were pretty fluid about relationships. Jameel had confirmed it before he went back.

One morning, when Selena and Rob had tired of conversation and gone to bed, Rani had had a long talk with him. Most vampires, it seemed, had multiple relationships, or had sex on the side if they had a main relationship. Jameel had said that living so long changed the rules. Jealousy and possessiveness was frowned on—although that didn't stop people feeling them. Rani hated possessiveness, so this was good news. She was also relieved to hear that non-monogamy was common. She hadn't quite believed Leah.

Rani preferred not to examine anything too closely. Everything was changing. She almost wished that she hadn't realized she was in love with Rob. It was better not to dwell on things. Her body was different. For one thing, she was turned on all the time. Rani wondered if it was, in fact, *because* she'd become a vampire, and maybe that was why she fancied both Rob and the Count. Maybe it came with the territory—like hating bright light and craving blood.

She sat on the wall outside her flat. It was a cloudless full moon, and the moon was toasty. The air felt fresh and clean. She looked up through her sunglasses, staring the moon full in the face. Vibrant rays reached out to her. It's better just to go with the flow, Rani told herself, realizing the moon would still be there tomorrow whoever she slept with.

Rani stood, stretched, and resolved that she was going to catch up on her backlog of work. She'd been stealing time for a couple of nights. Rani had wanted to be around Rob, so she'd skipped work and hung out at the club. The next night, Rob was off so Rani wanted to get all her work out of the way.

Gulsin had left a list of urgent orders. Rani dealt with those first. Then, sitting at her desk with a cup of black coffee, Rani started on the post. Most of their clients ordered via the Web, so a lot of it was promotional stuff. Rani had opened and tossed a good few letters in the bin before she pulled out a card in the shape of a bat. On the front it said: *Batman Deliveries: Fast Discrete Nocturnal*. Rani smiled and turned the card over.

A new service from Count Enterprises. You've had just about everything I can give over the centuries, now let me deliver it too. A competitive service you can trust. Say ups yours to other delivery services. Stick with the firm you can Count on. Taking orders now.

Rani laughed at the thought of the Count taking orders from anybody, even for business. There was something else in the envelope, a handwritten invitation.

My dear Rani,
Some lovely vampires and I are planning an evening's entertainment on May 31st, the full moon. We would love you to join us. Please let me know if you can make it.
Yours truly,
The Count

Rani stared at the invitation for a while, running her fingers over the words. Then she looked at Gulsin's list. There were still some accounts to catch up on. She tapped the invitation as it lay on her desk. Perhaps she should be good, just this once, do the accounts. The phone rang. She answered it with her most helpful business voice. "Let's Talk Lingerie, Rani speaking, how can I help you?"

"I'd love to talk lingerie." The smooth, amused voice of the Count slipped out of the phone wire and caressed Rani's neck.

"Oh, it's you." Rani had a feeling her smile was translating to the Count's ear.

"Have you opened your post yet?"

Rani took the cordless handset to the window. She was sure the Count was out there somewhere, watching her.

"Yes, I have."

"Oh." The Count sounded coolly disappointed. "And you haven't called me? Oh dear..."

"I'm supposed to be working this evening." Rani peered out, looking up and down the street. No Harleys, no blood transfusion vans, no figures in cloaks.

"Work tomorrow. Tonight's the full moon."

Rani sighed, looking up at the sky. It was true. No one should be working on such a night.

"But I don't know what to wear. What kind of entertainment is it?"

The Count laughed. "Fabulous, I knew you'd come. As for clothes. Well, my dear, have you got something traditional?"

"You mean vampire traditional?" Rani clarified.

"Of course. Something black and floaty, oh and revealing."

Rani thought. "I don't think I've got anything like that."

"That's hard to believe. Hang on a minute." The Count went off the phone. Rani could hear him talking to someone.

"Rani, it's okay. Leah's got something for you. You can put it on when we pick you up."

That changed things. Leah was coming. "I don't know…" Rani hesitated.

"Thought you might like an evening out. There's only a few of us—me, Leah, and Maria. Come on, Rani. You'll even the numbers up. And you'll love Maria. She's completely inoffensive, honestly."

Rani had to laugh. "Okay, but what outfit is Leah bringing? Maybe I'll just choose something I've got already."

"Hang on. Leah wants to talk to you."

The Count put Leah on. "Rani? Hello, honey. Listen, the Count's absolutely useless when it comes to women's clothes. You need black underwear, a strapless bra, black stockings or tights. You can do your makeup because you can just step into this. Anything else you need to know?"

"No." Rani was surprised Leah was being so friendly.

"Okay, we'll be over there in an hour. Oh, and put one of your catalogues to one side will you? I checked your website out. *Very* interesting merchandise!"

The phone went dead.

Rani promised herself she'd make it up to Gulsin about the accounts. When the doorbell rang, she was ready, save any outer garments. She buzzed Leah up.

"Maria and the Count are waiting in the car," she said, handing Rani a short, black, strapless chiffon dress.

Rani gasped. "It's beautiful."

"Um-hmm. Sure is," Leah said in a sultry voice as Rani

slipped off her robe. When Rani had stepped into the dress, Leah came round behind her and zipped her up. "Oh, that certainly works for you, babe," she said. "And it fits like a glove. I'm so clever! Take a look." She indicated Rani's reflection in the mirror. Rani had to admit the dress did look good on her. This Leah wasn't like any Leah she'd met before. Maybe she had an evil twin.

"Come on then, let's go. You're going to love this evening," Leah said, her dazzling smile framed by magenta lipstick.

The Count parked his Benz outside a dome-like round building in Camden. Rani still didn't know what the event was. She was getting an idea from the people waiting to go inside. There were more cloaks than at a Count Dracula looky-likey convention. There were also a lot of floaty black dresses, long dark wigs, pale makeup and other Hammer Horror classics.

"It's a vampyre convention," Leah whispered. "That's vampire with a Y."

"Humans who love vampires. This is going to be fun," Maria said to Rani with a wink.

The Count locked the car with a flick of his key fob. "Well, ladies, and Maria, I think we'll fit right in, don't you?" He smiled.

Rani looked like she'd stepped right out of a Bollywood vampire flick. The Count had the same cloak and tux on that he'd worn at the ball, with a blood red shirt. Leah wore a low-cut, full-length rubber dress, split to the thigh. Maria, a dykey looking woman with short brown hair, was dressed like a Goth in a black shirt with drooping sleeves and tight black vinyl trousers.

The four joined the short queue.

"These things are surprisingly popular," Maria said as they crossed a foyer and walked down a long ramp lit by theatrical candles—flickering electronic lights made to look like naked flame. Music got louder as they walked deeper into the bowels of the building, and then they emerged into a circular space. There was an inner and an outer circle. Corridors like the one they'd just walked down led off the outer circle at intervals. The space was dark and eerie, despite fairy lights and lanterns everywhere. It smelled strongly of damp stone. The inner circle was a dance floor packed with people dressed like vampires from films or like Goths. More people walked around in the outer circle, leaned over railings watching the dance floor, or made their way to other places via the long corridors.

"This is wild!" Leah smiled, taking it all in.

"Typical vampiric scene," the Count remarked.

A tall man dressed in a cloak walked past and smiled, revealing very large and obviously prosthetic fangs.

"There are some strange people here," Rani said.

"How can you tell the difference?" the Count asked in a superior way. "All *people* are strange if you ask me."

"We didn't. In fact, I specifically remember telling you I didn't want to hear any of your anti-human tirades," Maria said firmly.

"I was about to stick up for these vampiric types, actually," the Count protested. "They're the only ones I have any time for. At least they seem to get us."

Maria ignored him. "What do you think?" she asked Rani.

Rani shrugged. "Haven't made my mind up. Who are these people? They're not vampires then?"

Maria looked around like she was feeling the air. "Maybe one or two. I think they're nearly all human."

The Count stood close to Rani. Her body responded immediately. "Let's see," he said scanning the crowd. "Some of them call themselves HLVs: Human Living Vampires. That one over there..." He waved toward a man dressed in jeans and a leather jacket talking to a blond woman also dressed in ordinary clothes. "He's a blood vampire: drinks human blood. The woman he's talking to, she's his 'donor.' She makes the cuts herself with a lancet. Won't let anyone else do it."

"Does he need the blood?" Rani asked.

The Count shrugged. "He says he does."

"How do you know?"

"I'm pulling it out of his mind," the Count said, as if it were obvious.

"He knows he's not supposed to, but the Count's such a bad boi," Leah murmured, squeezing between Maria and Rani.

Maria rolled her eyes. She was obviously used to their games. Rani realized she was in a game sandwich. Leah slipped her arm through Rani's. "Now, observe that group over there."

She pointed daintily to three people hanging out on the edge of a dark corridor. Two of them were kissing passionately against the stone wall while a woman watched passively. "The voyeur, she's a psychic vampire, feeds off human energy. That one gets off on sexual energy, anger, hysteria, all the amphetamine emotions. She doesn't like depression or anything sedative. Then there are vampire lifestylers, like our friend with the impossibly large fangs." Leah tipped her head toward the tall guy who had smiled at them earlier. "He's not an HLV, just a lifestyler. He's got a coffin in his bedroom, baroque-style decoration in his home, and several cloaks in his wardrobe."

"Are you pulling all that out of his head?" Rani asked doubtfully.

Leah smiled and tapped Rani affectionately on the end of her nose. Rani's mouth opened in surprise. She caught Maria's eye. Maria was laughing.

"No, darling. We went to his house once. Trust me. It isn't a story you want to hear," Leah said cryptically.

A large guy dressed top to toe in leather walked along the passage toward them, spraying people from a brass plant spray. A thin red mist glistened in the mottled light when he depressed the trigger.

"That's Gerard. He's one of us," Leah whispered into Rani's ear.

The Count held his finger out as Gerard reached them, and Gerard sprayed the red liquid onto it. The Count put it into his mouth and then grimaced. Gerard winked, sprayed the air above them, and moved on.

"Theatrical blood, yuck," the Count complained. "God, I need to get the taste of that out of my mouth. How about we go find some donors?"

"Oh, yes." Leah squeezed Rani's arm with excitement.

"How about it, Rani? Feeling hungry?" the Count breathed into Rani's ear.

She tried very hard not to think of the last time he'd said that. She might start to flush, and she had learned that vampires could feel the heat of blood rushing to someone's skin.

"I don't know...." She hesitated.

"Take this." The Count handed her a small, flat, silver semi-circle. Rani pressed the button on the top and felt it slide forward. A blade popped out underneath.

"You can't use your teeth," the Count explained. "And they might want to make the cut themselves. If they do, just make sure you get the knife back!"

Maria declined hers. "I'm not in the mood tonight."

Rani decided on the spot to stay with Maria. She wasn't sure about the whole place—humans pretending to be vampires, human-vampires, vampires pretending to be human. It was messing with her head. She waved the knife away. "I'll just hang with Maria."

Leah raised her eyebrows. "I see. Don't do anything I wouldn't," she purred before following the Count off along the passageway.

Maria leaned back against the wall, sighed, and smiled at Rani. Rani relaxed. There was something about Maria she liked, something familiar. Maybe it was because she looked so dykey.

"Want to go get a drink?" Maria asked.

Rani nodded.

At the end of a corridor was a bar that opened out into a triangular space. The buzz of conversation overtook the music here as people gathered in groups to chat. Rani got two bottles of sparkling water, and then they wandered out again.

There was corridor after corridor off the outer circle. They felt like tunnels to Rani. She thought how easy it would be to get lost in them. Maria picked one, seemingly at random.

The smell of damp was stronger away from the body of people. The corridor led to a small, unoccupied space. There were some chairs stacked up against the wall, several lanterns hanging from the walls, and real candles stuck to a ledge by their own wax.

"Want to sit down?" Maria asked, pulling a couple of chairs off the stack.

Rani nodded.

"How do you like it so far?" Maria asked.

"Well, it's different," Rani replied. "Why didn't you want to get some blood?"

"Believe it or not, I'm not really hungry. I don't have a problem with it or anything like that. I sometimes think it's the most honest way to get blood."

Rani thought about that. "Do you feel bad about taking blood then, if people don't know?"

"No, I think of it like taking vegetables or fruit from plants. I don't harm the person. In fact, the way we feed is kinder than humans who eat meat. We don't kill anything to live."

Rani nodded. "I think of it like that too."

"It's not very practical, getting blood from conscious donors," Maria said. "Sooner or later, it would bring the vampire to the attention of human authorities. We can't afford to do that."

Rani got that.

"Vampires are quite soft-hearted really, I'm generalizing here, but it's true. I know loads of vampires who don't like to go out and feed, just in case they scare humans in any way. They keep the Count in business. You know the Count acquires blood, yeah?"

Rani did know. She tried not to think of the blood transfusion van, but she still got a flash of him holding the sachet of blood above her head. She got a sexual rush. To knock the image out of her head, Rani focused on Maria. She realized she had seen her somewhere before. "Do you know what? You look familiar," she said.

"Do I?" Maria thought for a moment. "Have you been out long? As a lesbian I mean?"

Rani nodded. "Yeah, ages."

"You might have seen me around then. I'm a bit of a lesbian junkie."

"What's that?" Rani asked, bemused.

"I just love the mortal lesbian scene. Have done ever since I discovered it in the 1920s."

Rani had to smile. "I really want to know what you mean by that."

Maria shifted a little in her chair. "God, where do I start?" She appeared to be thinking. Rani waited, listening to the music softened by coming through stone walls. In the eerie half-light, Rani thought she could hear the occasional drop of water hitting the stone floor. She listened intently as Maria picked a place to begin.

"After the war, the first World War, I went to Paris. I was fascinated by the mortal literary crowd—men and women. And during the early nineteen twenties, I went to literary evenings. I already knew Selena, the Count, and another vampire called Ursula who were in Paris, and they were very much involved with the human lesbian circle. Because I knew them, and because I was seen at literary events, soon I was being invited to select evenings in artists' salons.

"For several years, I hung about on the fringes of that world. I thought it was decadent and exciting. There was such an atmosphere of going against the bourgeoisie in France at that time. I was quite caught up in it. And of course, I didn't realize it, but I was becoming addicted to lesbian company. I knew I was bisexual. Most vampires consider themselves bisexual. It's not considered practical to limit yourself, what with feeding and sex being so tied up for us. Oh, I know, lots of vampires would insist feeding and sex are completely separate, but I don't agree. And I think that explains our bisexuality. Vampires are more tolerant than humans about sexuality generally," Maria said.

"I wouldn't know. I haven't met many straight ones yet, or bisexual ones, whatever," Rani said wryly.

Maria laughed. "You will. There are more than you think! Where was I? Oh yes, I considered myself bisexual, but I was absolutely fascinated by all these lesbians, many of whom were feminist—the first wave of feminism you know. Anyway, I dithered about till nineteen twenty-six when I fell in love with a human, and I had my first mortal lesbian sexual encounter. My oh my. Changed my life."

Rani smiled at the glowing look of contentment in Maria's eyes and infusing her smile. She'd felt something similar, the first time she'd slept with a woman.

"But you were already a vampire?" Rani asked.

"Oh yeah, I came in in eighteen seventy-five, so I was…" Rani waited while Maria did the maths. "Fifty-one years of age then. You know that expression don't you? Fifty-one years a vampire."

Rani nodded, appreciating the way Maria didn't assume she knew anything, and explained stuff in an unpatronizing way. She thought she'd learned more in the last twenty minutes than she had in months.

"So why did you say you're a lesbian junkie?"

"Because since then I've had this irresistible urge to seek out the company of lesbians. In the nineteen thirties, I followed the heady scent of lesbianism and feminism to Berlin. When things got heavy and very unpleasant, I came to England, and in the forties, I joined the Women's Land Army. In the nineteen fifties, I was lured to New York by tales of the new bars and clubs for perverts and deviants. They were good times, and hard times. Everyone was butch and femme then."

"Which were you?" Rani had to ask.

Maria pulled a face. "Well, I tried to be butch, but I wasn't very good at it. I was considered a bit of a sissy. But I would have made an even worse femme. Anyway, about nineteen sixty-nine, I went first across the border to Canada, then far away to Sweden where things were really starting to happen for women. I had to stay away from England and America, as my face was getting too familiar. That's the only problem with hanging out in the mortal world."

"Wasn't Rob in New York in the sixties?" Rani said.

Maria nodded. "Yeah, she made a good butch. Well, still does of course. She was there, and Selena, Jameel…"

"Do they just hang out with each other, all the way through history?"

Maria laughed loudly. "No, they go their separate ways as well. But the vampire world is much smaller than the human world."

"So what about the seventies? Were you still in Sweden?"

"Not by the late seventies. I was getting too well known on the mortal scene—discreetly, obviously, not in the public eye. As you know, that's against the Vampiric Code."

Rani nodded, the one thing Rob had done was tell her the rules, all of them. Rules were very Rob.

"In seventy-eight, I moved to Amsterdam, and then in eighty-five, I went right over to Sydney, Australia. Stayed there till the early nineties when London called me again. So you see, I really am a lesbian junkie."

Rani thought it was fascinating. There was so much she wanted to know, especially about Paris in the 1920s.

"So did you know Rob in the twenties? She was in Paris then wasn't she?" Rani thought she might get some answers out of Maria about that time. Rob was very tight-lipped about it. All she knew was that Rob had been living in Paris with Selena, and that the Count had also been on the scene.

"Psst."

Rani and Maria turned their heads sharply in the direction of the snake-like sound.

"Psst," came again from the shadows outside the doorway. A white-gloved hand appeared in the dim light, holding a card.

Maria looked amused, but made no move to the doorway. When neither of them appeared to collect the note, a disappointed-looking Count Dracula lookalike stepped into the room and handed the note to Maria. It was the tall lifestyler who had showed his fangs to them earlier. He turned with a swoop of his cloak, not waiting for an answer, and left them.

Maria read the card.

"I've been summoned," she said, a twinkle in her eye. "The Countess Leah calls."

Rani raised her eyebrows, and Maria laughed.

"Don't get excited. It's more likely to be gossip or a harebrained scheme she wants to involve me in."

As they walked back along the dark corridor toward the inner circle, Rani asked Maria, "Is Leah a real countess?"

Maria's shoulders shook in front of Rani in the dim light. "No!" she called back over her shoulder. "The Count is though!" she added cryptically.

As they reached the outer circle, the Count himself stepped smoothly in front of Rani from another corridor.

"I've been waiting for you. Come on," he said, his warm breath scented with blood and red wine.

Rani's fingers were encased by the Count's. The tingle of electricity started a gentle rush along her arm, bypassed her heart, and headed straight between her legs. She looked into the Count's eyes and knew she'd been wanting this moment since the phone call hours ago. The Count turned and headed for another of the myriad of tunnel corridors, pulling Rani along. The walls seemed to flash by, the bare stone an orangey-yellow. At that moment, Rani loved the fact she was a vampire. She loved feeling this turned on, feeling so alive. She smiled to herself. She had guessed the Count would do something like this. She felt deliciously pleased she was right.

The Count pushed open a door at the end of the tunnel,

and cold air rushed toward Rani, sharpening her senses. She smelled the air, realizing how much stronger her sense of smell had become. In the first hours after midnight, the sky was deep and the air cooler. This was the time for strenuous activity, and Rani had some in mind. The Count led her into a small walled garden area. As they walked across paving, the scent of chamomile, sage, and thyme drifted upward.

"Would you care for a seat, madam?" The Count indicated a stone bench in a corner of the small courtyard. "Or would you prefer to stand? If I remember, you quite like it standing up."

Rani answered him by undoing first the black bow tie and then the Count's collar, exposing his neck.

"Straight to the point!" The Count's voice was a low growl in his throat, but his head went back as Rani kissed the hollows above the Count's collarbone, then slowly, lightly worked upward toward the jugular. He sighed as Rani's lips hit the first pulse. Rani felt the blood surge beneath her lips, but then the Count reached out and held Rani, stopping her biting into the skin. Rani felt the control in the Count's body. She was gratified to see how much control it took. The Count started a slow smile, and Rani watched the familiar look of self-assurance replace the quiet struggle on the Count's face. He lifted Rani's hand and brought it to his lips, kissing it softly, then he turned the palm and lightly bit the wrist pulse.

The Count pulled the blood into his mouth, holding Rani in his arms. Rani was shocked at how much pleasure she got from having her wrist sucked. There seemed to be a direct line to her clitoris. The sharp scent of sage filled her nose. Rani was held up firmly at the waist and she relaxed, slowly, sweetly moving in a general direction toward orgasm. Oh, yes. This was exactly what she'd been waiting for.

Mozart's "Requiem aeternam" cut through the air, well, a very tinny version of the beautiful, haunting music was coming from the Count's jacket pocket. Rani opened her eyes as the Count stepped back, took his mobile out of his pocket, and answered it. Rani blinked, unable to believe someone would answer a phone at a time like that.

"What?" The Count's tone was short. "So? What are you doing back? You're not supposed to be back for another two days." He walked away from Rani, listening. "Oh, don't be ridiculous. He must have been seeing things." There was a pause while the Count listened. Rani stood silently. Quite frankly, she was still in shock.

"I don't believe a word of it." His voice got much quieter. He glanced carefully at Rani and then turned away. "I'll tell you this though, if there's any more trouble over this, I'm not getting you out of it. If I were you I'd make sure that drama queen was just seeing ghosts."

He listened again, and then Rani heard him arrange to meet the caller in half an hour. He put the mobile away, covered his face with his hands, took a deep breath in and out, and then faced Rani with a very apologetic expression.

"I'm afraid I have to go. I've got a problem with my business. One of my guys just got back from America, and he ran into some trouble."

Rani felt like her whole body was an extension of her clitoris. She couldn't believe the Count was going to leave her like this.

The Count walked over to her, a cheeky grin on his face. "I'm sure we can pick this up another night."

Rani gave him a look that would have withered a less assured person. She was annoyed about the situation, and she was annoyed she had to follow the Count back inside, as she wanted to say good-bye to Maria. Rani had had enough for one night.

The only thing that picked Rani up was Leah's digusted face when the Count told her he was going off to a business meeting. Maria came over warmly, but Rani declined her invitation to hang out with them. Leah turned her back on the Count, who walked away with a smile and a wave to them all. Leah put her arm through Rani's. "So, sweetcakes, what are we three going to get up to now?"

When Rani told her she was getting a cab, Leah's face dropped, then she looked suspicious. "You're not going off to a secret liaison with the Count are you?"

Rani smiled enigmatically. "Of course not."

Leah narrowed her eyes. "I don't care, you know. I just like to know everyone's secrets." She smiled her python smile, and Rani completely believed her.

Halfway to Stoke Newington, Rani changed her mind. There was no way she was going to sleep. Her body was on fire. She was fed up with being annoyed at the Count and had turned her mind to the more practical problem of what to do with her pent up sexual energy. She got out her mobile.

"Rob, it's me, baby. Whatcha doin'?" Outside the cab window, houses and shops flashed by, bathed in diffuse orange street light. "Well, I was just thinking of you, thought maybe I'd come over, what do you think?…Yeah…me too, baby. Listen, you might want to go and get someone to eat. You're going to need all your strength, honey."

Rani pressed End Call and leaned forward to the driver, sliding the glass window open.

"Can we go on to Wood Green, please? Sorry, I've just changed plans."

The driver tutted, but one glance at the meter restored his good mood.

Rani's had just got better too.

CHAPTER SEVENTEEN

Rani had me up all night. She said she'd been working before she got a cab to my house, but I found that hard to believe, unless her work had been to look at erotica. Maybe fingering all that lingerie had turned her on. She grabbed me as soon as she walked through the door and tore most of my clothes off, stripping me down to my boxers. I was ready to go for it by then, but Rani put some Lovers Rock tunes on loud, sat me down, and gave me my own private lap dance. She had an amazing dress on that showed off her breasts and hips, and she used it. Nothing turns me on more than a woman who knows she's sexy, and Rani sure as hell knew it that night. When I couldn't bear it any more, I pulled Rani to me on the sofa and sucked hard on her neck, figuring she'd want it hot and fast. She did, coming almost instantly.

I sat back against the sofa, satiated, a little out of breath, but happy. Rani stretched, gave a long sigh, and got up, moving languidly toward the kitchen. I thought she might feel sleepy now, but when Rani reappeared, she was carrying a bottle of wine and a bottle of water, and I knew I was in for a longer session. I had no idea how long...

She had me next. Feasting greedily on my neck, taking so much of me I was glad I'd gone out and got a quick feed before she'd turned up. It was good though. I came without even thinking about it, quickly and easily.

Rani's mood shifted after that. She was very tender, holding the wine glass to my mouth, insisting on feeding me, even though the wine kept dribbling down my neck and chest.

She drank the drops from my skin, one by one. I lay back on the couch thinking I was very pleased she'd decided to come over.

I licked the salt off Rani's skin, returning the favor, except I didn't limit myself to her neck and chest. I ran my tongue over every inch of Rani's lovely skin, discovering and rediscovering all her sensitive spots, taking a very long, very sweet time about it.

Rani suggested we have human sex, a devilish look on her face I couldn't resist. I was happy to oblige using my fingers and thumbs. Rani climbed on top of me, wet and open, and rode one hand in front, another from behind. Her capacity for pleasure was amazing. There was no real end, no breaks. Just changing pace, speeding up, and slowing down. Orgasms divided the time, but one moment just melted into the next, like a continuous caress. Rani was insatiable, and after a couple of hours, so was I.

Funny how sex can be like that—spin it out and it turns into a drug. Maybe it was my energy mixing with hers. She stole a little more of my heart that night. I was high that Rani was so into me. I was high on pleasing her, would have done anything she asked. She got out her dildo and harness and strapped it onto me. I've always preferred vampire sex, but I would have put one on and swung on a rope over a ravine if she'd asked me to.

There was no sleep. After a while, no stopping. We kept at it all through the day. Rani had me doing it in all kinds of positions: standing up against the full-length mirror, flipping front to back, me on my knees—her on top. I was worried I was going to put my back out at one point, on my knees pumping for a good half an hour, her weight spread across my waist. I told her it was a lot easier lying down, using my fingers. Rani laughed and moved very slowly, very lightly, smiling down at me with her eyes half open till I forgot any back pain, forgot any moment past or future, forgot anything except Rani moaning loudly, digging her fingernails into my shoulders, and coming looking into my eyes. She was beautiful, and I felt damn lucky to have her.

That night, I was glad Rani had become a vampire. She made a good one.

Chapter Eighteen

"This better be important. I was right in the middle of something." The Count was short-tempered and probably sexually frustrated, Todd decided, trying not to stare at the lipstick plastered all over the guy's neck. Todd cleared his throat. "Why don't you sit down, boss?" he said.

The Count strode across his office to a long wooden cupboard, pulled open a door, and unceremoniously swigged from a large carafe of Nosferatu O+. He sat down, put his feet up on his desk, and stared unblinking at Todd.

"I just thought we should talk it over. And I thought you should ring Selena. Find out what's going on in Spain," Todd suggested. He needed to play this carefully. Get the Count on his side.

"What exactly did that fool Martin say?" the Count demanded quietly.

Todd faced his cold eyes. "I was delivering the blood, like you wanted. You know me, don't like to chat, but it's hard to get away from that man. He prattles on and on."

The Count nodded, staring up at Todd continuously.

"He starts talking about Jameel and his chicken boyfriend, how the place hadn't been the same since the chicken died and Jameel left for Spain, blah blah blah. Then he says he thought he saw the boyfriend in January, after Jameel had left."

"He thinks he saw a ghost?" the Count said scornfully.

Todd shook his head. "No, he didn't think it was a ghost. Saw someone like him, he said, taking money out of a cash machine."

"He was sure it was, what was his name?"

"Ben," Todd said. "No, he couldn't be sure. He was too far away. In fact, at the time he thought it was someone who looked like him."

"But that doesn't make a very good story, does it? So now suddenly he's sure it *was* the boyfriend, is that it?" The Count stood and stretched, getting ready to dismiss the whole thing as gossip.

"Maybe." Todd considered. "But that Martin, he was a good friend of Jameel's. He would have known Ben quite well. Well enough to ID him across a square."

The Count pulled himself up to his full five foot eleven. "You'd better pray it wasn't him."

Todd didn't need the Count to tell him that.

"That crackhead can get you convicted of murder. And I'll get put down as a bloody accessory. There's no way they'll believe I'm not involved. Not now I've helped you cover it up. I gave you an alibi for that night. For God's sake. I lied before the justice." The Count was furious.

"All we've got to go on is one dodgy sighting in San Francisco. The chicken junkie probably is dead. We should find out if there's been any more problems in Spain. I can't do that, boss," Todd said quietly.

The Count considered the situation. "Okay, this is the last favor you get from me." He threw the empty carafe of blood in the waste bin and went out the door without saying another word.

***

As the Count's footsteps echoed in the empty corridor Leah pressed harder into the darkness behind the door of the adjacent office. She'd only popped into the Depot for a case of blood. She and Maria were going on to a house party, and it was unthinkable to turn up to a vampire's house empty-handed. She hadn't expected to find the Count here at all. When she saw the Benz parked up, she'd suspected he was having it off in his office with Rani and had crept up to listen outside the door. She'd heard more than she'd bargained for. Who was the crackhead that could get Todd convicted of murder? What had the Count done to help Todd? And what the hell had any of that to do with Spain?

CHAPTER NINETEEN

Waiting...warm and hidden in the shadows, pressed into the darkness, invisible to the human eye. Waiting and watching....watching the little house, who comes in and who comes out. Patience. Takes patience, takes control, takes energy. Need to replenish energy, need enough for the whole night, need to be strong. Feeling wired, feel tired. Time to take more of the powder, the pure white powder that must be ingested, rubbed on the gum, enough to make a paste in the mouth. That's the correct and proper amount. It must be taken for speed and strength. The elixir: first it numbs, then it starts to flow inside, changing old, tired blood into pure energy. Gradually, it works its magic. It feels good when the old blood is replaced... feels good now the system is charged with power. Ready.

Action. The drag queen comes out onto the street. He looks around, sensing someone watching, but he can't penetrate the shadow around this doorway. He starts walking, walking fast. Start creeping now. First creeping softly behind, light as snowfall, quiet as a little mouse....a long shadow stretching from one doorway to the next. Cunning, cunning from the fox blood. Silent from the mouse blood. Flitting between the dark places. Eye on the drag queen running. Running is effortless thanks to the elixir ...running is like flying...two steps above the ground. Sure and steady...sure like he was sure, how sure he used to be, sure he was right. Now he's running.

Pressing closer behind. The happiness of pursuit... following and giggling. How funny it is when he runs.

Chapter Twenty

Selena stepped through an arch into a small, square room near the back of Medina Granadina, a Moroccan tearoom in Calderería Neuva.

She sat on a low, blue silk upholstered bench and leaned against the deep red fabric-lined wall. Incense was burning. Moroccan music played softly in the background. The floor and walls were tiled with geometric patterns. The octagonal table before her was decorated with polished dark wood marquetry work and topped with glass. Light filtered through brass lampshades on the ceiling containing fretwork in the shape of hexagons and diamonds, a band of large diamonds held alternate blue and yellow glass that colored some of the light hitting the ceiling.

She ordered a Hindu tea and sat back waiting for the guardian to arrive. She hoped the guard had sent her someone good. The situation was worrying her far more than she had let on to Jameel or Rob. She was impatient to get the case investigated and the culprit caught. She was annoyed that her contact in the guard hadn't told her who they were sending. And that the guardian had decided to go to San Francisco first. In fact, Selena was cross that she had to rely on a guardian at all. She felt she could have sorted out this situation herself, if she'd been allowed to. The other members of the Night Council had unanimously—*unanimously*,Selena remembered with irritation—decided everything must go through the proper channels. They had decided to nudge Selena out of the main action in case it compromised her position on the

Council. They had shoved Selena onto the sidelines when it was *her* old, dear friend at risk, and she wasn't happy about it at all. Oh yes, this guardian had better be good.

She acknowledged the arrival of her tea with a smile, picking up the turret-like teapot and pouring tea into the etched glass sitting on a gold-rimmed saucer. She took a sip. The warm flavor of cinnamon covered her tongue. She closed her eyes, enjoying the mixture of spices and black tea. Replacing her cup on the saucer, she accidentally knocked the teaspoon to the floor. She swore under her breath and ducked under the table to retrieve it.

As she stretched her fingers toward the spoon, a pair of long, denim-clad legs ending in worn tan boots stopped at her table. Selena straightened to take in a face with smooth, dark brown skin stretched over high cheekbones, full lips the color of blackberry juice, Pilot sunglasses, and a blue baseball cap. Selena's eyes ran over the toned but solid physique, dark blue 501s over heavy tan boots, tan pilot's jacket creased with age, pale blue work shirt beneath. Selena glanced at the crotch, and felt a flutter as she confirmed she was staring at a handsome butch.

"Habla usted Inglés, señorita?" The butch's voice was low. Confident, but soft. Her Spanish pronunciation was good, though Selena picked up an American accent.

"Indeed I do speak English," Selena said.

"Well, ma'am, guess I'm the person you came to meet. The captain sends his regards, and so does Aunt Jo." Now the guardian was speaking English, Selena picked up a Southern accent.

"Do you mean Aunty Jo?" Selena clarified.

The butch stood silently, any trace of expression on her face invisible to Selena's scrutiny. After a moment, the guardian replied, "I do mean Aunty Jo, my apologies, ma'am."

"Well, then, you'd better have a seat." Selena slid along the bench, hoping the guardian would choose to squeeze in next to her. She did, removing her sunglasses and laying them in front of her on the marquetry table. Selena noted the guardian was blessed with a pair of jet black eyes fringed by the kind of lashes that could sweep the floor.

"I'm Selena."

"Yes, ma'am, the captain said." The guardian smiled politely.

Selena smiled back in amusement. "And do I get to call you anything?"

The guardian shook her head, as if to shake sleep out of it. "My name's Skipp. Beg your pardon, ma'am, still jetlagged I guess."

Selena understood. The journey from San Francisco to Malaga was a two-nighter. Avoiding sunlight meant four separate planes and two stopovers.

"Jameel will be here soon. Is there anything you want to tell me before he comes?"

Skipp studied Selena. Selena waited, feeling a little nervous as the black eyes swept over her face.

"The captain briefed me that you're into something classified, so you have to keep a low profile. But you want to be kept informed. Is that right?"

Selena nodded, pleased her instructions had been passed on correctly.

"If you don't mind, ma'am, I'd rather brief you at a later time. I'd like to speak to the victim first."

Selena felt Skipp was holding information back. "Jameel wouldn't like being called a victim."

Skipp raised her eyebrows, but said nothing. Instead, she picked up the tea menu and studied it. A click of heels on the tiled floor heralded Jameel's arrival. Skipp stood to greet him.

Once tea was ordered, Skipp insisted on hearing about everything from the beginning. "Don't leave out any detail. Tell me about anything that seemed out of the ordinary."

Jameel described his bill being paid at the bar, back at the beginning of April. Skipp made a note, while Selena was annoyed Jameel hadn't mentioned it before. After they'd been talking for a good half hour, Skipp summed up, reading from her notes.

"Okay, Jameel. You travel to Spain in December, following the death of your boyfriend in November. Nothing happens for a couple of months. At the beginning of April, someone pays your bill in a bar. Two weeks later, you come home to find someone has placed a postcard in your housing suggesting a meeting. You go to that meeting, but no one shows up. You start locking your house, concerned that someone had been inside in your absence."

Jameel nodded.

"On May fourth, you go to Los Espejos, a club in central Granada with two mortals, Carlos and Juan. You have sex in a bathroom with another mortal, name unknown, and approximately thirty minutes later, the man is found dead in the same bathroom. You return home and find your blackout material has been sabotaged, and a shard of mirror lying on your bed. You are sure you locked up your house on that occasion. Following this incident, you travel to London on May sixth to visit friends. While there, you arrange an evening's entertainment at the Strand Hotel for yourself, Ms. Selena Fitzgerald, Rob Perdoni, Ms. Leah Jacobs, Ms. Rani Shah, and a person identified only as the Count."

Selena started to giggle, but Skipp looked so serious she stopped.

"At five thirty on May eighth, you all vacated the hotel. You were on the street waiting for your cars when a vehicle swerved off the road onto the pavement. You, Selena, and you, Jameel, tried to escape back into the hotel entrance, but a sharp object on the vehicle cut into your arm, Selena. Otherwise, there were no injuries. The vehicle disappeared, without any of the six vampires present getting a vehicle identification number."

Selena and Jameel looked at each other. Were they being told off? Selena glanced back at Skipp. Her face was as impassive as ever.

"You did note, Jameel, that the driver was wearing a Halloween type mask caricaturing a vampire. One week later, you return to Spain, Jameel, and you, Selena, accompany him. On your arrival at the airport, you are presented with a bunch of lilies, containing a note that reads Deepest Sympathies in Spanish." Skipp paused. "Is that all accurate?"

"Yes, I think so," Jameel said.

"Anything you want to add?"

Jameel looked hesitant. "This is probably just me being jumpy, but I thought someone was following me earlier, when I went on my run."

Skipp frowned. "Did you see anyone following you?"

Jameel shook his head. "I just had a strong feeling someone was there, right from when I left the house. I kept looking, but I didn't actually see anyone." He tossed his head. "I was probably imagining it."

"Hmm." Skipp wrote something on her palmtop, but didn't ask Jameel anything more. She turned to Selena. Selena sat up.

Skipp tapped the tiny computer, ready to input more information. "Selena, we've established your whereabouts from May sixth onward, as you were already in London when Jameel arrived. Can you tell me where you were in April?"

Selena shifted under Skipp's steady gaze. "I was in Mexico."

"Can anyone confirm that?" she asked levelly.

Selena thought. The only people who'd seen her in Mexico were mortal.

"Only mortals. I spoke to Jameel, Rob, and the Count though."

"Hmm." Skipp made another note in her palmtop. "I'll need a list of the mortals, later. You traveled to London, when?"

Selena liked Skipp's investigating voice. It was to the point, yet polite. "Twenty-second of April. I wanted to go to the ball on the twenty-fifth."

"And you stayed there until you left for Spain on May fifteenth?"

Selena leaned forward, teasing. "You know I did."

"Just checking, ma'am." Skipp did something to her palmtop that made it ping.

Jameel gave a sideways glance to Selena. "Right, if that's all, Officer," he said beguilingly, "can we round this up and go have some fun?"

Selena raised her eyebrows just as beguilingly into a question mark.

Skipp leaned back in her seat and shot them a broad, shy smile. "Sounds good. So where can a person get a feed round here?"

CHAPTER TWENTY-ONE

"Selena, it's for you-hoooooooooo." Jameel's singsong call rang through the little house to Selena's bedroom. She looked at her watch and groaned. Good God, it was four p.m. Throwing a flimsy robe around herself, she walked to the living room and saw the Count's bleary face looking at her from the monitor.

"Have you seen the time?" Selena asked.

The Count grinned happily. "Sorry, did I get you up? Is that a robe you're wearing? It's hard to see. Still looking good in next to nothing...I think. Perhaps you can remind me in person, next time we meet."

Selena ignored his flattery. "What are you doing up so early? It's three o'clock there isn't it?"

"Sure is. Completely overcast here. Means I can get going with a particularly exciting surprise I've got lined up."

"Oh, yes?" Selena was suddenly awake and interested.

"Trust me, Selena. You don't want to know about this one. Not yet anyway."

"Oh," Selena said, disappointed. "What did you want, then?"

"Just checking up on you guys. Everything been okay since you got back to Spain?"

The Count was being unusually solicitous.

"Just one strange incident. Nothing too alarming."

"You're both all right though?"

That concern was genuine, Selena could tell.

"Yeah, we're fine. Jameel thinks someone's watching

him, that's all."

"Selena, phone me if I can do anything. I won't let anybody hurt you or Jameel. You know that."

"Okay." Selena paused. "Listen, Dominic, is there anything you know about this you're not telling me?"

The Count's head tipped from one side to the other, leaving a blurry trail on the screen.

"Of course not, Selena. Why would I? Anyway, gotta go. Places to go, people to do."

Selena gave a wave she hoped would translate on the Count's monitor.

***

Rani woke feeling the joys of early summer. Rob, still asleep beside her, deserved a kiss, she decided, and she tenderly planted one on Rob's lips. Rob stirred but wasn't shaken.

Rani slipped out of the covers and jumped into the shower, singing to herself. She soaped herself all over, luxuriating in the sensation of the hot water and her own touch.

It was like she'd grown a different body in the past two months. Her sense of smell was more powerful, and she was physically stronger as well. Lifting things was way easier. Her sense of touch had gone through the roof. Everything seemed heightened, more sensual, and definitely more sexy. Rani realized her misgivings were lifting. Back in April, she had almost regretted her decision to come into the Life.

She still couldn't think about her family and mortal friends without feeling pain, and something else—guilt. She realized she felt guilty that she wasn't going to die, but they would. Maybe it would lift soon and she could start seeing more of them. Her mum was hurt that Rani hadn't been round much. Anyway, she wasn't thinking about that now. Rob and Rani were driving down to Brighton for a dirty stopover.

She was dressed and poised to wake Rob with a kiss when the buzzer went.

"Special delivery for Ms. Shah," a voice said on the intercom. Rani went downstairs and opened the street door. She smiled when she saw the delivery woman was wearing a shirt with Batman Deliveries printed on it. She accepted the small package and watched the woman return to a Batman Deliveries van parked right outside the house. She shut the door and eagerly opened the package, wondering why it had come to Rob's address and not hers.

Inside was a velvet lined jewelry box containing a single key. She was standing in the hall, puzzling over it when the doorbell rang again. She opened it straight away to find the Count grinning broadly on the doorstep, looking very hot in his gray Armani suit. Rani glanced upstairs and then said softly, "You've got a lot of making up to do."

The Count smiled even broader. "I know," he said, giving Rani a look that melted clean through her thong. "That's why I'm here. Did you get your package?"

Rani nodded.

The Count's eyes twinkled. "I've bought you a little gift." He swept his left arm to the street, and Rani saw a shiny red sports car parked across the road.

"What do you mean?" Her voice was almost a squeak she was so excited. The Count couldn't have bought her a sports car, could he?

"I thought it was time you upgraded. Once you've had a superior ride, I think a person finds their old model a little sluggish. Is that what you've been thinking?" The Count eased closer to Rani and ran his tongue over the delicate skin behind Rani's ear. Aware that Rob was just upstairs, Rani half-heartedly pushed the Count away. All the same, with the car seductively winking at her and the Count blowing in her ear, she was getting very damp in the thong area. She'd just started to reward the Count with a passionate kiss when a voice called from the stairs.

"Rani?"

"Speaking of sluggish," the Count muttered, pulling away smoothly.

Rani had just rearranged her clothes when Rob appeared beside her in boxers and vest, her hair tousled, frowning at the Count. "Yeah, what do you want?" Rob's voice was sharp.

"I came to talk to Rani," the Count said pointedly.

"Oh really? Come to insult her family again?" Rob folded her arms. She was clearly still mad from the soirée.

"No," the Count said coolly. "I've come to make it up to

her."

Rob pursed her lips together in that sulky way of hers.

The Count smiled at Rani. "Like I said, I'm so sorry we were interrupted the other night. I wouldn't normally leave a girl so frustrated…"

Rani was horrified. She couldn't believe the Count had just said that. Rob was still staring at the Count, but then she turned to look at Rani. Her own eyes held Rani's for a second before she turned and walked away.

"I've got to go now," Rani said to the confused Count, shutting the door practically in his face.

Slowly, Rani walked upstairs. She had not wanted Rob to find out like this. Rob was in the bedroom getting dressed. Rani followed her in, not sure exactly what to say. Rob didn't say anything either. Just pulled on her jeans, zipped them up, and started buttoning up a shirt, all the time looking at Rani. Rani badly wanted those eyes to soften.

"Okay, I saw the Count the other night," Rani admitted hesitantly.

"When?" Rob's voice was as cold as her eyes.

Rani dreaded saying when. "Saturday."

Rob stopped buttoning her shirt. "*Last* Saturday."

Rani nodded.

"The night you came over here, *that* night. The night you couldn't get enough?" There was no tenderness in Rob's words, no joking sexual banter. From her mouth the words sounded like an insult.

Rani stiffened. "Yes."

Rob bit her lip. She stared at Rani until Rani wanted to run away. "How long?" Rob asked. "How long have you been seeing that count?" There was hardly any o in the Count's name the way Rob said it.

Rani swallowed. "What's the matter with you?" She changed tack. "Vampires are non-monogamous aren't they?"

Rob's eyes flashed. "Didn't take you long to find that out," she said bitterly. "You haven't answered me. I want to know how long?"

There was something about the way Rob demanded to be answered that annoyed the hell out of Rani. Rob didn't own her. She'd brought her into the Life, not married her. She turned and walked toward the kitchen.

"Where do you think you're going?" Rob shouted, following fast behind her.

Rani felt Rob's hand on her arm. She shook it off. "Don't ever touch me like that, you kutha. I don't answer to you or anyone else."

Rob stepped back. "Clearly," she said quietly. "And by the way, don't call me a dog."

Rani stalked to the kitchen and put the kettle on. She was regretting ever telling Rob Punjabi swear words. After a moment, Rob came and stood against the doorframe. She sighed. "Has this been going on since the ball?"

Rani didn't even turn. She carried on making coffee, putting the grounds in the jug, pouring water, getting her espresso cup out.

Rob took her silence as confirmation. "When were you going to get round to telling me?"

"Why would I tell you? You're a vampire. Read my mind!"

"Vampires don't do that. I don't do that. I'm too honorable," Rob shouted in the prissy way that made Rani's blood boil.

"Oh yeah, you're the perfect bloody vampire, aren't you?" Rani turned. "Except you don't like *your woman* sleeping with anyone else."

"Not *anyone else*, just that thing. That count."

Rani screwed her eyes up. "Why?" she shouted. "Tell me the hell why? Why do you hate the Count?"

Rob clenched her teeth but said nothing. Rani had had enough. Rob needed to be honest with her if she expected total honestly in return. Rani may have only been a vampire a few months, but she'd had plenty of relationships. And she knew possessiveness when she smelled it.

"Why?" Rani said again. The word rang crisply through the tiled kitchen.

Rob just stared at the wall. She reminded Rani of a schoolchild being confronted by a teacher, stubbornly refusing to admit to anything. Rani turned away, disgusted. She poured her coffee and took it to the front room.

She was halfway through her first cup before Rob appeared. Her face had softened slightly. She sat on the edge of the sofa. "Rani," she began, clearly trying to control her voice, "I hate the Count, and the Count hates me. It doesn't matter why."

Rani blew air out through her teeth. Rob ignored her and put a hand over her face, smoothing down her own cheeks. "We fell out a long time ago."

Rani shook her head. Rob was treating her like a child.

"I think this Count business is a smoke screen, I think you're possessive, Rob."

"What?" Rob obviously didn't like that idea.

"I don't like being controlled."

The steel had come back into Rob's eyes. She looked at Rani like she hated her.

"You don't know anything about the Life, or what vampires can be like. I don't believe how ungrateful you are! I've been there for you from the moment you turned. And this is the thanks I get."

Rani reeled from Rob's words. "I didn't know I had a debt to repay." Her voice was ice cold.

Rob frowned. "You don't. I didn't mean...." she trailed off, looking anxiously at Rani.

There was a long silence. Then Rani put her coffee cup down. "You may have *turned* me. You don't own me." She said each word nail hard. She walked to the hall and grabbed her bag, her coat, and the shiny new key.

"Rani." Rob was standing in the doorway to the front room, searching her with her eyes. "Don't go," she said as Rani let the flat door swing behind her.

Rani kept her head facing front, all the way downstairs. She refused to look back as she walked onto the street. She walked purposefully to the red Maserati Spyder.

Oh my God! Rani was astounded she had the key to such a beautiful car. From the side, the car was all silver wheel spokes and red paintwork. She walked in front of it and decided the car looked like a sporty tomato with a big, smiling face. She stole a look from behind and liked the car's chunky bottom with four perky exhausts.

Rani opened the driver's door and slid onto the black leather seat. Keen to get moving, she turned the key in the ignition and the car purred like a lioness asleep in the sun.

With barely a glance in her rearview mirror, Rani pulled out and took off down the road. She swung onto the North Circular and headed for the M1. She was ready to put some serious miles between her and Wood Green. Oh yes, she was going to check this baby out all right.

***

At nine o'clock, Jameel, Selena, and Skipp walked down through the cool woods on Alhambra Hill to Campo del Principe. The open-air restaurants were popular on warm nights and consequently good for a feed. Skipp wanted another meeting. Jameel suggested they hold it in the grounds of the Alhambra, the Moors' red palace, giving Selena and Skipp the opportunity to see close up the beautiful, impressive Islamic architecture. The Alhambra was beautiful at dusk.

They entered through the towering gateway—Torre de la Justica. Skipp and Selena explored the palaces while Jameel waited in the Patio de los Arrayanes, relaxing in front of the pool. A long rectangle of blue-green water spread pliant before a run of seven arches with a tiled roof and a tower rising above. Floodlight falling on the water sent a reflection shimmering onto the screen work as a cool breeze stirred the elegant pool.

Jameel appreciated the Moors' love of arches and fretted screen, the intricacy of carvings in wooden ceilings and of the stuccowork in plaster. He loved the pools and fountains, enclosed gardens, the privacy, and the sense of interior space afforded by so many windows, large domed ceilings, and tiled surfaces.

Carlos and Juan had educated Jameel about the Moors in Granada. The seven centuries of Moorish rule had been, according to them, a benevolent occupation. Although the government was Islamic, other faiths were tolerated. Muslims, Jews, and Christians lived peacefully in a cultured society. There was an emphasis on art and education. Trade and agriculture flourished. When Christians took over in 1492, harsh times followed. Jews and Muslims were expelled—first the Jews, then any remaining Muslims were offered the choice of conversion or expulsion. If they chose expulsion, they had to leave behind their children and their property. The road the

Moors and Jews walked out of Granada became known as Paseo de los Tristes—Passage of the Sad.

When Selena and Skipp had visited the interior of the Palaces, Jameel took them to a secluded area in the Partal Gardens. They sat on a bench by a stone pool covered in water lilies. Date palms rose majestically near the red walls of former servants' quarters. A hibiscus bush, resplendent with blooms, ensured their immediate privacy. The smell of cypress drifted on the night air.

Despite the calm and beauty of the gardens, Jameel was impatient. He wanted to get down to the drag club, where his evening would really begin.

He pulled out a nail file and ran it across his nails. "This won't take long will it?" he asked, crossing his legs and swinging the top one. "Only I've got a bar full of strangers awaiting my entrance. My Doris Day is legendary." He turned to Skipp. "Imagine, if you will, 'Move Over, Darling' done Hindi film style. I don't know a song that can't be improved by a few bindis and a twirling sari."

Skipp stared at him. Then she flipped open her palmtop. "Okay, folks, this is where we're at. Our chief suspect is the vampire called Todd Williams. His movements have been hard to check, as his employer, the Count, is unreliable. But from information I have been able to collect, he was in Spain at least once in April. He was eyeballed at the Bloodsuckers' Ball event you attended, Selena, in London on April twenty-fifth, which means if he was the perp at the Espejos club on May fourth, he would have had to come back to Spain immediately. He could have found out from your friend, the Count, that you were in London, Jameel. I need to establish where he was during that second week in May. Now, did either of you tell the Count that you were returning to Spain?"

Selena nodded. "Yes, I did."

Skipp studied her. "Did you give him any flight details?"

Selena thought for a moment. "No. I didn't even say what day we were leaving."

Skipp nodded and made a note in her palmtop. She stared at the little screen for a while, and then she looked up. "That's the main thing I need to establish—how your movements were tracked."

Jameel didn't like the thought of anyone tracking him. Skipp made it sound very serious. Up till now, things had been unpleasant, but Jameel wasn't really frightened. In fact, he hadn't taken it seriously. He thought everyone, Selena especially, was overreacting. For some reason, now Skipp was here, it all seemed much more scary. *Having a guardian around should be reassuring. Maybe if they'd sent a nice beefy man in some sort of uniform.*

"I need to talk to your friends, Carlos and Juan," Skipp said.

Jameel shrugged. He supposed all kinds of people would be interviewed. He tried to concentrate, but he wasn't really listening. He was thinking about his drag act and wondering how he could mock up a tree and get it onto the tiny stage at Bar La Diferencia. If so, perhaps then he could persuade Pedro, the cute technical guy, to stand behind it on a stepladder with a watering can and simulate monsoon rain. Jameel just knew his life would be complete if he could lip synch round a tree in a wet sari.

"There is something else I want to run by you guys. Something I found out in San Francisco," Skipp continued.

Jameel sighed and began to file the nails on his other hand. He was admiring the color—Gold Haze—and was happy with the way it sparkled in the dim light. Selena nudged him, knocking the file out of his hand.

"Pay attention," she said.

Jameel tutted and bent to pick up the file. It had fallen right under the bench. He heard something swoop past his head and then Selena screamed. He sat up, alarmed, and saw with horror something that looked like an arrow sticking out of Selena's shoulder. Blood was pouring out of the wound, and Selena's face was contorted in agony.

Skipp threw them both to the ground, shouting, "Hit the deck."

"Can you tie up that wound?" she asked Jameel.

Jameel looked blank. "What with?" he asked.

"Try your pantyhose," Skipp said. "

Jameel opened his mouth in horror. Skipp grunted and took her shirt off. Selena's eyes were fixed to Skipp's biceps as Skipp tore the shirt into three strips.

"I saw a flash over there," Skipp said. "I'm going after the perp." She threw the torn strips at Jameel and vanished into the night.

Jameel was very scared now they were alone. Selena was in terrible pain, he could tell, and the guardian had just deserted them, leaving him to try to apply medical aid. What a thing. It wasn't nearly so much fun playing nurse in real life.

Selena gave tiny cries as he wound the material around her shoulder. He wrapped it as carefully as he could, not wanting to hurt her. He didn't know what to do then. Blood was seeping through already. He knew they needed to get the arrow out of her shoulder, heal up the hole, and get some blood back in her system. He couldn't do all that outside the Alhambra. He didn't even know how to get arrows out of someone's body. Okay, it wasn't going to do any good just crouching on the ground.

"Come on, Selena." He tried to help her up. She leaned unsteadily against him. Jameel knew someone could fire another arrow at any time, but he started walking anyway, half-carrying Selena.

It took ages, but he got Selena on the road back up to Albiacín. A car pulled up sharply, and Skipp was suddenly beside him. She lifted Selena easily and put her onto the back seat. Skipp started rewrapping the bandage, pulling it so tightly Selena cried out.

"Careful, you brute!" Jameel said sharply. What was Skipp's problem? Couldn't she see she was hurting Selena?

"If I don't get this tight enough, she'll lose too much blood," Skipp said flatly.

Skipp got behind the wheel and started driving. Jameel looked at Selena. She was obviously getting weaker. He'd seen vampires bleed to death. In the terrible hunted times, when mortals still believed in them, humans had done some cruel things, stabbing vampires with sharpened sticks and leaving them to drain their lifeblood into the soil. Or leaving them outside where sunlight would get them. Jameel shuddered, berating himself for remembering that now.

"You didn't steal this car did you?" he asked Skipp to distract himself.

"No comment," Skipp grunted.

No distraction there then. Jameel leaned back and held Selena's hand, praying she would be all right.

***

The red Spyder burnt through miles like a hot knife skating through butter. Rani had been testing the car for two hundred of them, and she was rising to the challenge so far. She'd finally had to refuel, both the car and herself. She'd made the acquaintance of a fellow traveler, who was having a crafty cigarette in the bushes surrounding the service station car park. On the pretense of blagging a cigarette, Rani had swiftly helped herself to a pint of blood, healed the smoker, and left him. Now she sat in the Spyder, smoking the cigarette and contemplating her route.

She loved the Spyder's cabin. In front of her, the speedometer, rev meter, and other gauges looked like they were straight out of a racecar with a black inner circle, white outer circle, and bold red gauge. To her left, a teardrop-shaped clock sat above a sophisticated-looking navigation system. She had no idea how it worked. She pressed a button above the screen, and opera music soared through the interior. "Nessun dorma," she realized as the words flashed across the tiny screen that had been the navigation system seconds before. Obviously, it was dual purpose. For some reason, the music reminded her of football.

Spots of rain splattered on the black paneling and on Rani's skin. She hit a few more buttons before the electric hood popped over her head with a comforting simplicity. The light summer rain revitalized Rani, and she thought she'd head back down South. Not to see Rob. She wasn't anywhere near ready for that. Just to make sure she was somewhere safe before sunrise.

The drive was blowing away cobwebs. Rani felt a lot better than when she got into the car, several hours ago. She pulled out again and let the opera play. She didn't know how to switch it off anyhow.

The music swelled as the Spyder flew over tarmac, Rani's foot holding the pedal down until the speedo hit 120 mph. There was very little traffic and Rani had that open road feeling.

Something that sounded like a telephone ringing undercut the music, muting it very low. Rani glanced at the screen to see what was wrong and was surprised to see the Count's face in miniature, looking at her.

"I had a video phone installed," the Count's voice informed her out of the car speakers.

Rani kept her eyes on the road, deciding if she would speak to the Count or not.

"I'm glad you're enjoying the car. Does it really do zero to sixty in five seconds?" the Count asked.

"I'm still angry with you," Rani said to the windscreen.

"What on earth are you angry about?" The Count sounded genuinely confused.

"What were you doing coming to Rob's?" Rani demanded.

"Oh. Well, that was a bit cheeky of me, but I figured, we're all grown-ups. Why? Did Rob get her knickers in a twist?"

Rani slowed down a little, her focus split between the conversation and driving.

"Come on, Rani. Surely it didn't cause that much of a problem?"

Rani sighed. "It caused a big problem. But that was because I hadn't told her about us."

"What?" The Count paused. "Tut, tut, Rani. How naughty you are, keeping secrets. Ha! I wish I'd stayed around for the explosion."

Rani was very glad he hadn't.

"I had no idea Rob didn't know. You should have told me."

Rani knew the Count was right about that.

"It's amazing how the mortal mind works. Oh, I know you're not a mortal now, Rani. Don't look at me like that, darling. You've got to admit you still think like one. Why on earth didn't you tell Rob you were seeing me? It's not like you were doing anything wrong."

Rani heaved a sigh. The Count was right. She hadn't been doing anything wrong.

"Where are you now?"

"Somewhere near Leeds," Rani answered.

"That's perfect. Well, point the car toward Manchester.

I've taken the liberty of booking you a room for the night."

Rani frowned suspiciously at the screen. "I don't know."

"Oh, come on, Rani. You've got to sleep."

"Single room is it?" Rani asked pointedly.

"Well, no. Do you want it to be?"

Rani didn't answer.

"Rani, you can't punish me for something that isn't my fault," the Count said persuasively.

"That's true," Rani muttered quietly.

"Okay, Hotel Chez Moi, room number one sixty-nine. I wanted a plain sixty-nine, but *that* was a single room. À bientôt."

"Song to the Moon" swelled through the car, replacing the Count's voice. Rani thought for two seconds then started looking for exit signs.

Within an hour, she was walking along the corridor of the hotel to her room. An hour's anticipation had changed her mood from guilt and anger into pure lust. The Count had been right. Rani hadn't done anything wrong, and Rob was out of order to make her feel that way. It really wasn't her problem that Rob didn't like the guy. Rani felt a stir of anger deep in her gut remembering Rob's stubborn refusal to explain the animosity between them. She knocked on the door, and turned the handle without waiting for an answer.

The Count looked up from the bed. He was in the same suit but had loosened his collar. A blue silk tie lay strewn across the duvet.

"Would you like a little refreshment?" he asked cordially, pointing to some bottles of blood waiting on the dressing table.

Rani shook her head and walked straight over, sitting astride him and pulling off his jacket.

"I see you've got other things on your mind." Rani tore open his shirt, and buttons popped into the four corners of the room. Rani's mouth was all over his face, kissing him, licking him, and pushing him back onto the bed. Rani was ready for sex and felt almost righteous about doing it with the Count.

She sat up, enjoying the power she had to melt the Count under her gaze. Rani's hands moved softly down the Count's chest to his trouser waistband.

She popped the fly and pulled off the trousers and

socks, running her hands along the Count's legs. The Count swallowed, still lying back on the bed. Rani held his eyes and climbed on top, her skirt hitching itself up, her hand pulling her thong aside. She moved, slowly at first, still staring down, the Count watching from below. As her pleasure increased, she needed more and pulled the Count up to her, amazed at her own strength. She pushed her neck into his mouth and an orgasm rocked through her as the Count took her blood. Before she had finished pulsing, she pushed the Count's mouth off her and sank her own teeth into the sweet hollow between the windpipe and the lymph gland, hearing a gasp of satisfaction from him. The Count impressively continued pumping upward as he rode his own orgasm, and Rani took everything she could get.

Rani got up, adjusted her skirt, and turned to go. It was enough she'd had the Count, now she was ready to get back in the sports car and drive. A strange fury rolled inside her.

"Where are you going?" The Count was on his feet. He stood, clearly confused, his silicone appendage swaying up and down like a lewd nodding dog. The Count saw Rani looking and tried to stuff himself back inside his boxers. He only succeeded in creating a tent-like bulge. Rani shrugged.

"I've never seen you like this," the Count said uneasily.

Rani hadn't seen the Count so unsure either. He seemed almost...ordinary.

He stared at her for a moment. "Why not work out some of that mood on me?"

Rani felt a surge of satisfaction that the Count wasn't just going to let her walk out. She wasn't sure if that was enough though.

"I don't know what's going on between you and Rob," he said more smoothly, "and quite frankly, I'm not interested."

Rani laughed. "Really? Isn't that what you wanted all along, to get at Rob?"

The Count looked away. "Yes, perhaps, to begin with. But the last few times, I've been doing it for the sex alone."

Rani laughed harder. It seemed it was a night for revelations. She looked the Count up and down. "So what is it you want from me so badly?" She eyed the Count's impossibly bulging boxers.

The Count shifted, but when he spoke, his voice was cool and quiet. "All I want from you is sex."

The Count's honesty ignited the touch paper to Rani's independence. It was just what she needed. Full of sudden lust for herself and her increasing power, she went over to the Count and walked him backward to the bed.

The Count's eyes widened as Rani took little sensitive bites from his neck and chest. Slowly, his eyes glazed; his breathing grew rhythmic. Rani worked the Count, keeping the image of Rob in her mind defiantly. She had no idea what it meant—being with the Count now that Rob knew. Rani didn't know if that would mean they would split up. She didn't know if she cared. She did know she would never let anyone control what she did.

CHAPTER TWENTY-TWO

When Rani walked out, I drove into Central London and took a walk along the embankment. I was mad, but I still needed to feed.

In a lonely spot, a guy asked me for money. It seemed a fair exchange. I took hold of his mind and began drinking. I couldn't stop thinking about Rani and the Count. She'd made a fool out of me. I was furious she'd tried to blame her lying on me. I remembered how patient I'd been during her transition, and it twisted in my stomach. I'd been so careful and responsible, thinking her actions reflected on me. Well, I wouldn't think that any more.

Suddenly, the guy was sagging in my arms. *Oh God, I must have taken at least a pint and a half.* I healed his neck and checked his pulse. Luckily, it was strong. I stuck three twenties in his pocket, hoping he'd buy himself some food with it.

Guiltily, I hung around to make sure he woke up okay. It gave me time to berate myself thoroughly.

I only moved on when I was convinced no permanent harm had been done. And then I ran. Light summer rain began to fall. It fell cool on my face as I jogged.

I forced oxygen through my lungs, my heart beating fast to pump blood around my body. I felt horrible. I wouldn't let it be like the time when Selena was seeing the Count, and I couldn't handle it. Shit! I must be the last monogamous vampire on the planet. Shame there wasn't at least one other; we could team up.

My breath was coming ragged now. I was up by Blackfriars

Bridge. I went down a set of steps and found a quiet place on the little shingle beach to watch the river. Drops of rain splashed onto the dark surface in a satisfyingly mournful way.

The dark river reminded me of the Seine. The jealousy burning in my gut brought back the 1920s, Paris, and Selena starting an affair with the Count. We were together. I was supposed to accept it. It wasn't even just sex. Selena was in love. It drove me crazy.

I was convinced I was losing her. She'd been my savior. I thought I'd die without her. I was young and easily hurt. The vampire world is not a nice place to get jealous in. No one understands. It's one of the worst things a vampire can do. It's not in the code, but I don't know why they don't write it in. Vampires pride themselves on being tolerant, but my God were they disapproving of me! I got no support for my jealousy, and it just got worse, till I couldn't be in the same room as them. I caused scenes and made ultimatums—which Selena turned down flat. I made an idiot of myself, and vampires began to shun me. Then the final shame came when I lost control and attacked the Count.

There was a court case. They were kind to me, under the circumstances, especially the guardian Brunell. He was the first vampire I met that seemed to understand. I didn't want to share her. He got me to see sense, and in the end, the guard turned everything around for me because I joined up. Stayed in for four decades, by which time the Count was history, Selena and I were back together, and most important of all, I felt good about myself again.

My mobile started chirping in my pocket. I pulled it out, not wanting to talk to anyone, but then I saw it was Jameel.

"Hey, honey, you've got amazing timing," I told him.

"Listen, Rob, something's happened. Someone fired an arrow at Selena…What?"

He trailed off and I heard some American say in the background, "Not an arrow, a bolt."

"Selena's got a bolt stuck in her. We're trying to get it out," Jameel came back on.

"What?"

"Someone fired a bolt at Selena," he said clearly. "We have to get it out because she's losing a lot of blood. We think she'll be all right. Listen, Rob, we need some more blood. I've got four bottles here, but she'll need some tomorrow. Can you get some more couriered out to us?"

I took a split second to decide. "I'll do better than that. I'll courier it myself."

"Oh, Rob." Jameel started crying. It choked me up. "Will you? Oh, honey, will you?"

"Yeah, darlin'. I'll get the first plane I can. I'll make sure no one hurts you or Selena."

"I know you will." Jameel was crying full on now.

"Can I talk to Selena?" I asked.

"No, she's not up to it just now. Rob, I'm really pleased you're coming."

"Okay, you gonna look after Selena for me?"

"Of course I will. No one looks after a femme better than a queen." That was more like the Jameel I knew and loved. "Phone me and tell me what flight you're on, Rob darling. I'll meet you at the airport."

I ended the call and started walking to the car. On the way, I dialed Leah's number. Hopefully, I wouldn't have to call the Count. Leah answered on the fifth ring.

"Hello, sweet boi. What can I do for you that you haven't had done already?"

I didn't usually mind a little harmless flirting with Leah, but I wasn't in the mood. "Hello, Leah. I need to go and pick up some Nosferatu. Can you okay it for me?"

"Of course, Rob. When do you want to collect it?"

"Tonight? I need eight bottles."

"You might as well have a case, dear. I'll arrange it for you. Mike's over there tonight. I'll get him to put some aside with your name on it."

Leah was being very obliging, and no banter with it. She must have picked up on the seriousness in my voice.

I started running the rest of the way back to the car.

***

On Jameel's sofa, Skipp ripped Selena's sleeve, pulling the material away from the wound in her shoulder.

"She's not going to be happy about that," Jameel said. "She only bought that T-shirt last week, in London. It's irreplaceable you know."

Skipp frowned. "I've got to get at the wound, Jameel. And I can't take her top off, can I? That would be embarrassing."

Jameel wondered who was going to be embarrassed. It certainly wasn't going to be Selena. Not the same Selena who went topless at Greenham Common for five years. Skipp was trying to clean blood away from where the steel bolt protruded two inches out of the top of Selena's chest.

"Got any Scotch?"

Jameel fetched his ten-year-old Malt, thinking they could all use a drink. A terrible situation like this deserved nothing but the best.

Skipp took the Malt and poured it liberally onto the wound as Jameel stared in horror. Selena made a faint hissing sound. At least she wasn't completely unconscious.

"Got any cocaine?"

What did Skipp think he was, a bloody pharmacist? A funky pharmacist at that. Jameel did just happen to have a little wrap. He handed it over to Skipp, who opened out the packet and dusted Selena's skin all around the wound. Then Skipp got a metal multi-tool gadget out of her pocket. She opened it out and selected a blade.

"What are you doing?" Jameel screeched.

Skipp heaved a sigh. "I have to cut this bolt out of her. Something's stopping it pulling out," she said like she was explaining to a child.

"With that?" Jameel pointed disparagingly at the tool.

"This is as sharp as a scalpel." Skipp ran the blade over her own finger. "See?"

Jameel watched a thin line of red appear where Skipp had run the blade. She healed the cut immediately.

"No need to show off," Jameel said to show he approved.

Jameel held Selena's hand as Skipp cut into her shoulder. She cried out and squeezed till he thought his bones would break. Skipp was mercifully swift. Three cuts and the bolt was out, along with a lot of blood. She poured more alcohol into the wound, gave Selena a swig as well, and placed her hand firmly on the bleeding hole.

"I've got to stop taking bullets for you," Selena said to Jameel through gritted teeth.

Jameel was glad to have something to laugh at. Skipp lifted her hand. The blood was beginning to clot.

Skipp picked up the bloody bolt and examined it. She wiped the end clean. It had a very nasty looking triangular head with three sharp sides. "This broadhead tip looks like silver. That doesn't make sense. Silver's much softer than steel. Hell, this is a contradictory case."

After a moment, Skipp continued. "I thought I saw something tonight, in that raised bit of gardens above us, but when I got there it was empty. Someone had been there though, someone who drinks blood." Skipp pulled an evidence bag out of her pocket.

Jameel peered at it for a moment before he realized he was looking at a dead field mouse.

"Ahh!" he shrieked, jumping back.

"Blood's been completely drained out of this poor creature." Skipp said matter-of-factly.

Selena shuddered and closed her eyes.

For goodness sake! Fancy showing that to Selena when she was in such a state! Jameel couldn't believe how insensitive butches could be.

***

Mike greeted me at the depot as I strolled through the main door.

"Got your case. Just need you to sign a chit up in the office. Want me to load it while you go sign?"

I liked Mike, even if he did work for the girlfriend thief. Speaking of whom...

"The boss about?" I asked.

Mike shook his head. "Won't be in tonight."

I didn't want to think where he might be. "Hey, did you get that Internet thing all sorted out?" I remembered to ask.

Mike laughed wryly. "Yeah. Well, the guard believe it was nothing to do with me anyhow. They're looking into it, and so am I. I got my theories who put my face up there."

"Yeah?"

• 187 •

From the look on Mike's face, I wouldn't have liked to have been the person who set him up. If indeed that's what happened. You never could tell with the Count's people.

I walked to the office, eager to get away again. I knocked and got no answer, so I pushed open the door. Leah was sitting on the desk, a pink slip of paper perched on her knee. I couldn't help noticing she had black fishnet stockings on, and I knew they were stockings because I could see all the way up to her suspenders.

"Just wanted to make sure you got what you called me for," she purred.

I took a breath, not wanting to be rude. "I'm in a bit of a hurry."

"O-h." Leah managed to stretch the one syllable word into two, as if I'd made an indecent proposal.

"Leah…" I began walking toward her, suddenly nervous.

"I'm amazed Rani's let you out all by yourself. She's more of a vampire than I realized. I'm impressed."

Rani's name burned through my gut like I'd swallowed sunlight. I wondered if Leah knew they were probably together, right now. I didn't want to ask her. Sure, she wouldn't care, like every other vampire on the planet. I reached out for the pink slip, and Leah held it out to me, then she folded it up and put it down her top.

"I think you need to work for what you want, Rob."

She was attractive. I'd always thought she was sexy. I couldn't get a plane till tomorrow anyhow. What was stopping me? Maybe that was all I needed…a little extracurricular activity myself. Still, I hesitated.

"Tell me something, Rob. How come, in thirty years, you've never sucked me? Don't you find me attractive?"

"Of course I do," I said.

"Ah." Leah sighed gently. Her breasts heaved; the paper rustled. "I'm glad. So…" She leaned back against the desk. Her dress lifted so far up I would have won a competition to guess the color of her knickers. "Why don't you get your little piece of paper?" She pointed her breasts in my direction.

I slipped my hand down the front of her dress, searching for the little pink slip and finding two very erect nipples.

"Come here, baby." Leah took hold of my other hand and

took my pulse at the wrist. A self-satisfied smile came over her face as she gauged the rate and power of it. "Is that all for me?" she asked innocently.

I knew she knew it was. She looked beguilingly up at me, and her lips glistened in the dull light. My body moved closer to hers as if on its own accord, and I laughed, knowing she was practicing her magnetism. Her mouth found mine. She slipped her tongue between my lips, darting like a snake. She felt sweet, soft, and wet.

I was doing good, doing what everyone else seemed to do, carried away and enjoying it—until she started to bite me. That's when it stopped feeling right. "Er...Leah…" I mouthed into her head.

She came up. "Hush." She put her finger on my lips. "Rani won't mind. She's probably with my boifriend right now."

So she did know. I kissed her finger. "Leah, you're attractive, I fancy you."

Leah looked serious. "Why do I think a but's coming? Or to be more precise, why do I think my butt's not going to be coming?"

I laughed. "You know me. I'm weird. Anyway, I only found out about Rani tonight."

Leah studied me, amused. "Really? You *are* strange. If that was me, this would be the best, the sweetest time to suck someone else."

I pursed my lips, feeling like a stranger in my own country.

"Keeping secrets, eh? What a little minx you've brought in, Rob." Leah sounded impressed. "You know, you might not feel good about it now, but I bet a lot of people will thank you over the next century for bringing that one in."

I stared at Leah. I knew there was no point in trying to work her out. Just when you thought you had, she seemed to make a point of changing tack. "Yes, Rani will end up the perfect vampire, no doubt." Leah was sweet though, underneath her polished bitch exterior. I gave her a little kiss and pulled away. There didn't seem anything else to say, so I headed for the door.

"I think you'll be needing this." Leah threw the pink slip toward me.

Mike smiled as I approached.

"All the paperwork sorted out, Rob?"

I tossed the slip on the counter. Minutes later, loaded with the case of blood, I headed for the street.

CHAPTER TWENTY-THREE

Jameel was true to his word and picked me up at the airport. As soon as we got back to his house, I rushed in to see Selena. She was propped up on the couch in the living room, looking pale and tired.

"Hello, gorgeous." I hugged her close. She winced.

"You need to be gentle with me. I seem to remember you were quite good at that," she joked.

"Thank the goddess you're okay. I've been really worried."

She held my hand and smiled. For a moment, it felt like any day in the last century. Selena and me, secure in our love for each other. I felt that love inside me, as strong as I'd ever felt it. Damn! How can that happen? I thought it had gone. I stirred and let go of her hand.

"So where's Rani? She didn't want to come?" Selena looked disappointed.

Jameel coughed. "Rani doesn't even know the boi's here," he said snippily as he walked across the room.

I sighed in exasperation. That was all I needed, Jameel getting protective of Rani. He stopped at the couch and started fluffing Selena's pillows. I moved away. I'd already had a lecture from him in the car, and he had told me in no uncertain terms that I should treat Rani right. Sometimes I hated vampires. I knew mortals would be really different about this. *I* would be being looked after, if my friends were human. I made a mental note to check in with my mortal friends at the earliest opportunity.

"What's going on, Rob?" Selena was never too ill for

intrigue.

Jameel butted in. "Rani's having a little triste with the Count. Quelle surprise!" he flapped his hands in the air in front of him to punctuate his sarcastic French.

"Oh," Selena said in an understated way, not seeming surprised at all. She was probably being diplomatic. "That won't last," she added by way of consolation.

Hearing her say it, I knew she was right. I couldn't see it lasting either. "I don't want to think about it," I muttered.

Jameel caught my eye. "Rani kept it a secret till yesterday," he informed Selena in a hushed voice.

"Oh, Rob." Selena gave me a loving look. My heart swelled. It was good to know she cared about me.

There was a knock on the door. Jameel yelled, "Come in," and an athletic type strode through it. The jock wasn't so much tall as muscular. She had a pilot's jacket on that would have looked fantastic on me, with a pair of black jeans, a cool pair of boots, and a black bandanna. Instinctively, I stood taller.

"Lieutenant Rob Perdoni?"

I guessed this must be the guardian. "That's right. But I'm not Lieutenant Perdoni anymore."

"Skipp." She extended a hand. I took it. She had a firm handshake.

"That a name or an instruction?" I asked.

"First and last name," she said succinctly, without a hint of amusement.

"How long have you been in the guard?"

"Five."

"Decades?"

"Years." Something flickered on her impassive face.

I frowned. Selena had said this guardian was one of the best.

"So, what have you got so far?"

Instead of answering me, Skipp went over to Selena and asked politely how she was feeling. I saw some color come back into Selena's face, and she started acting all girly. Skipp was shifting around from one foot to the other, and I couldn't imagine many situations made that butch look awkward. I folded my arms and studied Jameel's painting of a swimming pool. It was very calming. After a quick conversation, Skipp came and stood beside me.

"If you don't mind, Perdoni, I'd rather not discuss the particulars of the case at this moment. I've come here to go over something." She nodded her head sideways, toward the next room.

I got that she had a hunch about something and it wasn't safe to speak. She patted a little black unit sticking up out of her breast pocket. Then she put one finger to her lips. I thought she wanted me to be quiet rather than to kiss her.

I followed her into the next room, where Jameel kept his PC. She glanced at the webcam, shut down the computer, and then reached behind and unhooked the camera.

"Hey!" Jameel protested futilely, as Skipp didn't even look up.

Instead, she fiddled about at the back of the hard disk plugging in her device, setting some controls on the front of it, and then ushered us out of the room again.

"I'm trying to establish how the perp or perps know your whereabouts," she explained.

It was good to be around people who talked the talk again. I suggested Jameel get some of the Nosferatu I'd brought in to Selena, figuring he would be more hindrance than help.

I cracked open a couple of beers, guessing Skipp'd be a beer butch. I was right. Jameel graciously accepted a glass of Rioja.

Skipp went through Jameel's house with another piece of test equipment. It was about a tenth the size of the ones I'd used in my time, but I knew it was a bug checker. A half hour later, Skipp had some results for us.

"Far as I can tell, the house is clean. But the computer wasn't." She raised the webcam. "Someone was spying on you using this. It's not that hard. Because you have a videophone, it meant they could listen in and watch any of your phone conversations, as well as spy on you anytime the computer was on. Even if you had the cam program shut down."

Jameel looked perturbed. I was amazed. I'd had no idea what Skipp was describing was possible.

"You know that people can use Web cameras for surveillance?" I asked her.

"Sure." She was very nonchalant about it. "I've done it

myself. Of course, you're restricted to whatever angle the camera's set at, and the audio doesn't reach very far. Probably not even to another room. I've done a hack check also, and someone's been through your computer, Jameel. The main activity though is around your e-mail folder."

"So can you find out who's been doing this?" I asked.

"Sure can, but I need some time and some specialist help to trace the signal. I'll send this info back to the CCS, that would be the Computer Crime Squad. In the meantime, I wanna go through your e-mails, Jameel, is that okay?"

Jameel nodded slowly. Skipp left us, heading back to Jameel's PC.

I fussed round Jameel and Selena for a bit. Truth was I felt a bit redundant. I'd come over, thinking my years in the guard would be useful. Trouble was, computers were in their infancy when I was in. I was useless around this kind of stuff. Skipp may have only been in for five years, but she knew the cou all right.

It's ironic I don't know more about computers really, considering they keep my savings account looking very healthy. Or the mouse does, to be more precise. I bought some shares in an early prototype, back when computers were still the size of small rooms. No one could have guessed one day everyone in the West would have one. Or that they would all need a little something to click with. The same investor had just persuaded me to put some money in a new technology. He called it smartphone technology. I couldn't see it catching on, but it was worth a punt.

"Who's Buffboy?" Skipp appeared in the doorway.

"Oh, he's just my cyber boyfriend. Really, you can't suspect him!" Jameel looked up from his wig catalogue.

"How did you meet him?" Skipp came and sat. She was holding several printouts.

"We met in a chat room."

"The Back Room?" Skipp asked immediately.

Jameel frowned. "Yes. Do you know it?"

Skipp laughed. "No, that ain't really my thang. I guessed because you visited it so often."

Jameel looked away, as if that was really none of Skipp's business.

"C'mon, Jameel, give it up. *When* did you meet this person, and why did you start e-mailing?" I was getting impatient with the speed of this inquiry.

"I don't know. Sometime in January. I liked him, and then we started e-mailing, just so we could flirt with each other. He's never asked me for any details of where I live or anything like that. I'm sure it's all harmless."

"Sure. But maybe you just happened to mention you were going to London, or that you went to a club in Granada," Skipp said.

Jameel thought about it, looking uncomfortable. "Maybe."

"Doesn't matter anyway," Skipp said. "Whoever's been hacking into your PC, buddy, has got any details in any e-mails you've sent or received, plus all the details from your contact book, including addresses, and they could have gotten your flight details because you booked on the Web and got a confirmation e-mail."

"Oh shit! Is it that easy?" Jameel asked, horrified.

"Yep. Wish you'd called me in earlier," Skipp said.

"So do I," Selena called out weakly.

Whether that was to save herself from getting hit by a bolt, or so she could have ogled Skipp for longer, I didn't know. Skipp looked pleased, either way.

"Buffboy," I said.

Skipp and Jameel looked at me expectantly.

"Didn't the name put you off?"

"Rob, you really must keep up. Buff means attractive," Jameel said dismissively. "She's not down with street language," he told Skipp.

I bristled. "*Buff* boy... Buff—Buffy. Didn't you ever make that connection?"

From the look on his face, he obviously hadn't.

Skipp looked thoughtful too. "A slayer. Well, that's very interesting. Fits with something I've been looking at. Our main suspect at the moment, as I'm sure you've considered, Perdoni, is Todd Williams."

"He's my hot favorite," I said. "He's got motive, opportunity, and he works for the Count."

"Exactly," Skipp said. "We've been keeping tracks on that organization for some time."

I laughed. "We were when I was in the guard. I have a huge file on the Count's activities, if you want to check it out sometime."

"Oh God, don't get her started," Selena called out hoarsely.

"Actually, Perdoni, I've read it. That file is kinda legendary in the guard. The detail is outstanding."

I grinned broadly. The jock was exactly the kind of guardian I would have wanted in my squad when I was in.

Skipp's mobile went off. While she took the call, Jameel whispered to me, "I'm surprised you haven't arrested the Count already."

"I'm not a guardian anymore, remember? Mind you, the idea of him caged up in a cell does give me some satisfaction."

"Whatever floats your boat," Selena muttered.

I ignored her.

Skipp lined up her palmtop next to her mobile, tapped some buttons, and laid them on the table.

"They're sending a document," she told us.

"You got an infrared link between your phone and your palmtop?" I guessed.

"That's right."

I was impressed with the kit guardians got to play with now. I got to dust fingerprints, maybe listen to phone calls and record the conversations on a tape machine the size of a TV set. That's why we had to hide away in basements. You couldn't slip one of those babies in your pocket and go unnoticed.

"Okay. Here's the thing, people. Buffboy's our man all right. The hacking traces back to whatever computer he's using. My guess is, it's a laptop. The phone numbers change all the time. But get this, a lot of them are in Spain, southern Spain, some of them even from Granada."

Nobody spoke. It wasn't good news.

"Jameel, I want you to try to arrange a meet. Will you do it?"

Jameel considered it. I could tell he was upset his cyber guy was implicated. Jameel wasn't having much luck with boyfriends. After a while, he nodded.

We watched as Jameel logged on. Even Selena dragged herself off the sofa, ignoring both Skipp's and my advice to stay and rest. She hated to miss anything. Unfortunately,

Buffboy wasn't logged on, not to Gaychatfun.com, not onto the Net at all, so Jameel couldn't even instant message him. Jameel sent an e-mail instead.

"Care to take a walk?" Skipp asked me discreetly as Jameel typed away.

I agreed. Selena didn't look happy about us going off without her, but we both said we would run if she tried to come with us. She looked as fed up as a young child who isn't allowed to play with the big kids.

"I'll tell you everything when I get back," I said, tucking her back onto the couch.

She made me promise, and I did. Even though we'd stopped going out, I found it hard to deny Selena anything. Old habits die hard I guess.

***

And now there are four. Four safely tucked up in the little house. One isn't well, though. How sad. Everyone say Ah. Jamie can't bear to be alone anymore. Silly boy, when will he realize he has to learn his lesson before he can forget the past? The past can be a friend or a terrible enemy. But four is too many. The watching must stop for a while. Instead, stay home and plan. Mmm, time for a pick-me-up. You are what you drink. Quiet as a little mouse, come here, my beauty...

There, that didn't hurt now, did it? And now the elixir. Ahh, that's made it all better. So, time to send a letter to the queen...The queen would like to meet me, how lovely. Oh yes, how lovely that will be. Perhaps we can take tea, or E, or K...

Now, which shall it be?

***

It was as warm in Granada at four a.m. as twilight was in England. It made me sleepy.

We were sitting on a wall in the Albiacín area. I liked the tiny streets, and the houses with white or sand-brown stone walls, arched windows, and terra-cotta tiled roofs. Blue and green painted plates were displayed on walls everywhere, often decorated with the pomegranate symbol of Granada.

There were old fountains and cisterns at every corner and buildings that were obviously once mosques. Rani would love this, I thought, and the thought twisted inside me.

Skipp looked out to the skyline. Beyond the Alhambra's dusky terra-cotta, the purple outline of the Sierra Nevada Mountains curved into an endless indigo sky. "What's the story with Jameel's ex boyfriend, the mortal one?" Skipp asked.

"You mean Ben?" I clarified.

She nodded.

"He committed suicide. Jameel took it very bad, even though they were already split up. He'd wanted to bring him in. The Night Council wouldn't agree to it. I think their relationship was pretty serious. I don't know if Jameel's got over his death yet."

"Hmm." Skipp took the information in. "I spoke to Jameel's buddies in San Francisco. They said the same kind of thing you just did. Selena thinks Jameel blames himself for the man's death."

"Does she?" It was news to me. The warm air stirred very softly, caressing my skin rather than cooling it.

"Do you think Todd Williams could have murdered Ben Mathews?" Skipp asked.

"Yeah. That's entirely possible. I think Ben had something on Todd. There was the whole business with the other drug dealer, the mortal one. Ben used that dealer a lot in the old days, told me once he used to be his main supplier. You know Ben slipped off the wagon?"

Skipp nodded. She'd done her homework.

"That was why the Night Council turned him down I think. So chances were, when he wanted drugs again, he went back to his old supplier. Todd didn't like Ben. He wouldn't even acknowledge him, though according to Jameel, he sold him drugs when it suited him. Todd could have hated Ben because he was human, or Ben could have had something on him."

"Right. Tell me what you think of this then. Jameel's buddy Martin told me he thought he saw Ben Mathews using a cash machine in the Castro in January."

I stared at Skipp. "He died in November."

"I know. It's not a very reliable sighting. Up till now, I've been looking for a vampire. Everything seems to suggest the perp's one of us, including information from an air hostess concerning a vampire she witnessed on the New York to London flight. The description fits a vampire, but not one I've been able to identify." Skipp stared out over the dark city below.

I followed her gaze. I preferred to think the perp was a vampire. I didn't like the thought that a human might be involved, and worse than just any human, a slayer. Those people were unpredictable.

We headed back. There was no further news. Skipp hung out with Selena for a while, filling her in. I left them to it and got an early night.

CHAPTER TWENTY-FOUR

Rani's neck hurt. And she hadn't had a wink of sleep. She'd stayed longer than she meant to with the Count. She'd left as soon as twilight struck. Not sure her body could take any more sucking, she wanted to eat, sleep…go over events in her mind, without anyone else breathing down her neck. However pleasant that might be.

She drove to her flat, stopping only for a feed. At last, when she was safely inside, she checked her mobile and her answering machine for messages. She figured she could cope with Rob when she was alone in her own space.

The odd thing was, she had no messages from Rob. That confused Rani. By the time she'd poured herself a tall glass of ice-cold sparkling water, she'd decided to text her. For the first time since their row, she started to worry a little. She hoped Rob was all right.

***

Todd knew Jameel's address. Even though Todd didn't deliver it in person Jameel had bottled blood delivered regularly.

Todd supposed a lot of people would find the cobbles and whitewashed walls of Albiacín charming. Todd thought its narrow streets were restrictive. He preferred wide open spaces, like the Midwest. Now that was a place you could get lost in. A place you could do what you liked in. These little streets made it easy to hide, though. Staring across at the house, Todd thought again about Jameel. He had caused Todd an awful lot of trouble, getting him hauled before the justice. Fortunately, they hadn't been able to prove he'd killed that drug dealing chicken.

Todd couldn't understand why they would even care. One useless chicken drug dealer—what was he to them? Whatever. If they got any proof, what with the other stuff on his record, Todd would be frying in the sun for sure. His case would be passed over to the enforcers. Todd wasn't going to let that happen. He was glad Jameel was suffering. He deserved to.

He pulled a photo out of his pocket. Well, maybe there was something he could do to notch up the pressure on the drag queen. Todd smiled. Planning something always made him happy.

***

Jameel woke feeling sick. He just wanted to up and leave Granada now. The others wouldn't hear of it. The butch guardian said whoever it was would track him down again. Jameel felt like a hunted animal. Also, it looked like his choice of boyfriend was appalling. One died. Well, that's what you get for going out with mortals, he supposed. Now the charming substitute had turned out to be a nutcase.

He slipped his feet delicately into his favorite fluffy pink mules and padded to the kitchen. It was still early. Jameel's gaze fell on the printout of Buffboy's e-mail. He had responded the next day:

Hey ScarletLady,
I wondered if you'd be brave enuf to meet? I'm excited already. Let's do it! I can't believe my luck — you've been here in Granada all the time! What R the chances of that? Hope u know Sacromonte. What about tomorrow? I'll meet u @ the Abbey, at 10 p.m. I'll be wearing white jeans and a black top.
Can't wait. Why don't you e me a number I can text u on tomorrow.
Buffboy

The others would be up, and Skipp would be here in an

hour for the Seventeen Hundred Hour Briefing, as Skipp had put it. They didn't talk properly, those guard types. The whole thing was turning into a military operation.

Jameel poured himself a glass of orange juice, noticing his hand was shaking. Well, when this was all over he was going to party, party, party.

At least Selena was going to be all right. After the extra blood had kicked in, she'd healed quickly.

He checked for post and picked up a letter. It smelled nice. Jameel's heart lifted. Hopefully, one of his friends had sent him something lovely and distracting. He opened it and pulled out a photo. His stomach turned to ice. Ben's beautiful smiling face shone up at him from Jameel's apartment in San Francisco. Jameel's eyes filled with tears, and his hand shook as he read the tiny piece of paper clipped to the photo, it was a quote from the code. "*I shalt harm neither mortal nor vampire.*"

Jameel swallowed, and read on:

Remember your oath, Jameel? Don't you think a vampire who hurts a mortal should be punished? Some might say you have blood on your hands.

Jameel felt the photo slip from his hand. Willing the room to stop spinning, he bent to pick it up, walked quickly to the kitchen, and threw everything in the bin—photo, paper, envelope, everything. He couldn't take any more questions. There was no need for the others to find out about this

CHAPTER TWENTY-FIVE

I was in position by 21:30 at the meeting place: the Abbey on Sacromonte. The Abbey was a dark stone tower rising behind an orange wall. Under other circumstances, I would have enjoyed the steady climb through Sacromonte village until the houses and white walls fell away, leaving a hillside studded with cave openings and a fantastic mirador of the Alhambra across the valley. I wasn't here for the view though. We had decided as a group that my role in tonight's operation was Obs—to be in place before the perp arrived, to identify him or her, and to tail as necessary. Jameel would arrive at 22:00, followed discreetly by Selena and Skipp.

I was trying to look like a tourist, complete with rucksack and big map. In case the perp was someone we knew, I was in disguise, wearing a blond wig (one of Jameel's short ones) covered by a tourist sombrero-type hat, plus a moustache built from stick-on facial hair. All of which were making me itch like I had a plague of fleas.

Skipp had kitted me up with a tiny radio receiver in my ear and a mic hidden behind my wristwatch so we could keep in contact. I was ready for action.

The hillside was very quiet. The only people around obviously lived here. My attention was taken by a man walking up the road. He was wearing black and white, but black jeans and a white T-shirt. I turned away from him and pretended to study my map. Really, I was getting a good look at him through the surveillance glasses Skipp had loaned me. If I looked forward, the glasses functioned normally, but if

I looked to either side, I could see behind me. They were designed for covert rear observation.

The man was wearing sunglasses, hardly necessary in the evening light, unless you were a vampire. He had a rucksack on his back too. *Possibly not from round here then.*

His face was very wrinkled, though he didn't look like an old man. In fact, as he got very near and I sneaked a look over the map, his face looked decidedly odd. Maybe he was a mortal with an unusual facial disease. He wasn't stopping at the Abbey though. Something told me to tail him. I glanced at my watch. It was 21:45. I would still have time to double back if he wasn't our man. I muttered into the mic that I was tailing a possible perp. "Roger that." Skipp growled low in my ear.

The wrinkle-face guy walked on for a few minutes before stopping at a bar built into a cave. He stood at the entrance talking to a guitarist. He looked like he was showing the guy some photos. Maybe I was tailing the wrong person. I was just about to turn and go back to the Abbey when the suspect pulled out his wallet and handed over what looked like a lot of pesetas. The guitarist glanced in my direction and I walked to another cave, this one a restaurant, and studied the menu. Flamenco drifted out from inside.

When I turned back to the bar, the suspect was sitting on a rock at the side of the road, playing with a mobile phone, texting someone. Skipp's voice told me Jameel was approaching the Abbey now. She also advised me to stay put; they had the Abbey covered.

Far off, I could hear what sounded like hundreds of people walking up a cobbled street, rhythmically. As the noise got louder, I heard hand clapping, singing, and flamenco guitar playing, along with foot tapping on cobbles. It was the nightly procession Juan had described, heralding the arrival of the gypsy flamenco performers, coming back to the barrio to hold the zambras. Juan had dropped in before we'd left to see if Jameel wanted to come out.

When we'd told him we were going to Sacromonte, he had told us how the caves of sacred mountain had been the homes of Granada's gypsy population for centuries, until the 1970s when most were persuaded to move to low-income housing projects. Some said the gitanos hadn't had a lot of choice in the matter. They didn't want to go, so they never really left the barrio. It was certainly where they still made a lot of money from tourists, holding singing, dancing, and drinking events called zambras in the caves.

Skipp interrupted my thoughts to tell me Jameel had had a text message telling him to keep walking up the hill. Buffboy was apparently waiting in a particular cave for him.

A blur to my right alerted me that my suspect was on the move. I followed at a sensible distance. A glance into the bar as I passed showed me they were getting ready for the mother of all zambras. Cases of vino were stacked up at the back, and empty chairs each side of the long, narrow room, were backed against the wall. I was temporarily distracted by the flash of copper—pans, spoons, jugs hanging from the ceiling and walls. The glare bounced off the whitewashed walls of the cave and shot straight at me.

As we left the Abbey and Sacromonte village firmly behind us, the light fell sharply away, engulfed by the dark of open countryside. The moon was dark, and there was no street light beyond the village, only the occasional dim flow from openings and doorways carved into the hill all around, like eyes and mouths carved into a Halloween lantern.

My suspect was walking swiftly along the thin, chalky path. Luckily, the path glowed white in the deepening night. Wind was beginning to whistle across the hillside now that we were farther and farther away from any buildings. I saw his white T-shirt head off on a side path that lead only to one small opening.

I kept going on the slightly larger path, itself only a track by now. The suspect didn't seem to notice me at all as I passed about fifty meters below him.

I kept walking for a few more minutes and then headed up the hill myself. I intended to creep round and come out over the top of the cave the suspect had disappeared into. Though it was dark, from the top of the hill, I could see back to the lights of the restaurant and bar. There was Jameel, and a little distance behind him, Selena and Skipp.

I came a cropper on the slope. The hillside was chalky and crumbly. The sparse grass on top was slippery in the cooling air. I started to slide backward and grabbed at a bushy plant.

Its sharp, serrated leaves cut into me. I ignored the pain and scrambled on up the track. I was also trying to ignore the hot, itchy wig sitting on my head like an uninvited cat, and the gum sticking the moustache onto my upper lip that was pulling it taut and making it feel completely immobile. I certainly had a stiff upper lip. I told myself sternly to stop moaning and concentrate on the job in hand. When I was in the guard, I had put up with uncomfortable situations for hours without noticing or complaining. *When had I lost the ability to do that?*

I stopped on the hillside a few meters above the mouth of the suspect's cave. From here, I could see the path all the way back to the bar. It seemed a good place to watch from. I checked all around. No one was about except Jameel a little way off walking toward the cave beneath me. I allowed myself a good scratch and decided to ditch the hat.

I radioed my position to Skipp, who acknowledged. Skipp and Selena were just coming up to the bar. I watched them, thinking Selena looked very mysterious in her headscarf and huge sunglasses. The scent of jasmine and the dusky smell of wood smoke drifted on the breeze. Skipp suggested I should hold position until Jameel went inside the cave and then go quietly to the entrance. I agreed. It looked like my suspect was indeed Buffboy.

I had a moment to think about what it must be like to live in one of the caves. Before I came up, I'd imagined they would be damp and cold. But the ones I had seen were more like stone houses. Juan had told me the cave walls could be one hundred meters thick, providing a soundproofed environment that kept a constant, mild temperature throughout summer and winter. He said the caves often interlinked, a warren of homes built into the mountain.

A sudden burst of music in my earphone made me look over to Skipp's direction. I could see a group of gitanas gathering tightly around Selena and Skipp. Skipp was trying to talk to me, but all I could hear was guitar playing and female voices.

"Come in, come in, señor. Come and listen to the music. Gypsy music, yes?"

"Over here, lady. Come here, you must come dance with us. You like. Come into the gypsy cave, señorita."

Selena and Skipp were surrounded by taffeta skirts, arms were pulling them into the bar, gitana women were blocking their path, cajoling sweetly and making it impossible for them to carry on along the hillside.

Jameel was just disappearing below me into the cave. I glanced back to the bar and saw there was no way they were going to get here any time soon. I started creeping down.

The entrance was deceptively small. Through the narrow opening, I made out a room that seemed to spread into the very depths of the hill. The walls were an orange-copper color, dimly lit by a pair of lanterns hung from hooks, each side of the wall.

Jameel had his back to me. Facing the entrance to the cave, was the perp, formally known as Buffboy. He had on a crude Halloween mask of a vampire and was holding a loaded crossbow at Jameel's chest.

I pressed myself back, round the corner of the curved opening, hoping to hell I couldn't be seen.

"Who are you?" Jameel had switched his open transmitter on.

"A friend." The perp's voice was bizarre, like the voice of an alien in a bad science fiction film. I suspected he was using an effects box to alter his voice. His voice was louder than Jameel's as well, seeming to come out of the walls of the cave—probably out of speakers.

"You don't look very friendly," Jameel said.

"Sometimes friends have to be cruel to be kind." There was something very chilling about this person.

"By the way, Jameel, you have been found guilty. And it's my job to punish you."

"Found guilty of what?" Jameel's voice shook.

"I think you know. Now put these on."

There was the snap of something metallic being caught.

"Do it," the bizarre alien voice ordered.

I had to get in there somehow. I couldn't risk barging in the front way. Jameel was only feet away from the crossbow.

Over my shoulder I saw a much smaller opening. I crept toward it, staring into darkness.

Something snuffled. I jumped, slipped, and fell backward onto a large plant, discovering why it's called a *prickly* pear.

Pulling prickles out of my bottom, I cautiously returned to the small cave and shined my torch…into the face of a donkey. We stared at each other for a moment, and then I had an idea. The donkey seemed to grin happily as I untied its tether.

As I gave it a little pat, I heard Jameel back in the cave, trying to buy time.

"Okay, I've put them on," he said. "Now, if you're going to fire that thing, the least you can do is tell me why."

"You made a wrong decision, didn't you, Jameel?"

"What do you mean?" There was a pause. "Do you mean giving evidence before the justice?"

There was another pause. Then Alien Voice said, "I know you told lies about me. Why did you do that?"

Hearing this person speak sent a chill through me. His grasp on reality was tentative. I needed to flush them out of their hole. I pulled the donkey toward the larger entrance, looking for some small stones.

"I haven't told any lies," Jameel said.

"Ah-ah." Bizarre Alien Voice made a sound like a game show sound effect. "That was the wrong answer. That was your only chance, and you lost."

Now was as good a time as any. I threw a handful of stones into the cave and backed off round the corner.

"What was that?"

I heard footsteps and then a rustle as the perp pushed past Jameel heading for the entrance. I gave the donkey a firm but gentle shove down the hillside.

The perp came cautiously out of the cave and looked down the path. From behind, I watched him clock the donkey and heard him tut. I could see a radio mic lead running along the back of his neck behind the mask. I crept nearer. He was still looking out. In a second, I saw why.

Selena and Skipp had pulled away from the bar crowd and were gaining on the cave. He raised his crossbow.

I leapt at him and heard a bolt discharge as I knocked him and the bow to the ground.

I landed heavily on top of him, winding him. I grabbed the bow and threw it behind me, back into the cave. He tried to roll me off him, but I hung on. I felt him grab my hair, and it came off in his hands. He screamed.

In the confusion, I tried to pin his arms down, but he was like an eel swimming in oil. He got one arm free and punched me. That made me mad, so I got a hold of his head and gave him a good smack against the ground. I heard the mask crack. Then I felt a sharp stabbing pain in my arse. That's when everything got very quiet…and dark.

CHAPTER TWENTY-SIX

Selena anxiously held the water to Rob's lips, hoping to see her eyelids flutter. Rob had been out of it for several hours, and Selena was starting to really worry.

Jameel paced restlessly up and down, his wrists still encased in steel handcuffs. He had long since broken through the link holding them together, but was waiting for Skipp to return with her special tool to cut off the cuffs.

Rob made a moaning noise and spluttered. Selena allowed herself to exhale. Jameel rushed to the sofa as Rob blinked at them through bleary eyes.

"Wha' happened?" she asked weakly.

"You were attacked," Selena told her. "You were injected with something." Relieved Rob had come round, she held Rob's face between her hands, and kissed her gently. The kiss was somewhere between a peck on the lips and a smooch.

"Horse tranquillizer," Skipp said as she came through the door into Jameel's front room. She was carrying a metal briefcase. "Ketamine to be exact."

"Special K?" Jameel clarified.

Skipp opened the case and pulled a bolt cutter from a holder. The whole case was kitted out for tools, all in their own clip or section. All polished. Selena was sure each one was exactly where it should be.

"Yeah." Skipp grunted, indicating to Jameel to hold out his wrist. She opened out the bolt cutter, slipped the jaws around the thick metal cuff, and closed them. Two halves fell away to the floor. "I have a basic drug test kit."

"Why doesn't that surprise me, Inspector Gadget?" Jameel teased her, holding out his other wrist.

Skipp continued. "It confirmed Ketamine was the stuff in the syringe Buffboy used on Rob."

"Huh?" Rob's words were slurred. "I got stuck wiv kitkat?"

"Nice to see you're keeping up with street terms," Jameel quipped.

Selena stopped running a cool cloth over Rob's face for a moment. "But a tranq shouldn't affect us like that should it?"

"There was enough Ketamine in that syringe to knock out an elephant." Skipp looked up from her briefcase. She came over to Rob and stood solemnly over her. "Perdoni, I feel I let you down. The perp got the better of me, and I didn't get your back, buddy. I apologize."

Rob tried to smile. "I managed," she slurred. "Someone fill me in please."

Jameel told Rob that Buffboy had forced him to put a pair of handcuffs on. When Buffboy had heard noises just outside the cave, he had roughly brushed past Jameel, pushing him aside. Jameel had seen him raise the crossbow and fire, just as Rob jumped him. Rob had pinned him down, but Buffboy had pulled a syringe from his pocket and slammed it into Rob's behind. Jameel had gone out to try to help them, but Buffboy had run off down the hillside in the opposite direction to Selena and Skipp coming fast up the small track.

Skipp added that Selena had seen the bolt coming, a fact Skipp seemed very impressed with, and had knocked both of them to the ground. However, the perp had got away despite Skipp giving chase. Skipp guessed the perp knew the hillside well.

"So now we're in a fix. We're fairly sure it's a man, but we can't be entirely sure of that. I got his voice on disk, but that was altered. We've got very little to go on. And now the perp's seen all four of us." Skipp glanced at Rob. "Anyway, Perdoni, how're you doin'?"

Rob shifted in the bed, wincing as she did so. "Dizzy, nauseous...my hand hurts, my bum hurts. Bits of me feel numb. And," she said with sudden horror, "I can't move my upper lip at all."

Laughter broke out. "Why're you all laughin' at me?" Rob complained.

"You've still got your drag king moustache on," Selena said. Bending over Rob, she pulled it off with one swift movement. Rob gave a cry of pain and looked plaintive.

"Poor baby." Jameel came and stroked Rob's hair.

"How *did* you get those cuts on your butt?" Skipp asked with a smile.

"Wha'? How do you know..." Rob was clearly horrified.

"Relax, Perdoni. Selena told me about them." Skipp was chuckling now.

Rob stared crossly at Selena. "What were you doin' fiddlin' with my bottom?" she slurred.

"We had to check what had happened to you." Selena bit her lip to stop herself laughing. "Don't look like that. I was only saying hello to an old friend!"

Rob weakly told them how she'd fallen into a prickly pear and cut her hand on another plant. The short explanation obviously left her exhausted.

"I want to get you into bed now. You need to sleep." Selena started pulling the cover off Rob. She and Jameel got Rob to her feet and walked her to Jameel's guest room. Skipp cleared the sofa, disposing of used antiseptic wipes in the bin.

When they came back into the living room, Skipp was holding up a photo and a scrap of paper.

"You wanna explain this?" she said sternly.

Jameel swallowed. "It came yesterday. Okay, I threw it away. So bite me."

Skipp put the documents in her pocket, frowning disapprovingly at Jameel. Selena put her hand on Skipp's arm. "Are you okay?" she asked.

"Sure." Skipp smiled at her concern.

"Do you think anyone will try to break in here while we sleep?" Selena asked.

Skipp shook her head. "Unlikely. The perp knows Jameel's got a lot of vamps around him. I could stay over though, if it would make you feel better?" She looked from Selena to Jameel for approval.

Jameel smiled and nodded. The more the merrier," he said. "I haven't even begun to let myself think about what happened tonight. And why someone is so desperate to attack me.

I'm going to bed." He sighed.

Selena gave him a fierce hug. "Hang in there, darling."

Skipp put her briefcase neatly in a corner, poured herself and Selena a Scotch, and sat on the sofa.

"I'll sleep here." She patted the sofa, glancing up but not holding Selena's eye. The cool, butch guardian looked suddenly flustered. Selena took it as a sign. A good one.

She sat close beside Skipp. "Sleep on the sofa if you like," she ran a finger down Skipp's cheek, "but there's no need." She met Skipp's eyes, wanting to assess her reaction. "Not when there's a nice, big bed in my room."

Skipp put her glass down and kissed Selena long and deeply.

All the horrible events of the night flew out of Selena's mind as she wrapped her body around Skipp's. She slowly undid Skipp's denim shirt, playing with the buttons as she fingered them open. Skipp started to flush, heat spreading through her body as her heart pumped fast, and blood surged through her vessels.

Selena smiled, her lips parting. Skipp caught her breath and stared fixedly at Selena's incisors. Selena licked them, one by one, the tip of her tongue circling provocatively.

Skipp grinned then and pulled Selena to her, nuzzling her neck. Selena's breath came in short gasps. She pulled back, placed her hand firmly on Skipp's chest, and held her at arm's length.

"Oh no," she breathed, "I don't want a four-minute wonder. You're going to have to work harder than that, baby, if you want me."

Skipp studied her, breathing deeply through her nose. To encourage her, Selena slipped a hand inside Skipp's shirt, running her fingers over Skipp's abs, chest, and shoulders. The skin, stretched taught over muscle, was buttery soft and smelled of cinnamon. Selena squeezed a bicep and gave a genuine "Ooh" of delighted surprise. "That's a hard one!" she pouted.

Skipp laughed. Selena grew serious as Skipp's incisors caught the light. The moment flashed between them. Skipp slipped out of the shirt and stood.

The folds of her faded blue jeans contrasted with her

hazelnut skin. She held out her hand and led Selena to the bedroom.

Inside the room, Skipp lifted Selena and laid her tenderly on the bed. She began undressing her, the brush of her fingertips causing electricity to jump across Selena's skin. Pleasure started to swell in Selena's belly; it flushed slowly upward.

Skipp came in for a kiss, and Selena couldn't hold back. Her tongue searched Skipp's mouth, and she sucked Skipp's lips between her own till Skipp broke off for air. Skipp mumbled something. Selena looked into her eyes, and what she saw there pulled Selena's throat back to Skipp's patient lips.

Selena denied herself nothing. She had no fear of Skipp. Her self-confidence was such that the only thing on her mind was pleasure. And consequently, all the little nerve endings, and all the major ones, were receptive.

Fire ran through Selena as she pressed herself to Skipp's mouth. Sensation built to orgasm; another started as the last throes faded. As Selena came again, she felt Skipp's ecstasy and sensed the stimulation of her blood in Skipp's body.

Hard as it was to tear herself away, she was hungry for Skipp. Her hand found Skipp's carotid artery. The pulse throbbed between Selena's finger and thumb. She sank her teeth into Skipp's neck, and the blood danced over her tongue, the life force in it tingling, the taste delicate and delicious.

Selena paced herself. Over several lifetimes, she had discovered the exquisite pleasure of the slow sip. Skipp's blood hummed through her, washing away all her tension.

After Skipp gasped out her third orgasm, Selena took her lips off her. Skipp's eyelids fluttered, revealing her burnished mahogany eyes, and she gave Selena a completely open smile. Selena smiled back and then laid her head on Skipp's chest.

Selena was content. There were many hours till sunset. Skipp had been every bit as good as Selena had imagined she would be. And there was so much exploring still to do. Selena was satiated and, for the moment, held in Skipp's arms. She was very content.

***

Stupid, stupid interfering vampires. How dare they

obstruct the immortal one. No matter. It is all part of the eternal plan. Obviously, all four have to die as a warning. After this, all vampires will get the message.

A little cunning is needed. Time to search out a cunning little fox...fox shouldn't be hard to find on this sacred mountain. A short time for preparation and then, then they can all come, come to the house of the immortal one. The house where they'll get a nice, warm welcome.

CHAPTER TWENTY-SEVEN

Jameel woke me saying he'd had another e-mail from Buffboy. I sat up on the couch. My head was foggy, and it ached with a slow, thumping pulse. He was so agitated, I forced myself to pay attention.

"He wants to meet again, he wants to meet again." Jameel repeated himself in a clipped voice.

"Calm down." I yawned. "In fact, sit down." I tried to pull him beside me. He wouldn't sit.

"In half an hour."

I stared at him blankly.

"IN HALF AN HOUR."

I groaned as Jameel yelled the timeline. Selena's door flew open, and she came into the living room, followed by Skipp. They both had stupid grins on their faces.

"What's up?" Skipp slipped into work mode instantly, though she retained the daft smile.

"I've had an e-mail. Buffboy wants us to go to a flat in Granada city, right away," Jameel said anxiously.

The stupid grins faded. "Show me." Skipp reached for the printout in Jameel's hand.

Selena finally noticed me, came over and felt my forehead. As far as I remembered, I'd been injected with horse tranquillizer, not had the flu, but I didn't comment. Her touch was cool. "Maybe Rob should stay here."

Skipp looked me over. "How you doing, Perdoni?" she asked bluntly.

I staggered to my feet. "Fine," I said. Well, I would be, as soon as the room stopped swaying.

"We need everybody," Skipp said. Though both Selena and Jameel looked at me doubtfully, no one contradicted her.

***

Todd was sick and tired of running round after the little toerag. First, those ridiculous shenanigans up the so-called Sacred Mountain with no result, and then Todd had stayed up all night outside his flat in Central Granada, waiting for him to come home, and had he? Had he hell.

The first pink of dawn had forced Todd away to the improvised blackout of his hotel room. Now, at first twilight, he was back. And the little creep better be home now. Todd was determined to tie up this particular loose end tonight.

He effortlessly unlocked the main door, tripping the single three-lever lock with one turn of his pick.

There was no one in the dark, communal passage. He stepped lightly up the stairs, looking for flat number four.

He put an ear to the door, listening. There was a scampering noise. Someone, or something, was home. He pushed the door gently. It swung open slowly.

The room was dark. No lights on anywhere. Todd's eyes took a moment to adjust.

"You! What are you doing here?"

The whiny voice was unmistakable. Though he was wearing the bad latex mask that crinkled and wrinkled, Todd was gratified to see the loose end was indeed home. Todd stood in the open doorway and smiled.

***

Rani had been up for a while, waiting for the sun to set. She had woken, then tossed and turned next to Maria for a while. She hated not being able to just get up and go. She now regretted accepting the Count's invitation to hook up with Maria and Leah. They'd taken E together and had a fun night. But it was the middle of the day, and she badly wanted to be alone.

She sat in Maria's large living area, flicking through an encyclopedia of lesbian and gay film and waiting for twilight.

The door opened. Rani turned as Maria walked into the room. She gave a sleepy wave and went to the kitchen area.

Rani carried on flicking through the book. She was turning the pages, but her eyes weren't registering on them. She was wondering what she was doing in the house of someone she hardly knew. And she was thinking about what Leah had said, very quickly when they'd had a brief moment alone… something about Spain.

"Here." Maria passed her a glass of bottled blood.

Rani shuddered and shook her head. She didn't feel like drinking, even though her body felt dehydrated.

"You'll feel better," Maria said.

Rani took a sip, just to avoid arguments.

"Can I ask you something?"

Rani faced Maria. She shrugged.

"Are you feeling okay? I thought you got quiet last night when we were all talking about how we grew up. You didn't talk about your childhood, I noticed."

Rani stared at Maria, frowning. What did her childhood have to do with anything? She didn't want to think about her family. When she did there was a splinter lodged in her heart.

"That's not the reason I'm feeling low."

"Oh." Maria nodded her head like a therapist. She had that same look, a look that said, *I understand that's what you're telling me, but I don't believe it's true.*

"I didn't say anything because there's nothing to tell," Rani said flatly. Why wouldn't this woman take a hint?

Maria looked concerned. "Okay," she said evenly. "And everything's all right with your family now. Since you came in, I mean?"

Rani started to feel restless. It was very annoying that she couldn't just get up and leave when she wanted to. "Yes, fine, fine," Rani politely yet perfunctorily answered Maria.

Maria studied Rani. "So have you spoken to Rob since she got to Spain?"

Every question Maria asked irritated Rani more and more. She tried to smile at Maria, liking the woman, but she felt invaded by her concern.

She saw the blinds had darkened. "No," she said quietly. "Anyway, gotta go."

She stood. "Thanks for last night," she called out over her

shoulder.

***

We were just stepping into the car Skipp had *borrowed* when my mobile vibrated. Skipp sighed. "For God sake. Perdoni."

I winced. My head was so fuzzy I'd turned my phone to silent instead of off. I saw it was Rani. Before I thought better of it, I'd answered. She sounded relieved to hear my voice. There was a little catch in hers.

"Rob, are you okay? Is everything all right out there?"

"Yeah." I didn't see any point in filling her in on crossbow bolts and horse tranquillizer. Or that we were just now heading into the lion's den.

"Well, be careful, honey. Leah told me last night that Todd is probably out there. She overheard the Count and Todd talking about a crackhead that could get Todd convicted of murder. It had something to do with Spain. She knows Todd left for Europe a couple of days ago."

"Todd's in Spain?" I repeated. Skipp looked sharply round from the driver's seat.

"Also, Leah found a mobile. She thinks it's a secret mobile the Count uses for business only. It had a text from Todd saying he was about to clean up their little problem. That text came last night."

"Why did Leah to tell you all this? " I said suspiciously.

"She's worried about Jameel." Rani paused. "And you, apparently. Is there something you want to tell me, Rob?"

I decided to hedge that question for now. "Thanks, Rani. I've got to go now, but I'll phone you as soon as I can."

"Rob, don't do anything stupid. Promise me."

"I'll be careful,"

"Okay, Rob. Ciao."

"Ciao, bella."

I took a breath and brought the others up to speed.

We were off the cobbled streets and onto wider roads now. Jameel was directing. Buildings were more modern and more built up.

Selena read a road sign. "Santa Paula, that's it over there."

Skipp pulled up outside an apartment block and switched

the engine off. "Got your phone switched off, Perdoni?"

I hadn't thought she was the kind of person that would remind a guy of their mistakes. "Yes." I shoved the phone in my pocket.

"Right, Jameel, Selena, you're with me. I'm going through the door first. No arguments."

No one gave her one. I knew I was on lookout, so no point me fighting for the honor of getting taken out first. They had decided it would be less dangerous for them if I wasn't in the flat. I'd had to admit I was too full of horse tranq to be very useful if it came to a fight, or if quick thinking was needed. Or perhaps if any thinking was needed. Pure dogged determination was keeping me upright.

The three of them stood outside the front door of the flats and Skipp buzzed bell number four. There was no reply.

Jameel pressed bell number two. The door clicked open. Lax security was obviously an international trait.

I slipped in behind them, looking for a position where I could see the front door *and* the door of flat four.

***

"Take that stupid mask off," Todd ordered.

There was no response. That annoyed Todd. He thought it was disrespectful.

"I've been thinking of how to dispose of you," Todd said, walking over. "At first, I thought I'd cut your throat. No one's going to think it's me. Not this time." He grabbed the latex mask and peeled it off, surprised at how pale the crackhead was, even for a crackhead. "But then I remembered how you wanted to be a vampire so badly." He mocked the idiot. "And I thought it would be nice to drain you of blood, the old-fashioned way."

Todd pulled back the head, exposing a neck so pale that the veins glowed blue. "Do you know how long it takes a powerful vampire to drain a human of blood?" Todd paused, though he really didn't expect any response. The little creep was probably saying his prayers. "Ten minutes," he said. "Ten minutes, and you're never going to bother me again."

Todd sank his teeth into the pale neck and sucked hard. A feeling of power and control surged through him. He thought about how he'd get rid of the body. He would have to make sure no one could ever find out how the corpse had died.

The stupid chicken was fiddling about in his pockets. Todd let him. He knew his strength was vastly superior. There was nothing here that could hurt him.

Suddenly, the darkness was shattered by a bright light that scorched Todd's retinas. Something searing hot slammed against his face. Todd screamed, covering his eyes. He dropped to his knees. He couldn't see. All he could feel was burning, agonizing burning.

***

Jameel froze behind Skipp. The door to flat four was open. Beyond it a sickening cry had come from the pitch black room. Now it was silent. Skipp edged forward, flicking on her slim, black torch. Jameel followed.

Skipp moved inside the room, her torch a mini searchlight cutting slices through the dark.

Jameel stopped in mid step as a swing of the torch caught a face he knew from his dreams, from his nightmares.

He'd never believed in ghosts, but if anyone deserved to haunt him, it was Ben.

He felt Selena tap her hand along the wall. She flipped a light switch, illuminating the room.

There was a figure on the floor, moaning in agony. Todd Williams was hunched over, his face terribly burnt. It was a mass of blisters and exposed flesh.

Jameel looked up again, expecting the ghost to have disappeared, but Ben was still standing six feet in front of him.

He looked awful—paler and thinner than Jameel had ever seen him, and he was shaking. Jameel was surprised. Weren't people supposed to look better after death?

"Jamie, at last. We've been through so much, but finally, we're together again." Ben's voice was reedier, more whiny than Jameel remembered. Plus, he sounded completely mad. Jameel started to get a funny feeling that Ben wasn't a ghost.

"My Scarlet Lady," Ben said fondly.

Oh my God, he's alive, and he's Buffboy. And he's been trying to kill me. Jameel tasted bile.

"Then... you faked your death," Selena said into the thick

silence, broken only by a low moaning from Todd.

"Shut up," Ben said rudely. "I'm talking to Jamie." His hand rested on a long switch screwed into a piece of MDF crudely fixed to the wall. Wires ran from it.

Jameel's eyes followed the wires to machines lining three walls of the room. It slowly dawned on him that they were upright tanning machines, UV cells, at least fifteen of them.

Enough to fry them all.

***

I'd heard a yell from inside the room, just before they all went in…and then nothing. I was about to go closer to investigate when I got a thought from Skipp.

Perdoni, find the fuse box. It's Ben. He's got a whole load of UV cells rigged up in here. We can't do anything till the electricity's off. Over.

The fuse box to flat four would be inside the flat, so I knew I had to find the main breaker for the whole apartment block. I couldn't see anything on the first floor, so I headed down the stairs.

***

"What's this all about, Ben?" Jameel bit his lip.

Ben stared at Jameel, his eyes enormous in his tight, drawn face. "You didn't want me." He sounded hurt. The expression on his face was as bewildered as a child's. "One day you said you'd bring me in. Then you threw me away. Just a piece of trash you couldn't use anymore."

"It wasn't like that," Jameel protested weakly.

"Shut up, Jameel. It was," Ben said sharply. "At first I just wanted to bleed you dry, to use an expression." He laughed. "So I died. It wasn't hard. Got a junkie high, 'bout my height, my build. Lured him home and filled him full of barbs. Lit some candles, knocked one over, and left. Sent you a note in the post, Jameel." Ben took a deep breath. "And voilà, one unrecognizable but dead boyfriend."

Jameel shuddered, remembering the awful moment he'd read Ben's suicide note. It shook him to know Ben had still been alive.

"Then I started bleeding your bank accounts. God, you're a stupid queen. I kept using that credit card for months. Even in Spain I was using it. But after a while, I missed you, Jamie," Ben's voice softened. "And I watched you again, like I did when we were going out. I followed you, Jamie." Then his eyes flashed. "And I saw you didn't miss me at all.

You even moved away from me, from everything we'd had together. And I had to track you down. You tried to leave me behind. But I found you. I sent you a postcard and I was going to forgive you.

I watched you turn up to meet your mysterious admirer and then I realized you didn't know it was me. YOU WEREN'T MISSING ME!" he shouted, his eyes wide. "You were always going to bars and clubs, seeing men. You weren't in mourning at all. That's when I knew I had to kill you."

Icy fingers were clawing a path through Jameel's stomach. Part of him wanted Ben to stop talking, to stop explaining. Yet he had to know.

"I didn't want to at first. That was the old, human part of me. But then I started becoming stronger and stronger. I was becoming immortal you see." Ben's eyes were wide and staring now. "None of you can touch me." He wagged his finger at them.

"The mistake you keep making is to underestimate me. Like he did." Ben pointed at Todd, now lying on his side. It looked like Todd had gone into shock.

"I saw him cut Ferdinand." Ben turned back to Jameel, soft and loving again.

"Remember, honey, I told you I saw them arguing? Well, what I actually saw was that nasty vampire slicing Fer's throat. All I asked for was a couple hundred bucks and a constant supply of drugs. Not much to keep him out of trouble. But he tried to trick me. Gave me bad E." Ben swallowed, remembering.

"I had plenty of crack, the night he gave it me, I was feeling generous so I gave it to my junkie buddies. You know what happened to them." Ben fixed Jameel's gaze.

Jameel recalled the deaths of three humans from ecstasy in San Francisco shortly after the drug dealer had been killed. He hadn't known they were connected.

"But I fixed him, didn't I?" Ben turned to Jameel. His face as eager as a child's to be acknowledged.

Jameel nodded sadly.

"I fixed him with your people. And I fixed him tonight."

Skipp moved ever so slightly in Ben's direction. "So you're a vampire are you?" she asked.

Ben glanced at her and laughed. "You leeches are so arrogant. Stay where you are," he ordered. "The next time you move, I trip this switch. You don't want to test me."

Satisfied Skipp wasn't going to move again, Ben continued. "You think you're the only immortal ones. Except you're not, are you? You can die, can't you? As you'll all find out in a minute." He smiled eerily.

No one moved. Jameel had never felt so helpless.

"So you don't drink blood?" Skipp's eyes were darting over the tiny animal bodies all over the floor. Mice, rats, and even what looked like a fox, stretched out, their heads hanging limp.

"I didn't say that," Ben said sharply. "I needed blood for the transition. Obviously."

Jameel realized with an ache in his heart that Ben was far away, in an alternate reality.

"Do you need Jameel's blood. Is that it?" Skipp asked.

Jameel thought that was a very stupid thing to suggest. Had Skipp gone mad as well? He noticed Ben looking at him sadly.

"I thought I did," he said. He breathed a long sigh that hung in the still air. "But now I know I am the one to cleanse him. I'm sure this won't hurt you, darling. Even if it does, it'll be over in a minute." Ben put his hand to the switch.

Now would be a good time, Perdoni, Skipp sent urgently.

***

I searched the ground floor frantically and found nothing resembling any kind of electrical fuse box. I was getting desperate when I discovered the door to the cellar. I forced it open, my head clearing finally as adrenaline kicked in.

I stumbled down the steps. Even with my torch, it was hard to see and the steps were damp and slippery.

I found a light switch, but nothing happened when I flicked it.

I shone my torch from wall to wall, hearing creatures scuttling away. Rats probably. It looked like someone had tried poisoning them, from the amount of dead ones I kept catching in my torchlight. It smelled like dead rats down there too.

At last, I saw a metal box on the wall. I ran toward it, trying not to stand on rat bodies.

Now would be a good time, Perdoni, flashed into my head, just as I reached for a large trip switch. I pulled it down.

***

All the lights went out.

Skipp rushed Ben, but instead of Ben being expertly subdued or arrested or whatever it was guardians did, a strange white light flickered and Skipp yelled out. Jameel didn't know if he could take much more of this. Now what?

He heard a match strike and saw Ben standing in front of the glow of a candle. "Solar cells," he said savagely to Skipp. "I've got plenty of them, charged up. I used the same one on you I used on him. That's why you're still standing. But don't you dare rush me again or I'll fry you as good as I did the bat on the floor.

Jameel could see Skipp's cheek glowing in the candlelight. She was gritting her teeth. Ben picked up a gun from a desk next to him and pointed it at Jameel.

"Back off, you stupid fools, all of you." He waved the gun around.

Selena spoke. "What are you doing with that gun, Ben? You can't kill us with that."

"Normally not, I know. But I can with silver bullets!" Ben said triumphantly.

Selena moved a step closer, obviously looking for any more solar cells. "You've been reading the wrong books," she said. "Silver bullets don't kill vampires. Sorry to disappoint you. Come on, Ben, be sensible. Give me the gun."

Ben just laughed. His hand shook. He pulled a paper packet from his pocket and poured white powder into his mouth. "There is nothing you can do. I am immortal."

"Please, Ben, stop it," Jameel begged him.

Selena and Skipp moved in on Ben. Selena said again, "Give me the gun." Her hand was reaching for it. Ben pointed the gun straight at her with shaking hands, then he turned it on Skipp, and then flashed it back and forth between them, undecided.

"I *am* immortal. I'll show you. Look." Ben turned the gun on himself and pointed it to his head.

"No!" Jameel screamed.

Ben pulled the trigger and blew a hole clean through his head.

He slumped to the floor, blood flowed into a deepening red pool. Jameel ran to him and cradled him in his arms.

"Dammit, Ben!" he whispered. He turned Ben's face, what was left of it, to his own. He was dead.

Jameel stroked his cheek. He could hardly breathe. He bent and tenderly kissed Ben's lips.

Selena quietly turned to Skipp. "What are we going to do with Ben?"

"I think we should leave it to the mortal police to deal with." Skipp's voice was solemn.

"What?" Jameel looked up. "We should bury him."

"They'll bury him," Selena said firmly. "We can't get mixed up in this."

"We need to get out of here." Skipp was helping Todd up off the floor. "You're under arrest, in case you have any doubts."

Rob appeared at the door. "What's the matter with you people? Why you still here? I heard that gunshot in the cellar. We need to leave. Now." She took Todd's other arm, and began marching him out of the flat.

"Selena, get Jameel out of here," Skipp called over her shoulder as they left.

Jameel felt Selena's hand on his shoulder. He was still holding Ben.

"Come on," she said firmly, trying to pull him away. Police sirens sounded in the still night getting louder.

Finally, Jameel let go of Ben and stood. Selena grabbed his arm and broke into a run, dragging Jameel behind her.

They ran down the dark stairs, turning away from the

front door as sirens stopped and cars pulled up outside.

The back door closed behind them as heavy footsteps thundered on the stairs above. They slipped through the yard outside and melted into the alley shadows.

Chapter Twenty-Eight

Skipp had to guard Todd till he was well enough to travel. As soon as we got him back to Skipp's rented rooms in Albiacín, I phoned Selena to make sure they got out all right. It was a relief to hear she was not only safe but one step ahead of me. She'd dragged Jameel up to Sacromonte to collect aloe vera for the burns.

Todd's face was a mess. Most of the skin on his face had been badly burnt. Some of it had blistered. Fluid wept out underneath while the charred skin looked hard and dry. I didn't know if we could heal something that bad. Our only real chance was to get a protective layer on it so someone could touch the damaged skin directly. Selena was sure the aloe vera stuff would do that. In the meantime, I had to do something.

I put my hands as close to Todd's burns as I could without touching them. I knew all it would do was relieve the pain. After a few minutes, Todd relaxed a little.

Even if we got his face fixed up, I didn't fancy his long-term chances. He was already on a warning for murder. Now there were vampire witnesses to the fact he'd tried to kill Ben, and witnesses to Ben's testimony about the mortal drug dealer in San Francisco. I thought it was likely Todd would be found guilty of murder and attempted murder by the justices.

I didn't envy Skipp's job. When I was in the guard, I never met anyone who got a kick out of handing someone over to the enforcers. It was part of the job, but not something guardians liked to do.

"Selena's one helluva woman," Skipp said unexpectedly.

I didn't say anything for a minute or two. When I figured I'd done all I could for Todd, I turned round. Skipp caught my eye, and then looked away.

"You can't compare her to anyone, that's for sure," I said eventually.

I got up from Todd and walked over. "Want me to fix that for you?" I indicated Skipp's cheek, blistered and glowing a brown-red.

She glanced at Todd. "Okay." She turned her cheek.

I put my hand close to the burn. "So is there a girlfriend waiting for you in wherever you live?"

"New York." Skipp grunted. "No. Don't go in for relationships much."

"Uh-huh," I acknowledged. "Is that how you got the name Skipp? Skipping beds?"

The redness in her cheek had subsided a little. I took my hand away. Skipp gingerly touched the burnt skin.

"No. On account of skipping towns. Even before I came in, I never liked staying too long in one place."

I leaned up against the wall, folding my arms. "Selena know about that?"

"Sure does." Skipp glanced toward me, still keeping an eye on Todd flat out on Skipp's bed. He looked like he was sleeping. "Reckon that suits her just fine."

Maybe it did. Truth was, I wouldn't have known what suited Selena anymore. It had been a long time since she'd confided in me.

"So what about that Sergeant O'Shay? Still giving the new recruits a hard time?"

"Captain O'Shay," Skipp corrected me. "Yeah, he's still barking at them. Put me up for this job, you know."

That impressed me. If O'Shay had recommended Skipp, he must rate her.

"It's bad enough I have to listen to two butches bonding. The fact you're both filthy guardians is turning my stomach. Pack it in unless you want me to throw up."

We both stared at Todd. Apparently, he was feeling better.

Selena and Jameel arrived then with the burn treatment. I recognized it as the plant that had cut my hand on the hillside. It was ironic a healing plant was disguised as an offensive weapon.

Selena took a look at Todd and Skipp, and started squeezing thick, lumpy sap out of the aloe leaf. She walked over to Skipp first. Presumably, if it was a tossup between a handsome butch she'd just slept with and low-life murdering scum, the butch won out.

Selena carefully applied the sticky gel to Skipp's cheek, while Skipp bore the touch in a rugged kind of way. It was a bit predictable. Especially as I'd relieved the pain only minutes before. I didn't spoil it for them. Instead, I began to worry about Jameel. He was standing immobile and expressionless by the door, staring at the wall with hollow eyes.

"How long has he been like that?" I asked Selena.

"Like a zombie? Since we left Ben's apartment."

"If he's a zombie, at least he's still a creature of the night," I said, hoping to raise a smile from Jameel. Nothing.

"You got this situation?" I asked Skipp and Selena.

"Sure," Skipp said. Selena nodded.

I walked over to her. "Come on, babe, let's get you home."

***

Almost as soon as we stepped through the door, Jameel snapped to life, but in a weird way. He started cleaning frantically.

I let him get on with it until he got the Hoover out and I had to remind him it was three in the morning. Maybe his neighbors wouldn't appreciate it.

We had a bit of a tussle over the Hoover. He ran away from me with it still on. I calmly walked over and unplugged it, which made Jameel very mad. He shouted at me and hit me in the face with his feather duster. It didn't hurt but it made me sneeze a lot. After I'd sneezed about twenty times, I realized Jameel had stopped shouting what an insensitive, annoying butch I was. He'd sunk down on the sofa, his hands over his face.

As I watched, his hands slid down and I saw the pain inside him well up in his eyes. I couldn't imagine what it was like to love someone and have them do to you what Ben had done.

He began to cry then, the slow, dignified crying of pure

grief. I saw how much he had loved Ben in the quiet agony on his face. I heard it in the tearing breaths he took. I went to him and put my arm around him, holding him while he cried against my shoulder.

CHAPTER TWENTY-NINE

Rani didn't like being left out of the loop. Rob, and Jameel, and Selena for that matter, were all in Spain, and none of them would tell her what was going on. The Count contacted her whenever he felt like it. Rani had just about had it with vampires. She wanted to hang out at Ma and Pa's house, with everything the way it had always been. But Rani couldn't face being with the people she loved most when they knew nothing about her new life. She was caught between the mortal and the vampire worlds.

Well, there's no point in sitting around feeling sorry for myself. Rani decided she didn't have to wait for the Count to contact her. *He forgets I know where he lives.*

She easily found her way back to the house where the ball had been held. But when she was standing on the steps in front of the huge front door, she hesitated. *If Leah answers, I'll pretend I came to see her.*

Gathering her courage, she rapped the knocker. The sharp sound penetrated the quiet of Billionaire's Row. It reverberated for a moment, and then the same dead silence fell once more.

Rani waited for ages, expecting the large door to suddenly and slowly creep open, but nothing happened. She was walking away when a calm voice asked, "Can I help you?"

Rani turned and stared, confused. There was no butler, no Leah, no Count...only Adjoa, the woman she had last seen speaking to Rob on the night of the ball.

"I was looking for the Count," Rani said hesitantly.

"Oh," Adjoa said. "Well, Rani, why not come in?"

Rani thought that maybe the Count was inside. She followed the ancient vampire through the hallway and into a comfortable sitting room.

Rani took in the natural fittings: a wood floor with a seagrass rug, beautiful black wooden carvings, and African prints in modern frames on the walls. She sank into a deep armchair.

"Why did you expect the Count to be here?" Adjoa asked.

"Well, this is his house, isn't it?"

Adjoa shook her head. "No, child. This is my house. I just let Leah and the Count use it for their little party."

"Oh." Now Rani felt stupid. She remembered the room then. It had looked different, but she was sure this was the room Leah had been feeding her snake in. Well, whatever. She was in the wrong house. Rani stood to leave. "I'm sorry to have bothered you."

Adjoa extended her hand gracefully back to the armchair. "Sit down, my dear. I'm pleased you came by. I've been wanting to talk to you. How are you enjoying the Life?"

Rani opened her mouth to speak but didn't know where to start. Adjoa studied her. Rani studied back. Even though she was looking at a youngish face, Rani could see the years in her eyes. She was beginning to be able to distinguish vampire ages.

After a silence, Adjoa spoke. "I thought Rob would have brought you to see me by now."

"Why?" It sounded to Rani like being sent to see the headmistress.

"We have a custom. New vampires come to talk to the oldest vampire in the region. So they can ask questions, so the community can make sure the new ones are taken care of, are coping with the transition. I should have been at your swearing in ceremony, but Rob wanted to take care of it herself."

Rani stared at Adjoa for a moment, then before she could stop herself, she burst out, "Oh, she's so controlling!"

Adjoa raised her eyebrows. "Has Rob not told you all about our customs?"

"She's told me the rules!" Rani said crossly.

"Well, they're important," Adjoa said diplomatically. Then, almost to herself, she muttered, "Okay, it seems Rob needed more help than I thought."

Rani tried not to feel insulted. Adjoa made it sound like *she* was too much of a handful for Rob.

"Oh, dear." Adjoa sighed, then leaned closer. "Try to be understanding to Rob. It must be hard for her, considering how she came in."

Rani looked blankly at Adjoa.

"You do know about that, don't you?" Adjoa sounded concerned now.

Rani hit the roof. "I don't think I know very much, Adjoa. I know about the Night Council. I know about enforcers and guardians. I know I shouldn't take too much blood and shouldn't harm anyone. But I don't know anything about Rob, or about why she hates the Count. I've asked and she won't tell me. Nobody tells me anything!" she said petulantly.

Adjoa put her hand on Rani's arm. "You poor child. And everybody has so many questions when they come in. It must have been driving you mad."

Tears sprung to Rani's eyes. "It has!" She took a deep breath, feeling very hard done by.

Adjoa's deep brown eyes were full of warm concern. Rani felt instantly comforted and wished with all her heart that Rob had brought her to see this woman months ago.

"Rob had a difficult time coming in," Adjoa said.

Rani sat back, hoping finally for some answers. Adjoa's rich, kind voice transported Rani back to the beginning of the twentieth century.

"Rob lived in Tuscany in the early nineteen twenties. She worked as a servant for a family in her village. One day, she was told the family had rented out their small house up on the hill to a couple from Paris. She was to look after the couple. She would have to live in, but it was only for six weeks. Rob agreed.

The couple were the Count and a vampire called Ursula. Ursula had a thing for young, mortal women. Women who looked masculine especially. She kept her liaisons discreet, and as far as I know, didn't take or give blood with any of them. But she obviously forgot herself with Rob.

The Count went away for several days, and while he was away, Ursula exchanged blood with Rob. Something she hadn't asked permission to do. When the Count returned, he and Ursula left for Paris, leaving Rob alone.

Maybe they panicked. Whatever their reasons it was a cruel thing to do. Somehow Rob made it through the transition alone, and then got herself to Paris. Rob went to see Ursula, but Ursula turned her away, making it clear she never wanted to see Rob again. Rob didn't know any other vampires except Ursula and the Count, neither of whom would help her.

She found refuge in the arches beneath the Seine, hiding out of sunlight by day and trawling the streets by night. No one had told her only to take a little blood when feeding, but she instinctively did so. We know she did because there were no reports of humans drained of blood. Anything like that would have come to the attention of the Night Council.

Rob became a recluse for a while, shying away from everyone except when she needed to feed. Until the day a mortal girl, a young woman chose Rob's refuge to die in. Rob could see the woman was dying of starvation. She tried to help by stealing bread and leaving it by the young woman's thin body. But the girl was too weak to eat it, and it was clear she wouldn't last the night. Rob, not knowing any better, decided to bring the young woman in to save her life.

Somehow, she managed to take and give blood." Adjoa paused, reflecting back. "So the community gained Antoinette. And now there were two vampires brought in without permission, though the Night Council didn't know about either one at that time."

Rani's eyes widened as she realized Rob had lied to her about not bringing anyone else in before her. She didn't say anything.

"While Antoinette was recovering, Rob saw Selena feeding one night along the Seine. She was too scared to approach her but looked out for her after that. Several nights later, Selena called out to Rob in the shadows and somehow got her trust. She made Rob promise to visit her. Rob was half-feral by this time and hardly spoke, but she did go to Selena's house.

As soon as Selena found out about Antoinette, she took her away from the arches. Rob was fit and well, and looking after herself, but Antoinette was still transitioning and she was vulnerable. Selena brought her to me, and I raised her as my daughter.

Rob and Selena fell in love, and after a short time, Rob moved in with Selena and was gradually introduced to the Paris circle. It was painful for her at first, I understand. She felt especially awkward around Ursula and the Count, but as she got to know everyone else, it got easier.

Ursula was reprimanded of course for bringing Rob in without permission. Though there is nothing in the code that says a vampire must help a new vampire through the change.

Rob had to see a justice too, though it was only a formality as we knew she hadn't knowingly broken the code. All the same, she was mortified to find out she had done wrong."

Rani and Adjoa shared a smile at this.

"So that's why Rob hates the Count. Surely it was more Ursula she should hate?" Rani wondered.

"Rob thought the Count made Ursula desert her. Only the Count knows if that's true."

"And Ursula presumably."

"I'm afraid Ursula's not with us anymore," Adjoa said quietly.

Rani didn't know what to say. It was the first time she'd heard of a vampire dying.

"Rob told you about the Count and Selena?"

Rani shook her head.

Adjoa seemed disappointed. "I really thought Rob was over all that. Still, I suppose it's only been eighty years."

Rani looked horrified at the idea of taking more than eighty years to get over something.

"Selena and the Count had a romance around that time. Rob didn't like it. There was some trouble. I think Rob is still embarrassed about it. I would have hoped she'd have told you all this."

It was starting to make sense to Rani why Rob had stubbornly refused to tell her about her past. Her sense of honor wouldn't let her prejudice someone against the Count, no matter what an awful person Rob thought he was. Rani also suspected Rob hadn't wanted to tell Rani about breaking the Code or getting jealous about the Count and Selena. She realized whatever Rob *hadn't* done, she'd seen Rani through her transition, and she'd done it with care and with patience.

Rani felt a sudden surge of warmth toward Rob She really hoped Rob would get in touch.

***

Within a day, the five vampires in Granada had to haul ass to Brussels. Selena, along with Jameel, and Rob were all required to give evidence at Todd's trial, which was held at the European guard headquarters.

Selena was nervous, even though she'd had to give evidence before the justices several times before. After the heavy political trials of the 1980s, the Night Council had taken a decision that all trials would be closed to the public. Todd's trial was therefore in a small room in the center of the guard House.

When she was called, Selena opened the plain gray door and walked to the witness chair.

Three justices sat directly in front of her. Todd and his representative sat behind a desk on her right, and the speaker for the Night Council (the vampire equivalent of a state prosecutor) on her left.

The speaker, a serious looking woman, stood up. "Selena Fitzgerald, please tell us what happened in Granada on the night of the twelfth of June?"

Selena told them clearly what she had heard and seen, including the bite marks on Ben's neck.

Todd's representative got to his feet. "Ms. Fitzgerald, you say the lighting was bad and that you had to leave the apartment in a hurry to avoid the mortal police. How can you be sure that the deceased mortal had bite marks on his neck?"

Todd wasn't even looking in her direction, but Selena got a strong compulsion to say she wasn't sure. She felt something really bad would happen if she told the justices the truth. It took all her willpower to say, "There was at least ten minutes in full light when I was standing about three feet away from him. Close enough to see the blood dribbling down his throat."

"Thank you, Selena." The representative dismissed her with a weary look.

Selena stole a look at Todd as she left the witness chair.

He was staring ahead, expressionless. There was not a fleck of light in his eyes. Selena was glad to get out of the cold, gray room.

After the hearing had closed for the night, Jameel headed off to the gay bars near the Bourse and Skipp was stuck on guard duty. She nodded over to Selena wistfully when Selena left the guard house with Rob. Selena waved and cursed her attraction for butches who could always be relied on to do their duty.

She went with Rob to a little bar in St. Gery, a trendy area of Brussels full of people living alternative lifestyles. They sat at a little square table; a bistro-style candle in the middle of the table twinkled at them as they sipped raspberry beer.

The bar was situated on the corner of two streets. Two of the walls were windowed, leaving the punters voyeuristically open to passers-by. The remaining walls were hung with surreal paintings. The bar itself was painted dark red and burgundy.

They discussed Jameel for a while. Rob felt he was doing okay, but was worried about leaving him.

"Lois called. She wants me back at the club." Rob shrugged apologetically.

"It's okay, Rob. But I have to go to Paris for a few days." What Selena couldn't add was that she had to attend a Night Council meeting—the one that would ratify the justices' verdict on Todd.

"I'll talk to Jameel. Get him to come with me," she decided on the spot. "If he wants to go straight back, I'll join him in Spain as soon as my business is concluded."

Rob screwed up her eyes thoughtfully. Selena was sure Rob had her suspicions about what she called "Selena's secrets," but she was too much of an ex-guardian to comment. "Well, I'm relieved you can go back to Spain. I think Jameel needs some looking after." Rob smiled.

Selena told Rob about the compulsion she'd felt not to give evidence. Rob confirmed she'd felt it too.

"I wasn't surprised. When I was still in the guard, we were investigating the Count's firm for using mind technology. They were experimenting with control techniques back in the sixties, so God knows what they can do now. Maybe your boifriend can tell you," she added with a cheeky grin.

Selena lit up, thinking about Skipp. They hadn't had a chance to see each other properly since the night they'd slept together.

"So, you two an item then?" Rob was smiling, but Selena picked up mixed feelings.

Selena shrugged. "Skipp's coming to Mexico for a holiday as soon as she can arrange leave."

Rob searched her eyes. Selena felt the weight of her love for Rob sitting opposite her again, just the two of them. She wished Rob would understand how she felt about her. Sometimes she despaired that Rob would ever let go of her mortal concepts.

"Remember how you used to come visit me in Brussels, when I was stationed here?" Rob murmured, her voice smooth and sweet.

Selena leaned in and kissed her. It felt easy, like crushing berries between the teeth on a hot summer's night. In the middle of enjoying the moment, Selena felt Rob pull back.

"When will you get that I'll never stop loving you?" Selena said quietly. When she was sure Rob had heard her she let her go.

Rob's eyes were wide. She sat back. Selena loved the way Rob's emotions were written all over her face. She could almost see Rob thinking.

"But you're going to still see Skipp?"

Selena raised her eyes to the ceiling. "Rob, are you going to come and move to Mexico?"

"No."

"See. And I'm not moving to England. Been there, done that, too cold." Selena took a breath, and then continued more gently. "Yes, I'm going to see Skipp, if she wants to, but don't you know, Rob? You and me, that's for life."

"Is it?"

Selena could have cried, looking at Rob's confused face. But she couldn't help Rob work it out. She'd tried doing that for years. One thing she knew, she couldn't be someone she wasn't. Maybe Rani would be that person for Rob, someone who wanted monogamy. Though that didn't seem very likely.

"What about Rani? Could you just walk away from her?" Selena asked.

"No. Of course not," Rob said as quickly as she'd said she wasn't moving to Mexico.

Selena laughed. "So what *do* you want, Rob?"

Rob stared at her like she might find the answer in Selena's eyes. Selena smiled at her, knowing there was nothing Rob could do now that would make Selena stop loving her. She was too deeply woven within Selena's heart.

"I don't know. All I know is I need to get back to England. At least I won't have to put up with the Count probably. He'll have his own trial to think about, I guess."

Selena nodded. "The Count's only interested in two things, Rob: sex and money. You're so different. I don't know why you let him get to you so much. By the way, I saw Antoinette."

Rob looked uncomfortable. "How is she?"

"She's doing really well. She'd like to see you though."

"Would she?"

"Yes. It's only natural. She's got lots of questions, and she's only seen you once since you brought her in."

Rob thought it over. "I'll get in touch with Adjoa."

"And you make sure you come to see me in Mexico. It'll be lovely, the four of us: me and Skipp; you and Rani." Selena beamed at Rob.

Rob looked horrified. Selena knew Rob would think that was a terrible idea.

CHAPTER THIRTY

The night after I'd given evidence at Todd's trial, I took a walk in the early hours.

I stood looking at water sparkling under streetlight in the St. Katherine area and remembered sitting by the river with Rani, way back in February. It started to hurt inside; missing her. I pulled out my phone.

When I heard her voice, I blurted out straight away, "I'll be home in a few days."

I expected her to say, "So what." Instead, she said, "Thank God for that. I miss you, Rob."

"I miss you too. This has been really horrible, you know." I wasn't sure if I meant being apart, the stuff with Ben, or all of it. I decided not to elaborate over the phone about crossbows or nearly being tanned to death.

"Everyone's been worried about you," Rani said softly.

I wasn't sure who she meant. I couldn't imagine his cloakness being worried about me.

"I've been worried about you," Rani clarified. She sure was sticking her neck out. Actually, the idea of her neck being stuck out gave me a rush. The sudden closeness of her voice flushed sexual feelings through me.

"Well, you can stop worrying. I'll be back soon and we can have a long talk. I'm sure we can work everything out."

"Can we?"

The hope in Rani's voice lifted me.

"Yeah, I think so. As long as you don't lie to me any more" I told her, my voice soft.

She sighed "Okay. I agree. I don't lie to you, and you don't lie to me."

Now what did that mean? I decided not to pursue it at that moment. "I'll see you soon, amore."

There was definitely a catch in her voice that time. Guess I hadn't called her amore in a while.

"As soon as you can get here, meri jaan."

If Rani was being sweet to me in Hindi, things were looking up.

***

They were all bundled up in Maria's old Mini. Rani was amazed Leah had agreed to be seen in the car, let alone drive it. The three of them were en route to a lesbian benefit dance in Brighton. Rani had been at a loose end when Maria had rung with the invitation. It had sounded fun. Rani hadn't been to a human lesbian event in ages.

They were passing through the sprawling suburbs of South London. Sinking back into the upholstery, Rani looked out the window, sighing with contentment. Leah was in complete control of the little car, driving steadily, stopping at traffic lights, and generally not heading straight for oncoming traffic. She was a confident driver. Smooth R&B was playing on the car system.

"Can you turn this tune up?" Rani asked.

Leah obliged. The car seemed to move along in the rhythm of the tune. Rani felt the music fill her, soothing her.

She looked out the window watching streetlights diffusing everything beneath them with the characteristic pale orange of city light. At sky level, the cloudless southeastern sky was a vibrant violet. Rani fixated on dull sequins of starlight, like pinpricks into a brighter, lighter world lying beyond the sky's border. Craning her neck to the northwestern sky, Rani drank in the inky indigo, dark and deliciously deep.

A beautiful sky for the dark moon. Rani realized this was the first new moon she hadn't felt like she was going to explode. Since her first blood, each time the moon disappeared from the sky, Rani had got a prowling, growling anger inside her worse than any PMT she'd experienced in her mortal life.

Rob had been surprisingly patience about it, telling her people got all kinds of symptoms when their bodies were getting used to the Life.

Maria sat in the passenger seat in front of her. Rani sat forward, unconsciously putting her head between her and Leah.

Maria had said on the phone that Leah had only agreed to come when she'd heard Rani was coming. Rani was still trying to work Leah out. Maybe she felt Rani thinking about her, because she caught Rani's eye in the rearview mirror and smiled. On the other hand, Rani was sure Maria was going to be a good friend. She'd called Rani a few days after Rani had left her flat, and Rani had been able to talk some things through with her. Now Maria was discussing psychology with Leah.

"If I had to pick one, I'd pick Ulrichs over Freud. With Ulrichs's ideas about a female mind in a male body and vice versa, at least things got easier for a while. With his theory, homosexuals weren't criminal or insane. And that was a big step up."

"At least lesbians existed with Freud," Leah said.

"But, Leah, you have to think about what it was like in the nineteen twenties and thirties. We were the scum of the earth, baby. Anyway, don't get me started on Freud!" Maria threw her hands up. "With Ulrichs and Havelock Ellis, there was no blame on us. That's my point. Homosexuality was congenital. In other words, not our fault. But with Freud, there was something wrong with us again. In his case, penis envy. Of course, he was right about that, as it goes."

"What!" Rani and Leah chorused in disbelief.

"Well, every lesbian has one now doesn't she? She just keeps it in a drawer." Maria could hardly keep a straight face for laughing.

The heated discussion continued until they were well into Brighton. It petered out when they had to start looking for the venue.

"That's my summer residence!" Rani said grandly as they passed the Pavilion with its domed roofs and Raj-influenced architecture. The others laughed at her joke.

The car passed along the seafront with the pier stretching

out to sea and the impressive Regency hotels. On the way to Hove, they found the community hall they were looking for.

The benefit was unpretentious and friendly. Women on the door were welcoming. One of them kissed and hugged Maria, exclaiming at how good she looked.

The event was a fundraiser for a radical lesbian group Maria had been heavily involved with about a decade ago. The group had been active around Section 28, the mortal UK Government bill that made it illegal for any organization to promote homosexuality. Nobody was ever sure exactly what "promoting homosexuality" meant. It was sad that ten years on, the group were still raising funds to get it repealed.

The dance was in full swing. Women crammed the floor making moves to a collection of music from different eras and across music styles. Maria said this was common for a women's disco. Rani was only just on the lesbian scene ten years ago. Leah didn't know, as she'd been radically separatist and didn't go to human events then.

The atmosphere was infectious. No one was being cool. In fact, no one seemed to care what they looked like. Maria was buzzing from seeing her old friends. There was a lot of hugging and screeching. Rani loved the community feeling. It made her think about her own mortal friends, and her family. She still had a lot of time with them, she realized. She decided she wasn't going to waste any more of it.

A large woman in her forties spotted Maria and grabbed her in a big hug.

"Maria, look at you! You don't look a day older. What are you doing, drinking blood?" she joked, delighted to see her.

Leah and Rani exchanged a look while Maria changed the subject to some action the two women had done together that involved spray cans, billboards, and balaclavas.

Leah grabbed Rani's hand and pulled her onto the dance floor as a sixties number came on. Leah couldn't believe Rani couldn't jive, so she taught her. They jived their way through several numbers till Rani was slipping under Leah's arm and catching her arm behind her back.

They danced through every tune, and by the end of the night, Rani could not only jive but swing, and Leah had learned to bhangra. Maria stole the occasional dance and everyone got on the floor to a tune called "We Are Family," which Maria explained had been a lesbian feminist anthem.

In the car heading back, they stayed on a retro tip. Rani was driving, as she wasn't drinking. Maria put on a seventies CD. The high-pitched boo boo and funky bass guitar of a disco tune filled the car, and soon they were grooving in their seats and singing along.

The music was so loud and they were having such a good time it took Rani a while to register her mobile was going off. Maria hit the volume control, and they heard Leah's mobile ringing too. By the time Maria had plugged in Rani's headset for her so she could take the call and carry on driving, her own mobile was ringing.

"Hi, Rob, you won't believe this. All our mobiles have rung at the same time," Rani said, excitedly.

"Actually, I do believe it," Rob replied in a sober voice. "The verdict's come in. Todd's been found guilty."

Rani switched the music right off. "So what does that mean?" she asked Rob.

"He's already been picked up by an enforcer. If the Night Council ratify the sentence, it will be carried out tomorrow."

"Where?" Rani found herself asking questions, though she wasn't sure if she really wanted to know.

"Only the enforcers know that. I don't think we'll be seeing Todd again. Anyway, how are you doing?"

"Are you serious, Rob? Todd's going to be killed?"

There was a long pause. "Well, yes...probably."

Rani felt sick. "I don't believe in capital punishment," she said in a small voice, feeling helpless, and belatedly wondering what kind of society she'd bought into.

"Oh, baby." Rob's voice was gentle and kind. "I think everyone's feeling sick right now. What can I say? There is a campaign against using enforcers. If you want to get involved, I can hook you up with some people. Anyway, what are you up to?" Rob was clearly trying to change the subject.

"I *was* having a good time, with Maria and Leah."

Rob laughed. "Why doesn't that surprise me? I'm glad you are, darlin'."

"What about you, where you at?" Rani wanted to picture what Rob was doing.

"I'm in a bar with Selena and Jameel. We're just having a quiet drink, catching up on old times." She lowered her voice to a whisper. "Mixing with the mortals."

Rani laughed.

"Well, I'll see you tomorrow." Rob slipped that bit of info in right at the end.

"Come on home to me, baby," she said.

For a while no one spoke. Rani could only guess at the shock going through the vampire community. Losing somebody wasn't an event they had to deal with very often.

"What is this, a wake? Stick some music on, Maria," Leah called out from the back. Maria obliged, and tinkling piano music filled the car. Rani recognized Wuthering Heights. She'd first heard it at her seventh birthday party.

Leah's voice rang out in an uncannily accurate impression.

Glancing in her rearview mirror, Rani saw that Leah was also doing actions, for a second it was as if Kate Bush herself had transported onto the back seat.

As the little car strained up the M23 to London, they reached for the high notes of the chorus. Three vampires singing along to a song they all knew.

Facing the clear road before her, Rani let nostalgia fill her heart. She imagined one day she would have decades, maybe hundreds of years of memories. For the first time, the thought didn't scare her.

ABOUT THE AUTHOR

Crin Claxton is the author of *Scarlet Thirst* and *The Supernatural Detective*. Hir short stories have appeared in numerous anthologies and magazines, including *Erotic Interludes 3,4*, and *5* from Bold Strokes Books. S/he has recipes in *The Butch Cook Book*, and hir poems have been published by Onlywomen Press and La Pluma.

Crin is a technician and lighting designer for theatre. S/he was Festival Director for YLAF (York Lesbian Arts Festival) 2007-2009. S/he's a qualified medical herbalist and lives in London.

Books Available From Bold Strokes Books

Kiss The Girl by Melissa Brayden. Sleeping with the enemy has never been so complicated. Brooklyn Campbell and Jessica Lennox face off in love and advertising in fast-paced New York City. (978-1-62639-071-3)

Taking Fire: A First Responders Novel by Radclyffe. Hunted by extremists and under siege by nature's most virulent weapons, Navy medic Max de Milles and Red Cross worker Rachel Winslow join forces to survive and discover something far more lasting. (978-1-62639-072-0)

First Tango in Paris by Shelley Thrasher. When French law student Eva Laroche meets American call girl Brigitte Green in 1970s Paris, they have no idea how their pasts and futures will intersect. (978-1-62639-073-7)

The War Within by Yolanda Wallace. Army nurse Meredith Moser went to Vietnam in 1967 looking to help those in need; she didn't expect to meet the love of her life along the way. (978-1-62639-074-4)

Escapades by MJ Williamz. Two women, afraid to love again, must overcome their fears to find the happiness that awaits them. (978-1-62639-182-6)

Scarlet Thirst by Crin Claxton. When hot, feisty Rani meets cool, vampire Rob, one lifetime isn't enough, and the road from human to vampire is shorter than you think… (978-1-62639-317-2)

Desire at Dawn by Fiona Zedde. For Kylie, love had always come armed with sharp teeth and claws. But with the human, Olivia, she bares her vampire heart for the very first time, sharing passion, lust, and a tenderness she'd never dared dream of before. (978-1-62639-064-5)

Visions by Larkin Rose. Sometimes the mysteries of love reveal themselves when you least expect it. Other times they hide behind a black satin mask. Can Paige unveil her masked stranger this time? (978-1-62639-065-2)

All In by Nell Stark. Internet poker champion Annie Navarro loses everything when the Feds shut down online gambling, and she turns to experienced casino host Vesper Blake for advice—but can Nova convince Vesper to take a gamble on romance? (978-1-62639-066-9)

Vermilion Justice by Sheri Lewis Wohl. What's a vampire to do when Dracula is no longer just a character in a novel? (978-1-62639-067-6)

Switchblade by Carsen Taite. Lines were meant to be crossed. Third in the Luca Bennett Bounty Hunter Series. (978-1-62639-058-4)

Nightingale by Andrea Bramhall. Culture, faith, and duty conspire to tear two young lovers apart, yet fate seems to have different plans for them both. (978-1-62639-059-1)

No Boundaries by Donna K. Ford. A chance meeting and a nightmare from the past threaten more than Andi Massey's solitude as she and Gwen Palmer struggle to understand the complexity of love without boundaries. (978-1-62639-060-7)

Timeless by Rachel Spangler. When Stevie Geller returns to her hometown, will she do things differently the second time around or will she be in such a hurry to leave her past that she misses out on a better future? (978-1-62639-050-8)

Second to None by L.T. Marie. Can a physical therapist and a custom motorcycle designer conquer their pasts and build a future with one another? (978-1-62639-051-5)

Seneca Falls by Jesse Thoma. Together, two women discover love truly can conquer all evil. (978-1-62639-052-2)

A Kingdom Lost by Barbara Ann Wright. Without knowing each other's fates, Princess Katya and her consort Starbride seek to reclaim their kingdom from the magic-wielding madman who seized the throne and is murdering their people. (978-1-62639-053-9)

Season of the Wolf by Robin Summers. Two women running from their pasts are thrust together by an unimaginable evil. Can they overcome the horrors that haunt them in time to save each other? (978-1-62639-043-0)

The Heat of Angels by Lisa Girolami. Fires burn in more than one place in Los Angeles. (978-1-62639-042-3)

Desperate Measures by P. J. Trebelhorn. Homicide detective Kay Griffith and contractor Brenda Jansen meet amidst turmoil neither of them is aware of until murder suspect Tommy Rayne makes his move to exact revenge on Kay. (978-1-62639-044-7)

The Magic Hunt by L.L. Raand. With her Pack being hunted by human extremists and beset by enemies masquerading as friends, can Sylvan protect them and her mate, or will she succumb to the feral rage that threatens to turn her rogue, destroying them all? A Midnight Hunters novel. (978-1-62639-045-4)

Wingspan by Karis Walsh. Wildlife biologist Bailey Chase is content to live at the wild bird sanctuary she has created on Washington's Olympic Peninsula until she is lured beyond the safety of isolation by architect Kendall Pearson. (978-1-60282-983-1)

Windigo Thrall by Cate Culpepper. Six women trapped in a mountain cabin by a blizzard, stalked by an ancient cannibal demon bent on stealing their sanity—and their lives. (978-1-60282-950-3)

The Blush Factor by Gun Brooke. Ice-cold business tycoon Eleanor Ashcroft only cares about the three Ps—Power, Profit, and Prosperity—until young Addison Garr makes her doubt both that and the state of her frostbitten heart. (978-1-60282-985-5)

Slash and Burn by Valerie Bronwen. The murder of a roundly despised author at an LGBT writers' conference in New Orleans turns Winter Lovelace's relaxing weekend hobnobbing with her peers into a nightmare of suspense—especially when her ex turns up. (978-1-60282-986-2)

The Quickening: A Sisters of Spirits novel by Yvonne Heidt. Ghosts, visions, and demons are all in a day's work for Tiffany. But when Kat asks for help on a serial killer case, life takes on another dimension altogether. (978-1-60282-975-6)

Smoke and Fire by Julie Cannon. Oil and water, passion and desire, a combustible combination. Can two women fight the fire that draws them together and threatens to keep them apart? (978-1-60282-977-0)

Love and Devotion by Jove Belle. KC Hall trips her way through life, stumbling into an affair with a married bombshell twice her age. Thankfully, her best friend, Emma Reynolds, is there to show her the true meaning of Love and Devotion. (978-1-60282-965-7)

The Shoal of Time by J.M. Redmann. It sounded too easy. Micky Knight is reluctant to take the case because the easy ones often turn into the hard ones, and the hard ones turn into the dangerous ones. In this one, easy turns hard without warning. (978-1-60282-967-1)

In Between by Jane Hoppen. At the age of fourteen, Sophie Schmidt discovers that she was born an intersexual baby and sets off on a journey to find her place in a world that denies her true existence. (978-1-60282-968-8)

Under Her Spell by Maggie Morton. The magic of love brought Terra and Athene together, but now a magical quest stands between them— a quest for Athene's hand in marriage. Will their passion keep them together, or will stronger magic tear them apart? (978-1-60282-973-2)

Rush by Carsen Taite. Murder, secrets, and romance combine to create the ultimate rush. (978-1-60282-966-4)

Secret Lies by Amy Dunne. While fleeing from her abuser, Nicola Jackson bumps into Jenny O'Connor, and their unlikely friendship quickly develops into a blossoming romance—but when it comes down to a matter of life or death, are they both willing to face their fears? (978-1-60282-970-1)

Homestead by Radclyffe. R. Clayton Sutter figures getting NorthAm Fuel's newest refinery operational on a rolling tract of land in upstate New York should take a month or two, but then, she hadn't counted on local resistance in the form of vandalism, petitions, and one furious farmer named Tess Rogers. (978-1-60282-956-5)

Battle of Forces: Sera Toujours by Ali Vali. Kendal and Piper return to New Orleans to start the rest of eternity together, but the return of an old enemy makes their peaceful reunion short-lived, especially when they join forces with the new queen of the vampires. (978-1-60282-957-2)

How Sweet It Is by Melissa Brayden. Some things are better than chocolate. Molly O'Brien enjoys her quiet life running the bakeshop in a small town. When the beautiful Jordan Tuscana returns home, Molly can't deny the attraction—or the stirrings of something more. (978-1-60282-958-9)